THE LION OF AFRICA I
Wings of the wind

THE LION OF AFRICA I
Wings of the wind

To my dear brother, Michael

[signature]
www.sovereignbooks.com

Olushile Akintade

Copyright © 2008 by Olushile Akintade.

Library of Congress Control Number: 2005909276
ISBN: Hardcover 978-1-5992-6976-4
Softcover 978-1-5992-6975-7

All rights reserved. No part of this book may be reproduced or transmitted in any form or by any means, electronic or mechanical, including photocopying, recording, or by any information storage and retrieval system, without permission in writing from the copyright owner.

This is a work of fiction. Names, characters, places and incidents either are the product of the author's imagination or are used fictitiously, and any resemblance to any actual persons, living or dead, events, or locales is entirely coincidental.

This book was printed in the United States of America.

To order additional copies of this book, contact:
Xlibris Corporation
1-888-795-4274
www.Xlibris.com
Orders@Xlibris.com
30473

DEDICATION

This book is dedicated with love to almighty God—
the One I hope to please.

ACKNOWLEDGMENTS

I am surrounded by wonderful friends and family that define my success. My Father, you may be in heaven but your legacy lives on in me. My mother, Veronica, my sweet mother, a child is normally a gift to parents but God gave you to me. Segun, Bukky, Kola, and Funmi, you guys where on earth before me and for that, I will always give thanks for the lessons you teach me. You are the best family ever! The one who holds the key to my heart, Tope Alli, only God knows what you love in me for you possess the qualities of a strong, beautiful, and loving maiden. Thanks for pushing me when I would I have given up.

I offer thanks to Believers Assembly, OAU: In an endless tradition of God's Word and the Miraculous!

I owe my spiritual growth to Lenox Road Baptist Church. The pastor, Rev. Cohall, many preach the Word. You live it! Rev. Downer and Rev. Rattray: my mothers who love me unconditionally. What would I have done without the choir and their love and support?

To my publishers, Xlibris: thanks for everything.

Beyond what words can express, I owe it all to God. Jesus, I try to explore my wonder of you. Didn't do a good job but will try more in future texts.

I pray that Christ bless this work and accept it as my humble offering to stir hopes in many.

Olushile Akintade

PREFACE

When I gave my life to Christ, I wanted to share my faith with others. However, I didn't want to offend anyone and risk losing those dear to me. I found myself hesitating and keeping silent. Ashamed of my cowardice and frustrated by it, I tried working in my local fellowship. Maybe there'll be some comfort and fulfillment there.

One cool afternoon, my desires to hold the faith of a martyr birthed the Wings of the Wind.

While writing Samuel's story, I learnt that works don't please God and only faith does. He gives us the courage to speak when we are called to stand and voice our faith. How unworthy I am of His immeasurable grace. When we surrender wholeheartedly to God, He alone perfects and completes us. Each of my character play out a differently as I search for God's will. The lord placed it in my heart to write, as inefficient as I can, what I've written.

My main desire for you dear reader is to pray before you venture into this book. There are a load of things I try to pass across the way I feel it and hope you get to feel it the same way, and even more. May Samuel's story make you hunger for the real Word—Jesus Christ—the Bread of Life. Finish reading this imperfect work and pick up the Bible that home it all.

Beloved, do surrender to Christ, who loves you for you. As you drink from the overflowing cistern of life, the Lord will rekindle your heart, and was over your spirit as He walks on the Wings of the Wind.

Olushile Akintade, 2008

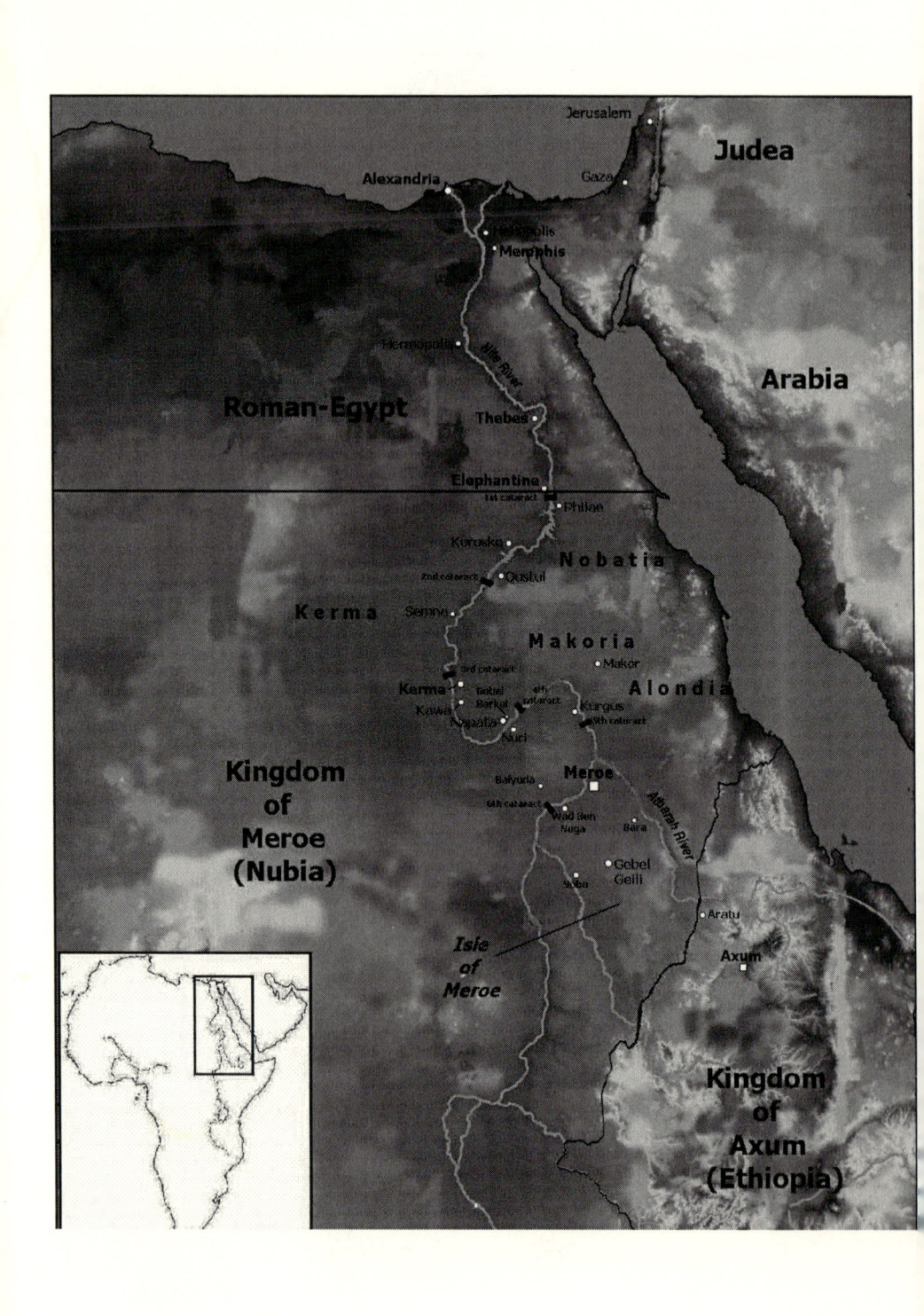

Judea
Jerusalem
Gaza
Alexandria
Heliopolis
Memphis
Arabia
Hermopolis
Nile River
Roman-Egypt
Thebes
Elephantine
1st cataract
Philae
Koroska
Nobatia
2nd cataract
Qustul
Kerma
Semna
3rd cataract
Makoria
Makor
Kerma
Gebel Barkal
4th cataract
Kawa
Kurgus
Alondia
Nagaata
5th cataract
Nuri
Kingdom
of
Meroe
(Nubia)
Bajrwia
Meroe
Atbarah River
6th cataract
Wad Ben Naga
Bara
Gebel Geili
Soba
Aratu
Isle
of
Meroe
Axum
Kingdom
of
Axum
(Ethiopia)

1

When I tried to understand all this, it was oppressive to me
Till I entered the sanctuary of God; then did I understand destiny

It all began, as long as I could remember, on a very hot day when the Sun scorched at its brilliant radiance. These were the days when no man was to cross the boundary that separated the existence of mankind from 'The Shadow of the forest.' Once more, all I could do was to wander beyond it—into the domains of the very thing that could end my life, and damn my soul to the abysmal depths of solitary darkness—where one waits for all eternity with no hope of restoration.

Birds chattered love songs that could wrench the very heart of an unfeeling soul to tears, streaming and ever-flowing. The winds rushed along in a gentle caress as I listened to decipher the mystery of these incomparable melodious harmonies. My resolve is not to give up exploring. Bony legs of mine held the grasses in discourse for a brief moment and only drifted away in bid of its master. Then and there, beneath the excellence of plant trophies, I stood amazed at its splendor and magnificence. Tree branches wounded up with twirled leaves to bed gardens, able to hold the weight of anyone bold enough to overlook its perceptible sustenance. And why should I be robbed of climbing up to the garden when my breath is alone hindered by its utter elegance and sophistication? On the moss-filled floor are spots of light reflections, shimmering from the blazing Sun that scalded so wickedly once I leave the covers of the forest to plunder beyond, in exploration.

Beauty is not always a produce derived from nature. To refine nature to something else would be to defile its purity, and authenticity. The perfectiveness of the rarest of African gems couldn't be compared to the exquisiteness of kingdoms orchestrated by Mother Nature. Tangible proofs stand so visibly all around us, right in our faces, yet the very creatures blessed to relish in its gracefulness are found to stir aloof in absolute and yet, inexcusable ignorance.

A glance above is enough to rapture a sleepy soul in its handsomeness; a stimulus wrung by the wind is enough to arrest the wanderer in its embrace; the quietude and comfort the surrounding trees minister to a weary heart is enough to birth hope and solace in its loveliness. Every whisper the breeze delivered, each sloshing stroke the tree branches caressed my Sun-burnt skin, the dancing color changes of the daylight source, the sweet melody that drifted from the smallest of birds, creating a sanctuary under the tree covers, these and many more constitute my own definition of beauty and loveliness.

In the foolishness of my innocence, I relished the beauty of life.

It wasn't long after my selfish exploration that the wind stopped in its course. Everything seemed still except for my soul which wandered on, being played on the symphonies. The dancing evergreen trees stopped in their obeisance to an unknown deity, momentarily depriving me of the showering rainfall of leaves. Birds that had enchanted me with their songs of blessings were strangely quiet. Even the raucous jangle of the grey-white monkeys in the far distance got drowned in the stifling quietude.

Something is coming!

For a moment my spider senses tingled. Danger suddenly lurked amidst the beauty that overwhelmed me. The twirling and wounding together of branches and trees formed images as the Sun's rays beamed down through the leafy spaces. The images, so distinct, that I couldn't distinguish reality from the visions of my fantasies. My eyes tried to acclimatize quickly to the inexorable form of danger my surroundings decided to bear. The trees met my gaze with a stern of apprehension while my pupils dilated in an infinite attempt to advance its focal point. Quite remarkable it is to listen to silence, for ambiance commanded stillness of its spiritless subjects.

In the midst of all, there was one: well-defined, pronounced, and not too far from the ground. It was two seemingly small cone balls that lay transversely, with crossings between them, dark and narrowed down like the fang of an adder. Momentarily, I trembled as it floatingly approached. Slowly, realization dawned on me for the visions cleared to reveal a lion, moving with an air of pride and dominance. It wasn't any lion.

It was the one.

The scar that cut across the left side of its horrid face was enough proof . . .

The Shadow of the forest!

The beast no living creature had ever witnessed its roars and lived to tell it.

I gasped for air that was very much in abundance and found myself unable to move. Hope drenched from me like water outpoured through a basket. I knew there and then, that there was no escaping this monster that had now plagued my village for decades. Its tales tainted the lips of village talebearers like it had existed for centuries.

The Shadow moved closer, eyes savoring, as life, from my spirit, slipped slowly away. A leaf got itself free from one of the trees and swayed slightly down. The enigma took a paw closer. The silence was so deafening that I heard the sound of the leaf hit the ground. Long have I questioned the demise of great warriors that had been preys of the Shadow. Now I knew different.

How could something so huge be so stealthy? How could one snap out from the enchanting, yet terrifying feeling its presence administered without shattering to bits? Only the symbiosis between the trees and the grasslands could explain why such a lion reigned in these regions, for it was now deemed as *Enkai*, the supreme god supernally in a lion form. Something else resonated within me, as I'm sure it had for everyone who stood in my shoes before: the inevitability of my fate.

Numbness spread all over as it took another step closer. Its thick brownish yellow coat rippled slightly in tone. Black manes covering the backside of its head ran down to its abdomen. My fear-full eyes dare muster courage to observe briefly.

Suddenly, the trees rose up slightly from their slumber and whistled in response to the blast of wind making its way with a fierce drive. Such a force it was that it loosened the reins of shackles that held my soul down from fleeing this quintessence of evil.

Go. Don't look back.

As if the winds gave me life, a whisper was enough to make me turn and run fiercely, knowing that I would be chased by the Shadow for trespassing its pride lands. Laibon, the tribe's religious leader, had announced these regions as the Shadow's domain long before I was born but my folly would have no heed to such warnings.

Cutting through branches and jumping over fallen logs, the expectation to be cut down any moment lingered on the sweat that ran down my skin. As I ran for my life, the Shadow followed in silence incomprehensible, obviously relishing the chase, for my legs couldn't have sustained me after a while.

How more tiring it is when every step is taken to avoid that which our understanding informs us as certainly unavoidable. The reservoir of strength that resides in the deepest reins of man is most times plagued by drought before the body gets to respond to the willpower to draw from its undeniable, and yet enriching vigor.
When the heart of man has resolved to fate, what can the body do? When the heart of man has embraced everything short of faith, what great calamity is due?
Man comes to wisdom when he realizes that the outside cannot inflict the inside unless his very heart gives up the fight before it commences. Man comes to understanding when reality dawns on his heart in relish of the indomitable excellence of his soul. Man comes to knowledge when that, which he retains within, serves as the root of reserved strength and not pride.

Leaping over the hedges that marked the boundary and turning about a tree, there stood my brother, Caleb, in the plains. For the first time, he looked nothing like the bully I had assumed him to be. The beatings I received from the swaying branches still remained alien to my senses due to the pensiveness of my flight. With lesser trees and more grasses now, the soon-to-be encounter was sure to be on an open field.

* * *

"Calebbbb!" Samuel cried out his brother's name. For the moment the Shadow stopped, seemingly sizing up its meal in incorrigible silence.

Samuel clenched onto his brother.

At the age of ten and five years, Caleb was already full-grown. His younger brother edged himself to him, taking comfort in the well-built muscles that made up his taut body and his six-inch height. No concern was it to the younger lad the bathe of sweat he had to put up with that smoldered his elder brother after an afternoon of unfruitful hunting. All he seemingly cared about was getting as far as possible from the enormous beast that stood a few meters away from them.

Every ray beam from the Sun blazed incandescently as they stood on the grassy plains. Amidst the fear that saturated the air—choking the life out of them, they were dazed at its stance! The stiff and wiry furs that covered the lion stood so rich and curly. Its skin, that would certainly be the riches' bidder for its quality, rarity and thickness, emitted the firmness of no possible penetration of any killing object. They tried not to look down at its huge paws that held the claws through which death is administered to anything that crossed its path.

Without thinking, Samuel uttered: "So death, this is thy victory, thy sting: to mask magnificently your messenger!"

As those words left Samuel he felt like someone had amplified those words before.

Somewhere! Some time ago.

Caleb glanced at his younger brother for a second clearly taken aback by his utterance and Samuel knew that he shouldn't have said such a thing when they were to become a feast to a no ordinary lion. Every ounce of strength had sipped away from Caleb and left a bland face. It was indeed impossible to prevent the piercing chill, which ran through them under the blazing Sun, at the stare of death.

Grimacing, they instinctively knew time was up as it pranced forward, after them. Samuel moved far back while his brother stood still. He thought he'd lost his brother as the beast ran up to them and pounced on Caleb. The grasses stood in witness of another innocent prey fallen to the hands of the ogre.

Caleb fell hopelessly backwards but tactfully thrust his legs upwards with so much strength that it threw the Shadow behind before it sunk its deadly claws into him. Springing up, Caleb immediately reached for his fallen loin's bag and brought out his father's whip. He whirled it round as the Shadow turned to have a quick tear at his younger brother who stood stunned and unmoving.

The weight and age of the king of the jungle didn't rob it of its slyness for it landed perfectly on its paws after the leg-thrust.

Caleb took the whip by his side, swirled and lashed it, wounding around the Shadow's neck, and yanked the quintessence of death away from his brother with all his might.

Blood flushed the Shadow's eyes and fury took its wits as it jerked its head terribly, almost wrenching Caleb's arm. Its fierceness filled the air with a shrieking sound that deafened and stunned its intended preys.

Caleb lost his grip immediately.

The whip came loose and fell to the ground.

The Shadow immediately charged towards Caleb, this time with the surety of dismembering his body into shreds. It leapt onto him and its hind paws rested heavily on his thighs thereby stopping Caleb's tactful leg-thrust again. Staring straight at death's cold eyes for the briefest of moments, Caleb caught a glimpse of horror and ultimately resigned to the fate that stood on him.

He knew it only took one strike and he would be joining his parents in the land where time had no boundaries.

In compliance with its prey's resignation, the Shadow raised its left paw to strike.

Suddenly, an arrow hit its right side and threw it off of Caleb. The long-forgotten young lad had prior taken Caleb's bow and arrow beside their father's loin bag and pulled at it with great strength.

Samuel was too smitten with shock as tears rolled down his face. Breathing heavily, he'd watched as the arrow he pulled hit its mark, his perspirations more from fear than what the Sun could administer. He cared less of how questionable such little force he applied on the arrow could have impacted its target enough to throw it off his brother. All he knew was for an instant, it all felt like a dream, and, like many of his dreams, he was guided by an unknown voice, and this time it was to pick the bow and arrow to shoot at whatever ailed him.

And that he did.

A slight struggle ensued from the Shadow and then . . .

It was still.

With heavy intake of air into his lungs Samuel felt the struggle slowly passing on. Rushing to the seemingly lifeless body of his brother, Caleb met his embrace with a slight squeeze, their bodies' reek of fear and trembling.

Caleb could have sworn he had almost crossed over to the other side at the mere terror of staring at the Shadow's cold eyes. He glanced at the evil that almost had its fill from his flesh and got up with his brother close to him. In his mind he juggled what had just transpired. Unfathomable it was how an everyday hunting turned to a battle for their lives at the turn of the second.

"How many times have I told you never to cross the boundary, Samuel?" Caleb pushed his younger brother away. "It seems you don't listen to anyone except yourself. I've never seen anyone so driven to the point of death by his folly."

"I was just trying to catch some butterflies when I saw . . ."

"Spare me the details. It's a bad child who doesn't heed advice." Caleb interrupted, angered by his brother constant insolence. His insatiable quest for adventure was becoming more unbearable and costly.

The stampede was still fresh in his mind. The wild cattle made it clear that they shouldn't be disturbed. Their territories were marked with feces and only animals stronger dare cross the landmarks.

If any strayed beyond it, the heavy grunting noises these hooved animals made are like twitching sounds of rattlesnakes in the desert.

Two animals did stray that horrible day.

The Shadow and Samuel.

One to quench its hunger.

The other to revel in folly.

"I'm sorry." Samuel pleaded with his face downcast. "I will not disobey you again."

Seeing how depressed he was, Caleb struggled within himself to draw his brother closer but knew this was one thing he couldn't let him off the hook so easily, especially when their lives almost got snuffed out.

"You just can't listen can you, Samuel? I don't know how we're still alive but that is the Shadow of the forest and no one has survived it before. You hear me? No one!"

Then again, he looked at the priceless victory that ensued from his brother's costly actions. He struggled within himself to appraise the bigger picture. Though hard to accept, great victory had ensued from his brother's recklessness. Caleb touched his younger brother's chin and lifted up his face.

"Look, let us reason together. If you refuse to be made straight when you are green, you will not be made straight when you are dry. We almost lost our lives for a moment there and that 'sting of death' thing you said made me feel like you would go to any extent to get attention."

"'Wages of sin is death,' father used to say." Samuel replied with slight throbbing as tears welled up in his eyes.

"Now that literally explains what just happened here. Sometimes, the sins carelessly committed could cost a life. You've learnt your lesson from such a one as this, hmm?"

A slight nod of understanding from crying Samuel and Caleb pulled him closer. He turned again to look at the Shadow; his face wore disbelief at the conquest.

Samuel loosened his grip of his brother and started hopping around suddenly in sheer display of joy. Caleb wondered what could be the cause of his brother's outburst of elation.

"The whole village will be more than happy to embrace the liberty this news will bring to them. The Shadow of the forest is fallen. We will be able to explore the fecundity the forest provides to lengths unknown. Nothing can stop us now." Samuel exclaimed.

"And to think that we, the ones considered as outcasts, brought this age-long threat to an end makes it even more unconventional, you know." Caleb added thoughtfully. "Worse! It was only a child that administered the blow that silenced this mystery. When *Ilmorani*, the warriors, and the elders get to know this, it would choke the very life out of them. Ah! I can't wait to see the expression on the Laibon's face."

"What do you mean?" Samuel interjected. He stopped hopping and wore fear on his face.

Caleb has always noticed how his brother's face paled over at the mention of the spiritual leader. He thought it was just out of reverence but now, more than ever, he sensed something different.

"What is wrong Samuel? Why do you always turn cold at the mention of Olanana, the Laibon?"

"Nothing, I just don't like him."

"You don't have to lie to me if you don't want to tell me. It's clearly written on your face that something bothers you at the mention of him. Besides, we've now come to the end of Olanana's evil reign."

"How can that be? The Laibon hasn't allowed the Orngesherr, the last age-set initiation, to take place from time knows when."

It is customary that when a man reached his thirties, meat is usually grilled and the first wife, if there is more than one, will shave her husband's head and the man will assume full independence to his own. It is a ceremony looked forward to by the whole tribe. The warriors will go out hunting and most times, if not always, the men to be initiated as elders will go with his warriors' age set to hunt for meat and above all, such a great pride if an age set speared a lion. A head piece made from the lion's mane will be worn during special ceremonies. Everyone regards it priceless for a soon-to-be elder to wear such a dignifying head piece at his initiation. Great chants and spirited dances are held by the age-set warriors in honor of such prowess. This ceremony usher men to the group of elders and chiefs that make political decisions for the tribe.

Unfortunately, such chants and beautiful dances have not being held from the time the Shadow roared its first in the region. Olanana, the spiritual leader, also called the Laibon, requested that the Shadow of the forest be killed as the price for the last age-set initiation. It has been said of how an entire age-set of warriors, made up of over twenty houses, perished under the claws of the Shadow after a hunting expedition.

"I see you don't know the prophecy that rests on the demise of the Shadow. Its better not take the wood out of the fire while the wind blows. You will know soon enough."

"Please, tell me." Samuel pleaded.

"It won't take long now. You will get to know." With a slight stroke of his brother's jaw line, Caleb continued. "Let's just say the stone which the builders have rejected has become the chief corner stone."

"That's one of father's sayings I don't understand." Samuel replied angrily.

"That's true. Father was speaking of a prophecy that came to pass years ago and in your case, nothing could be more befitting. Actually, it suits what just transpired here quite well."

"So you won't tell me?" Samuel pleaded again.

"No."

"Please?"

"Be patient now. Bees do not sting the one who doesn't run." Caleb pulled his younger brother closer and started tickling him by his rib-less waist.

Once more, the winds blew soothingly, nurturing them with its coolness as it carried their laughter away into the distance. The not-too-faraway-trees whistled in response and the Sun brazed their skins to form shadows of brothers in joyful sport.

"Besides, who taught you how to use the bow and arrow, let alone, aim and fire at such strength to take out a lion?" Caleb asked as he took a step closer to the fallen body of the beast. The shadow lay down on its left side with the arrow still sticking out on its right. He would definitely need to spear it through to make sure it's dead for good.

"You did!" Samuel answered.

"I don't remember ever teaching you Sam." Caleb pulled the arrow out of the Shadow. The gush of blood from the wound indicated that the arrow must have sunk deep. "Fetch me the spear. It's beside father's bag."

"But you should know that there are some lessons learnt without the uttering of words." Samuel continued. He turned to see where the spear lay. "I have watched you string, aim and pull the bow so many times that I leave eternity to count, if it isn't close to it.

"But it wasn't my pull that drove the arrow brother." Samuel turned to his brother and didn't get the spear. "I wish you were able to have seen me go at it with the bow and string. How it came off with such force I really don't know."

Their countenances mused on the past event. "'The roaring of the lion, the voice of the fierce lion and the teeth of the young lions are broken . . .' You remember those words?"

Caleb gave Samuel the arrow and touched his shoulder as they both walked back to get the spear. "Yes I do but there's end to the proverb you didn't recite and I can't seem to remember."

Caleb's words hung in the air as a growling sound suddenly rose. It raised the very hairs on them, tingling with fear.

The Shadow wasn't done yet!

In what looked liked the speed of light the lion came at them and Caleb spontaneously pushed his younger brother away. Evil's claws took more than a scratch of his right arm. The horrifying pain that spanned throughout Caleb's existence found its outlet through his mouth, scathing the trees of its leaves.

Samuel shivered terribly as he watched Caleb hold his bloodied right arm. He now fully believed that they were definitely fighting a god here.

After years of failed expeditions by the Ilmorani, great warriors and protectors of the tribal lands, to kill the Shadow, it was said no man could kill it. It would be considered goodwill to have gotten this much roar out of it and still be alive but now, once again, they face the creature that had never been denied of its preys.

Caleb couldn't find any logical explanation for the force the arrow hit its mark with earlier but it sure was some force.

He felt it!

He was under the Shadow when it threw it off of him. No normal living thing could survive such force.

That he was sure of.

But the Shadow obviously didn't fall into such categories of anything normal.

No living being could have pulled a bow to drive the arrow with such force either.

Let alone a child.

That was also clear in his mind.

He left all conclusions to the unseen.

Even though he stood there in resignation to what is to come, he hoped divinity will intrude their world again.

They had cheated death once.

Not again.

The viciousness that lit up the wounded lion's face heaved sure to take its toll on them.

Fear closed Samuel's eyes.

He found his heart praying for deliverance. But to whom should he pray to? He wondered. The Enkia, the tribe's god, or his father's unknown god? Are they the same or different beings? His little mind failed to comprehend.

The winds, ever so familiar, with its breezing sound brought the words of the village chiefs to memory:

"Whoever can smite the death mark of the Shadow will resultantly become the next head chief."

Samuel opened his eyes and looked at the Shadow having gained its deadly stance once more. Light flooded his thoughts. The death mark ran from its face to the left side of his abdomen. Its thick furs weighed upon it thickly but still didn't veil the sight of the fleshy scarred line that ran through its side.

. . . the death mark . . . left side . . . the lion's heart!

Of course! It all made sense to him now. The returning Ilmorani, both junior and senior warriors, from the expedition to kill the Shadow testified, on numerous occasions, that their arrows didn't take it down. No one had ever gotten the chance to aim at the Shadow's heart because you only had one chance and then it would be the Shadow's turn to attack.

It always disappeared so easily into the thick grasses.

Its cave had never been discovered.

Its movement, never been traceable.

He now understood how the several hunting of both the junior and senior warriors, was without success.

An idea brewed in his mind.

He looked at Caleb and for a brief moment they spoke without saying a word.

Caleb nodded in compliance.

He stood straight, held his red tunic to his teeth and tore out a piece in one swift movement and tied the bleeding place. Caleb looked at his brother again. He could almost whisper but he didn't. *"Whatever aided you the first time with the bow and arrow, will aid you again."*

Though he knew the Shadow will anticipate every move they make more carefully than before, they obviously had no choice. Still no explanation yet for the first strike against the Shadow in his mind but somehow he knew there wouldn't be room to find one if they don't survive this encounter.

In plethora of despair, today, of all days, Caleb fleetingly felt it appointed for this quintessence of evil to fall. He looked at his brother and intuitively knew that it was by his hands it shall be—*that foolishness might confound the wise, and the weak things of this world might defy the mighty.*

Samuel ran in one direction with the arrow in his hand to fetch the bow beside their father's loin bag while Caleb took off in the other direction picking up the fallen whip. The Shadow shot back glances from one to the other without tilting its head and reasoned on whom to attack first.

So it began.

Caleb stopped to watch as the Shadow went after his younger brother this time. It was like it knew now to rid itself of the young lad first. He swirled the whip again with his strong left arm, lashed it at the Shadow and could only yank the vicious animal's head to face him.

Samuel threw himself on the floor, raising dust into the air before taking up the bow. The bow fidgeted in his hands. He took his position on one knee and turned on his side to aim at enigma in motion.

"*Easy . . . steady . . . to your chin.*" He whispered to himself.

If the same force that impacted the Shadow earlier came out from these small, weak hands, then it wasn't completely insane to rely on it happening again.

But rely, he will.

Just one miss and he knew all will be lost.

Caleb looked in fright, as the epitome of evil freed itself of the whip again. The elements of life joined the trees to watch the Shadow try to oust its prey once more. As the raised dust cleared, Samuel released the arrow with all his might. His heart engaged in prayer but dread choked the words from leaving his mouth.

In an instant, it seemed the arrow came to life again.

Its tip lit up. With so great a force, it permeated the lion's left side, straight to the heart and threw it into the shrubs.

Silence.

Caleb held his shoulders slightly. Blood surfaced on the scratch the lion drew.

Everything happened so fast that a second more and the Shadow would have had more than a scratch.

Something beyond the natural just intervened again on their behalf. That killing force couldn't have come from his brother.

Just like the first one.

This time he watched.

This time he saw it all.

It seemed divinity had been taken from the Shadow of the forest for only that could explain its downfall.

Especially, when such fall from greatness comes from the least expected.

A child!

Caleb walked slowly to where the lion lay and knelt down slowly beside it.

This time it stayed dead.

He turned to look at his brother. For a second, he could have sworn seeing a being that shone brightly beside his brother before the vision literally faded away as his brother began shouting with inexplicable joy.

"'You will tread upon the lion and the cobra; you will trample the great lion and the serpent.'" Samuel cried out in dancing.

Caleb watched his brother and pondered in his heart what the future held for him. He had never seen anyone whose path was already laid out and written for substance like he saw in Samuel. He walked up to the dancing lad and brushed his head lightly with his hand, smiling.

"That's not the end of the proverb. That's not it at all."

* * *

Everything seemed peaceful as they approached the village. The purification ceremony will be that night and preparations had commenced already. Men were already at work, spooning fine wool to make their warm shuka for display, with varieties of checked colors, red being dominant. The women went about making sure that food and water will be in abundance at the village square.

Everyone draped themselves with red clothing all over only for the night to come and there'd be different displays of attires. The women will wear the best displays of attires as the Laibon approved them for the purification ceremony.

In a traditional moran costume, draped over is a gorgeous kanga red cape with patterned white designs, accented by an elaborate multi-colored collar. The accessories included matching bracelets on the ankles and necks, with red earrings of various designs. The matching bracelets and beads hang heavily as they perform the ceremonial dance.

In the meantime, Empikas, which is a warrior delegation, was going on at a clearing not too far away. Such meetings are always geared towards planning a secret lion hunting a few days after the meeting only that, in this case, the hunting will be later tonight.

Everyone knew that Empikas have been about the Shadow of the forest for over a decade. Protecting livestock from lions has and will always be a grave concern to the warriors. The survival of the tribe has been of great concern too since the Shadow roared it's first.

In the hot Sun no one noticed the two brothers as they dragged the Shadow down the forest path.

Not too far to the west, women and girls were gathered to practice the craft of beadwork. A woman was going round and inspecting the beads as little girls and maidens made them. She picks it up and shakes it. The sound of the jewelry symbolized admiration and played a major factor in the craft. She sometimes instructs her students to add more colored materials to their beadwork.

Caleb and Samuel stopped to take a breath as they looked up for a moment. Caleb wiped his brows of sweat with his left hand and looked at the place where the delegation was going on.

During the last mass circumcision of young males, the male faces were painted, partly with cow's blood, and they wore headdresses made out of wood and feathers. Caleb recalled watching the procession without participating. The Laibon made it clear that his family was not considered as part of the tribe. No wonder they were the only ones deemed unworthy to have their ears pierced and disked. He always found himself reminiscing and feeling so alone and left out. Even though it was clear his family and their tribe stood at both ends of a chasm.

Separate and impassable.

Children drew water not to far from the stream and can be sighted from a distance walking back to the village with cloths glued to their skin.

Their own loin cloths weighed drunk in excess of perspiration from the dragging of the Shadow. As they came closer to the intersection where the forest and the stream path conjoined, a child stopped not too far from Samuel and Caleb. Stunned to see what they dragged, she let go of the water vessel on her head.

It was something about the gift from his god. The vessel came down and hit the ground with a cracking sound. *'Wellsprings of living water . . .'* Samuel remembered one of his father's sayings. Resultantly, memories flooded Samuel's thoughts and it seemed he was taken back to that fateful night when his parents died.

It was the purification ceremony then, and all the children were at the village square waiting for their parents' cleansing so that the feasting will begin. It was customary for the purification to be held when the priest visited the Mugumo tree, a very special tree known to the whole region. The priest had to travel for days to reach this holy tree. It was under this tree that a priest once prophesied the influences of modernized foreigners that would come to the region long after he would have joined his ancestors.

One by one, the adults were cleansed in their mud huts made of cow dung, with each woman carrying water pots after being cleansed to the village square where the celebration will be. The purpose was to make the village holy, as a symbol of obeisance to the holy tree and also the readiness to be counted worthy for blessing when their ancestors' spirits hovers.

To Samuel, these were days filled with happiness.

No wanting.

Everything seemed peaceful and in order.

The moon once more proved its independence from the Sun.

His parents were in the hut, which was farthest from the village square. His father, Lusala, which means 'whip', a foreigner to the land, who escaped from slavery and stole away, returned to his homeland, Africa, only to doggedly preach a doctrine different from the land's beliefs. A doctrine that almost got him in death's palms numerous times as it came against the holy tree as the symbol to revere, and defied Enkai as the real god. After suffering beatings and being marked with scars, he won only one soul-his wife.

Lusala once told her that, *"sometimes to save another, you have to realize that all things are lawful, but not all things are expedient."* She had asked him what that meant and he told her that, *"the liberty we have must not become a stumbling block and that to save at least some, we must sometimes play a part in their culture."*

All the priest did during the ceremony was to give the men and the women materials needed for bathing, which symbolizes their cleansing. Afterwards, they go to the village square. The women carry a vessel of water to be used by individual families for the ceremonial feast. What Lusala suggested was that it would seem like they participated in the purification ceremony when they actually didn't. They never used whatever was given to them for bathing, but there were no means to validate that.

Having fully seceded from the bondage she claimed yoked her tribe Loiyan married the foreigner, Lusala, in defiance of her beliefs. No offense was greater than the one against her betrothed, the Laibon's son, Olanana, a man who had nothing but hate in his heart to kill the foreigner. On that night, Olanana was performing the ceremony as the new ascribed Laibon, after the mysterious death of his father, the previous spiritual leader.

Slipping away from the village square, stubborn as always, Samuel left his little sister, Lydia with Caleb and went into the bushes, heading straight for home. He walked for a while, feeling the cool breeze that arrested the dense vegetation around him. Shivering slightly, he gazed up, admiring the brilliance of the stars that blemished the dark blue blanket. Many times he would count the stars on nights like this until he lost count. It always amazed him how he couldn't figure the actual number of stars in a pre-determined region he marks out before counting.

Samuel learnt how to count from his father, who would spend late nights with him staring up to the skies and telling him stories.

A cloud or two sometimes pass in attempt to declare their worth of admiration. There've been times when he would acknowledge them and make acquaintances, but tonight, he was thankful that there was none.

If not for the brusque tone of Olanana, sneering the night, he would have kept looking up still when he got close to home, lost at the night's ensnaring yet delicate handsomeness.

"We have taken what we need for cleansing. What else is there Olanana?"

Samuel listened as his father addressed the Laibon and his five Templers. The Templers are warriors chosen to protect and serve the Will of Enkai.

"You can never be purified, stranger. You will always be an outcast," a smear of rage in Olanana's voice. "You came to enslave our minds, and hearts, and souls by your foul doctrine. You may have beguiled my beloved with your enticing words but never will I heed your blasphemies." He said disgusted. "You blot out ordinances contrary to our way of life and you expect us to accept it?"

"And what good has your way of life done for you?" Lusala responded. He was losing his cool to the wizard.

"I reckon it has held the village for centuries, way before your existence, but you portray goodwill spawned and rooted in evil." Olanana answered acerbically, close to frenzy.

"Can coconut be found on palm trees?" Lusala asked. "Don't you know that whatever mothers a thing, rightly determines its qualities. What else is there to do, Laibon, but to spoil men with philosophies and vain deceits after your tradition? You establish rudiments and laws that ironically lead men to bondage."

"And what would you recommend. You've been gone from these lands all your life. It's obvious you've been infected by the vile of foreign lands that's why you can't think or see clearly anymore. Even your children have names that hold no ties to their roots."

"As you well know that by custom, names are given with purpose. Just as the usefulness of cassava remains unknown unless unearthed, so also the purpose of a child till his defining name is fulfilled. So, on the contrary, the scales have fallen from my eyes since I left these lands and I see clearly now, more than ever before."

"What do you see Lusala? What do you know? The venture to change the way of life and structure of our people is to destroy us of our roots, and you claim you see clearly."

"Olanana, it was never my will to banish the heritage of these lands to oblivion and I wish you believe me that it never will be. I only believe that it's about time that darkness be lifted off these lands and the fierce Sun shed its light deeper than on our skins. The doctrine I proclaim takes its effect within, and then without. It bears no threat to wipe out centuries of our history, only to change the perspective to which we embrace and live."

"You are wrong. Enkai, inhabiting many forms, aids our existence and we know the path of life more than any other tribe or race. Every man has a choice to make and I've made mine. And so have you."

Kill him.

With an evil smile on his face, Olanana heard the words echo in his heart. It was time to rid himself of this intruder. He had consulted the gods for years but somehow hadn't felt the release to do anything about this blasphemer. At some point he thought he would die at the loss of his betrothed to him. Now, more than ever, he still loved his affianced and would relish the joy of killing Lusala.

Well it seems the laws you accuse me of is about to judge you and your doctrine. Under my priesthood, you have defiled the gods according to the manner of purification of the Tabora tribes."

"What?"

"And so you must therefore be locked in your home till the next ceremony will be held for your cleansing. If you will need any, that is."

"You can't do this." Lusala answered, startled.

"Templers, lock him in till he keels over to my terms."

Olanana held only one term in his hear.

Death!

"Don't you dare!" Samuel saw his mother voice out as she stepped out of the hut.

Olanana, as always, looked at her with a burning passion, still consumed by her loveliness that years had not even blemished. *'She deserves more,'* he thought in his heart, *'and I alone can give her.'*

"I can do however I please. Now! You! Come here." Olanana forcefully grabbed her and with a nod of his head, two Templers knocked Lusala down and dragged him inside only for the night to bear his groaning moments after.

"Please don't kill him." Samuel heard his mother beg as he stood in the shrubs obviously glued to the spot.

"Ah! But he once said that he would die for his beliefs. What better time is there than now? *'For my savior,'* he says. Ha!" Spitting on the ground, Olanana's face squeezed up in loathe.

"You are burning the whole house? Don't do this. This is murder. Please. Don't do this."

"And what is that we shouldn't do? His death or the house?" A glint of fulfillment lit Olanana's face as she struggled in his arms.

"Olanana, life is marked with mistakes and they do underline its borders, but this is inexcusable. Please, don't."

"You have forgotten that there has been no senior warrior initiation since the Shadow roamed the forest and I alone have the power to kill it for I am the chosen of our god, Enkai."

Looking at her, he felt anguish at the sight of her tears and thought in his heart that he would make it all right soon, after he rid the tribe of this wretched man. "Templers, hold her for me."

The Templers came closer with blazing torches on one hand and grabbed her with other. The other two stepped out of the house after venting their hate on Lusala while the last one just stood beside the Laibon without a flinch.

"As long as I'm Laibon, no one can stop me and anyone who dares will be destroyed, starting with the fool you call a husband. Very soon, his charms on you will wear off like the dawning of a new day. I swear it." He declared with assurance.

She watched as the Templers set the house on fire and struggled to set herself free. With the help of the wind the whole house was ablaze. Samuel watched in disbelief, unable to move as he saw the smoke rise up in the night.

"You don't understand, Olanana. I can never return. Please! You can still stop this."

"All defiance ends here!" Olanana looked at Loiyan as tears slid down her face. Lusala's cry could be heard from the inside.

She turned and met his gaze. "I will never be yours!"

The Templers holding her relaxed their grip a little as they moved back while the flames engulfed the house. Olanana looked at her deeply.

For the first time in years he realized that he had already lost her. There was a resolve in her eyes that blazed rhythmically with the flames.

Her heart was sold out completely and lay somewhere beneath the rubble of the burning hut.

Olanana took a step closer and grabbed her from the Templers. He turned her back to the hut and pushed her with so much force that it sent her into the flames to meet her companion.

The whole house came down before he could withdraw from the downpour and with it a piece of wood.

The wood struck the left side of Olanana's face before he withdrew. For a moment tears surfaced in those cold eyes as he watched the ruins of the house that held the burning remains of his acclaimed beloved.

No sound existed except that of the burning house.

"Templers, leave for the village square. Our business here is done."

"But my lord, your face, do you . . ."

"Go. I'll be right behind you." Olanana interrupted his most trusted templer, Kamau.

The pain of watching his parents die shocked Samuel so much that he felt the reason of living snatched away from him in an instant. He was too stunned to shed a tear.

Slowly, he knelt down on the shrubs, staring. His gaze shifted from the flames to the one who murdered his parents.

After a while, the Templers were gone.

Olanana turned and stared straight into the eyes of the little child. He could feel the boy shrivel under his gaze.

He would have to kill the lad after what he just witnessed. Olanana came closer to where the boy stood and stopped a few feet away from him.

He brought out his wooden scepter from the side of the wrap hold of his red tunic, determined to strike.

For some reason he didn't bring the scepter down.

He couldn't!

Samuel thought the priest was going to kill him and just stared into his eyes with tears rolling unstopped. It was like a gulf was right between them.

Not to be crossed.

. . . Somehow the boy was not to be touched . . .

Those same cold eyes now approached them.

The Laibon walked towards them. Aside from the same build with Caleb, the priest was much older and well scarred on the left side of his face. Samuel and Caleb tired from dragging the Shadow and had stopped to catch their breath. One by one, everyone realized what they carried and soon, a crowd of people, with their eyes dancing around gathered.

The news spread around the settlement. The Laibon stopped right in front of Caleb, Samuel and the fallen lion. With a wave of the Laibon's hand, the gathering crowd reduced their murmurings with unbelief written on everyone's faces.

"Who killed it?" the Laibon asked without taking his eyes off of Samuel.

"He did." Caleb announced placing his hand on his younger brother's shoulder.

Olanana, the Laibon, took a step closer towards the young lad, well aware of the effect he had on him. He willed Samuel to look up at him and when he did, he said, "And who do you pay obeisance to?"

Samuel looked at his brother in fear.

Caleb met his brother's eyes and saw so much fear and hate in them. Definitely, there must be a reason why his brother reacted this way in the presence of the Laibon.

"Who do you pay obeisance to?" the Laibon asked again, this time with his voice raised a little.

Samuel knelt down slowly on his left knee and in fear answered, "To the one true god."

The people cheered loudly.

The the last surviving chiefs, from the last age-set initiation, before the Shadow began its evil reign, approached. They could be made out by the blood mark on their foreheads and red chalk on their shoulders.

Olanana turned around and proclaimed: "My people! Prepare for the feast. The enemy of our lives, the living threat to our existence has been destroyed. Let the chiefs assemble tonight at the village square while I, the Laibon, prepare the conqueror for his initiation."

"Initiation?" Samuel whispered in disbelief. "Me? Initiation for what?" He looked up in dismay at his brother and finally understood what Caleb said earlier about taking the fun out of the surprise with regards to who kills the Shadow.

But Samuel felt no fun in this.

He's been alive for only a decade and throughout that time it was made clear to them how different and separate his family will always be to the whole tribe.

'Outcast!' they were once called, *'children spawned from the womb of division,'* the aged chiefs had remarked at the last purification ceremony. Now, he, an outcast, has been chosen to become head chief because it was from his hands the Shadow met its demise.

Samuel looked at Caleb, his eyes pleading with him to save him from this but Caleb looked back at him without a flinch.

He now understood what Caleb meant by the stone which the builders rejected. If Olanana couldn't kill him then, he reasoned he cannot now.

Caleb couldn't think of any better way to make the chiefs, the evil Laibon, and their entire tribe members stop the constant derision they pour out constantly on his family. But now Samuel will be head chief.

What better way to effect a change? Now an end will be put to the mockery and ostracism long-suffered by his kin. Once they survived the Shadow of the forest, he knew his brother will become the head chief of the ilingeetani, the senior warriors, according to the prophecy. Their father once said before, *'where the word of a king is there is power.'*

With power, Samuel will put things right.

He watched as women and children ran off in delight while a couple of men took the lion's body to prepare it for the feast. Though the lion will not be eaten by anyone in the tribe, it will be hung on many spears and skinned. The chiefs stood their watching a vivid twist of fate: the end of a great evil from the hands of the least expected.

"Now come with me young chief. Olanana slowly turned Samuel and led him away. Samuel shrugged from his touch and moved away from him.

Caleb acknowledged how Samuel looked at him like a sheep led to the slaughter and every fiber in his body wanted to stop his brother from going with Olanana, the Laibon.

"Refrain yourself!" Olanana said before Caleb even tried to intervene. "Don't waste your time. The custom requires the preparation for the chief's initiation."

Caleb hesitated as Olanana took Samuel away.

This time the hesitation came from within.

Since the last Eunoto ceremony, which is when warriors are initiated into the senior warriors' age set, the Osinkira, the designated Laibon's house, has been inhabited by Olanana and never visited by anyone. The mere thought of the many malevolent acts the Laibon had perpetrated frightened even the chiefs and warriors.

Now, his brother is on his way to the temple of doom and all he did was watch them leave. He could almost feel a hold on his spirit to let them go.

Out of all the reflections of both animate and inanimate objects the Sun would cast, the Shadow of the forest will no longer have one. Caleb knew this and slowly felt fear creep in at letting his brother go with another greater evil.

Olanana looked tall and brawny as he walked away. It seemed that the red wrappings that drooped over one shoulder burdened him as he walked. On his head was a round bead with a bird's feather sticking out on the left end. On each hand and foot were two beads. His bare legs look characteristically darker than any part of his face. It was said that he had the darkest foot soles in the village.

Rumors said he walked on hot coals in honor of Enkai during one of the needed rituals undertaken as the Laibon. Though his understanding rebelled against his resolve, a still small voice bade Caleb to let it be for now.

After walking on a small path that took them through shrubs and bushes, Olanana finally broke the silence by doing what he knew best.

Blot out poison.

"How do you feel to know you are to be the head chief who will lead the Tabora tribe into the next generation?"

"Unworthy!" Samuel answered, deflated.

"Probably your foul little mind does not comprehend the gift being bestowed on you when you're given the power to rule and do whatever you desire."

Samuel felt his inside twirl at Olanana's cold remark. It was true he understood why his brother let him go with this murderer. If he had only told Caleb what bothered him, he knew things would be different. Strange how he'd always felt to keep the secret that haunted him, more so now.

"Let me tell you something a lot of our tribesmen don't know. There was a prophecy a long time ago that someone, some child will be born into this region, '*another, but of the same,*' they said. He is destined to destroy and yet reform these lands."

Samuel couldn't get himself to look at him even when he kept quiet for a while.

"Personally, I abhor the idea of such a child and the prophecy borne by him. For who can destroy and yet reform? Who can destroy and yet reproduce the exact same thing?"

With every step they took, Samuel couldn't figure which was getting darker, the day, as the Sun began to turn in to rest, or Olanana's countenance. Samuel wondered if Olanana proposed a child evil because of a weird destiny to fulfill purpose, then to call him, the Laibon, evil, is an understatement.

"It would have been difficult to identify this child if not for the other prophecies that followed." Olanana continued without paying attention to the child beside him. "My father once told me that a wind would blow from the unknown, bringing foreigners that would influence our entire way of life. He also talked about the introduction of a rival god claimed to be greater than all other gods. Ah!" Olanana sighed, "My thoughts about it then were that it was all ranting of a folly.

"When your father was first spotted in these lands, I thought he was the first of other foreigners to come. When the years passed and he raised a family, it dawned on me that he was to be the father of foreigners and aliens to our lands."

Stopping suddenly, he looked at Samuel who had stopped a few feet right behind him. "There is a secret I know you have been keeping that haunts you terribly. I see it always in your eyes."

Samuel summoned a little courage and looked up to meet his gaze. Hot tears rich flooded his eyes.

Seeing what he deemed as fear in the young boy's eyes, Olanana's face broadened in a smile. "To think that you would avenge your parents' death makes it all too clear to me I won't live long once you become the head of the senior warriors." Lifting his hands, he stopped Samuel from responding. Olanana was certainly enjoying what he saw in this boy's eyes.

"This secret," he continued, "I myself share with you that memorable night. Suffice to say that it's about time I saved you from the misery that has had its fill of you through the years."

The clouds suddenly assembled in what looked like seconds and darkness slowly crept over the land. The winds, ever so angry, beat on the trees, giving a swishing sound. Samuel's eyes moved about in fright.

Before visibility became the almost impossible, Samuel realized that they were on the plain-the same one where he killed the Shadow!

Not too far from him he could still make out the exact place where the Shadow had fallen before darkness took out sight. He could slowly feel the gloom take hold as day turned to night.

Fear coursed through his body in a shivering sensation when he saw Templers, Olanana's faithful servants emerge from the upraised dust caused by the wind. His bladder gave way as the same horrific feeling that coursed through him during his battle with the Shadow resurfaced.

All five Templers held a spear except one.

He walked slowly and stopped right beside the Laibon. Kamau was his name. He was the Laibon most trusted disciple. In his hand was the arrow that Samuel used to kill the Shadow of the forest.

For the second time today, Samuel felt like praying. From childhood, he had never actually believed in the gods of the lands, but had revered the One his father spoke of.

'Blessed is the nation whose God is the lord' Samuel closed his eyes as he recalled one of his father's soothing songs:

Eternal God, who rules on high . . . Control the legions of the sky . . . And guide the human will . . . I pray thee guard our native land . . . Our empire shelter with thine Hand . . . And keep us safe from ill.'

The words flowed so clearly to him for the first time and Samuel knelt down in the cold darkness and continued the song in his heart:

'Mid the din of war and passion . . . Guide the issues of the strife . . . Crown the right and duly fashion . . . from the chaos of ordered life.' He gazed up to the heavens and felt the natural drive of every creature to its Creator.

He finished the song:

'Stile power confounding . . . which the way of Truth defies. Amen.'

Samuel knew that at that moment, something had changed. The written victory on Olanana's face was replaced by fear.

The next moment he couldn't see anything.

"God!" Samuel uttered.

His choice had been made.

Now he believes in the unknown God of his father.

The same unidentified being that aided him against the Shadow; the same that embodies the obscurities of the air and walks on the wings of the wind!

"Kill him!" Olanana shouted. "Now!"

Kamau drew his bow the same time the trees began wrestling with the winds.

'The day is gently sinking to a close . . . fainter and yet more faint the Sunlight glows . . .'

Another of his father's songs again.

'O brightness of thy Father's glory, thou . . . Eternal light of lights, be with us now . . . Where thou art present, darkness cannot be . . . Midnight is glorious noon, O lord, with thee.'

Kamau was set to release. In an instant, the whole area became so dark Samuel could almost feel it edged against his skin.

The priest and the Templers couldn't see themselves but were able to see Samuel. It was like a small light somehow radiated around him incomprehensibly.

Even the darkness could not understand it.

The young child felt his legs come free. The whole night was almost like a dream. Samuel knew it was time to flee, and that he did, for hope had shed its gleam.

"Kill him, I say." enraged Olanana, a heave of desperation in his tone.

Kamau released the arrow, which flew straight ahead for Samuel and missed him by a few inches.

He ran into the bushes erratically.

"Aah-h-h! He's just a kid," Olanana cried. "Find him and bring me his heart. No one will sleep in these regions until I have that infidel's heart hanging on my wall." He watched the Templers leave in a hurry as his hands shook on the beads around his neck, eyes as cold as ever.

2

The young lions roar after their pray and seek their food from God;
Rise up O creature and bid your master's call.

Words whispered by the unseen were alone enough to raise a resting lion far in the forest and soon, it was in the bushes running with strong majestic. The night was cool and the wind brushed over its rich fur so strongly, its eyes glowed in the dark. Within minutes, it was closing in on a young boy running hysterically through the forest.

Samuel gasped in fear with the sound of incoming warriors in quest for his blood. His breathing got heavier as strength left him. The fact that the Templers were closing in on him was enough to stop his heart.

His eyes briefly caught the movement of something not to far away from him.

It was like a dream to him when he saw the glimpse of a lion moving in on him, its resemblance, like the Shadow. With long fast strides it narrowed the distance between them.

Unable to catch his breath, he ran as fast as he could, moving through the throbbing bushes and swaying tree branches. The forests parted way behind him and he felt the lion edge closer. That alone knocked the wind out of him.

Turning to duck a tree branch, his feet caught its root and he lost his footings. Samuel hit the floor hard.

The lion stood over him and the night stilled itself.

*   *   *

Kimathi hunted all day to make a kill and bring home some meat for his wife, but now, with the sudden darkness engulfing the forest, he needed to head back to the village.

Why was he here anyway, he wondered. Rarely do anyone hunt alone. Something else always drew him away from his tribesmen. Unknown to him, the village was at that moment, getting ready for the feast and the initiation of his grandchild.

His mind couldn't stop recalling when he disowned his own daughter after she abandoned her tribe to cling to a foreigner. She got married to a man who, without restriction, opened his foul mouth to declare the land's norms vain and obsolete.

Wearied by memory, tears welled up in his eyes as he remembered his once beloved daughter. He had taken concubines to bear him more children after his wife couldn't bear more. With every damsel he took, none had been able to bear a singe child. Maybe that's why Loiyan was special to him since she was the only seed of his.

But he knew it was way beyond that. Loiyan was always free-spirited and lovely. She was adventurous and inquisitive, too inquisitive, to say the least. He would come home after hunting with the warriors only to find out his daughter had wandered off. She could be overbearing at times with too much questions loose on her lips. Sometimes she would run off and head straight for the forest. He could still picture her face. His daughter always said:

"*I want to know who's behind all this.*"

He asked her once who was behind what, and she replied him, "*Nature, Father. Nature!*"

He told her numerous times it was Enkai, the god who manifested in many forms, that was behind everything. She would respond by saying, "*then I might as well find out what form our great god is today, right?*"

Kimathi would go looking for her as she ventured to places culturally unfit for a female. Recalling still caused him so much pain.

Growing up wasn't easy for her. No one caught her fancy.

Nothing ever did.

Loiyan stopped heeding his words until one-day she came home, somewhat quiet and illuminated. At the age of fifteen, her countenance changed. She looked like she just stumbled on the secret doors to the treasury of wisdom and had drawn the waters of understanding.

The village tongue soon wagged about a stranger in their lands. He couldn't have been from these regions, for he dressed different, talked different and looked different. No one was to commune with him after his voiced disregard for the land's beliefs by merely bringing a different news about another god.

Meeting with the senior warriors one day, he was informed that his daughter had been seen with the stranger. That alone scorched him more than the blazing Sun could. His hands washed over his skinny head and then slide down his red tunic. Kimathi's bow rested on his back, secured on his left shoulder.

He could feel a strong bitter taste creep into his mouth as he stared into the night in disgust. That clouded, deranged man took the only treasure he had.

'*Take your chicks under your wings,*' a local proverb said, *'for the eagle plunders where it has not sown.*' But in this case, it seemed the chick itself suddenly grew wings and flew away with the eagle.

"Enough of regrets" he said into the night. "I better head back."

Kimathi turned to leave and walked a few meters. He stopped dead on his tracks. He sighted a squirrel teething into a nutshell. Thanks to the moonlight that framed a silhouette of it.

"Alas! I know that the saying is true" he whispered. *"At your wits end, look again. There lies your treasure. As strength becomes weakness, try again! There lies your strength's measure."*

The winds caressed the branches of the ever-green trees. Kimathi drew his arrow to aim at the barely visible life form.

The power of volition was suddenly bestowed on the squirrel, for it immediately looked down at him and then launched onto another tree, the arrow missing it by an inch.

"Ha! I will get you tonight. Be it my last kill, you are mine for the taking."

Kimathi cried out as he ran after the flying squirrel as it made way through the trees. He felt a new wave of strength surge through him with speed as he glanced up continuously at the animal gliding with a touch of simplicity and perfection.

"Caleb, it's been quite a while since Samuel followed the priest to his shrine for preparation." Caleb's last sibling remarked. "I'm scared. What could be taken so long? You know how insanity has been attributed to Olanana that moves him to edges beyond reason. I've heard he's inhuman and that he killed his father and that . . ."

"Oh please, Lydia. Stop been so dramatic." Caleb interrupted his sister.

"But what if his intent is to kill Samuel? What if . . . oh lord! I don't want Samuel to die, Caleb."

"Enough, Loiyan. I'll go to the shrine to see what might be keeping them so long, if that will make you calm down." He turned away from her and blamed himself for being so stupid to let his brother go with that evil priest. "I swear if Samuel misses to draw one breath into his nostrils, Olanana will surely pay with his life." The rising anger in his heart choked him.

Loiyan rushed to his legs and knelt down. "Oh brother, it's forbidden to visit the shrine without the summons of the Laibon himself. You know that. Everyone does."

"Then what do you suggest? That I leave him to the hands of that evil man? I can't do that." Looking at the way Loiyan held his leg tightly, with tears streaming down her face, compassion gripped his heart. He drew her up and carried her with his left arm like a baby. "Don't worry. I promise, I'll return with Samuel. Stay here and be ready for the initiation, for without a doubt, one has been chosen to be the first to be initiated into the last age set, and that I seek. Remember always that at all times, grace and peace."

"You grew to know them well. I didn't." Loiyan said sniffing.

"Our parents wished us well, Loiyan. Don't blame them for not being here. If you want to know them, read their parchments. I'll teach you." He dropped her gently and turned to make way to the shrine.

"How will that help me, Caleb?"

"Because all their life was lived according to it." Caleb said without looking back.

"Promises. I've had enough of them. Always something they said, or what they read. I wish I'd known them," she said to herself as her brother reduced in height and soon was out of sight.

Lydia remembered her grandmother's words: "if you want to know your parents, then you better know their god. All they said and did was from the parchment and believe me child, it radiated from them always."

Then, she didn't understand, and now, at the age of six, she still didn't. All alone, in their improvised home from the ruins of the fire that claimed their parent's life, the night seemed cool and peaceful. She stepped outside and beheld the sight of the sky-like a blanket spread to the very ends of the earth, where sight goes no further.

Lydia riveted in the rich blue deepness of it and foolishly reached out her hand to feel it. The winds blew gently over her red covering and did little to protect her skin underneath from the chill of the night. She felt light-headed from staring too long after the wind stopped sweeping the vegetation. The stars flickered ever so brightly as she turned away from it.

It seemed the night's beauty had administered changes to the surrounding. With a soothing wind, the trees afar off seemed to bow in procession to something.

Some deity, she thought.

When the winds stopped blowing, the trees became suddenly still. It seemed life had gone out of them. Filled with fear, she ran inside to take the parchments and head straight out to the village square where everyone would be waiting for what could be the possible end to their sufferings from the priest.

Running along the path to the square, Lydia felt like someone was following her. Every time she glanced back, her mind would play tricks on her and the fallen shadows of trees, contoured by the moonlight, slowly formed images running after her. By the time she got to the square, she was gasping for breath. She saw the chiefs gathered.

Unbelief written on their faces.

Or was it awe, she couldn't tell. They must be thinking that how could an outcast be crowned head of the last age set of the Tabora tribe? The chiefs still didn't approve and that got her scared for Samuel. Her bones could no longer support her from the run. She settled on the ground.

The dance began soon afterwards.

Male dancers stood in a row and made low grunting sounds with their throats and chests, each individual improvising new dance steps. Altogether, a wonderful, intricate, polyrhythmic song emerged. The grunting alone always seemed enchanting with the singers swaying back and forth. Too distraught to enjoy anything, she opened the parchment and foolishly tried reading the words with the moonlight.

3

But my enemies are lively, and they are strong;
and they that hate me wrongfully are multiplied

"There he is!"

One of the Templers had sighted the fallen body of Samuel. Kamau strode slowly towards the body and stood a few meters away, staring at the motionless frail body in the risen haze.

"Go." He commanded. "Bring him here."

The Templers ran towards to fetch the boy and could see that by every step they took, the haze blurred their vision all the more. The moonlight intruded the thickness of the night's darkness barely but didn't make through its doors.

Suddenly, a lion flew across swiftly, silently stopping them at their tracks. They couldn't see what had happened. It seemed every second stretched on like an hour. By a mere brush of wind, the haze cleared slightly to reveal one of them lying lifeless in the bushes upfront.

All sense was lost!

Naturally, they panicked!

The other three Templers trembled and drew back at the sight of such terror.

"Kamau, we can't go any further." One templer declared in obvious shudder. "You can fetch him yourself for all I care. I'm not taking a step further. This is where I draw the line."

Kamau walked up to him, watching fear creep into the eyes of the templer as he drew closer. "No." He replied, stopping right in front of him. "This is where I draw your life!" He lifted the spear in his hand and with a powerful thrust the templer's abdomen gave way in a pool of blood. Kamau broke the spear with a snap leaving an irretrievable piece inside.

A fatal wound.

Eyes shone in the night as others looked at him in horror.

"Now, if you two don't want to suffer the same fate, you had better cross that tree stump and bring that boy to me."

Sweat broke on their skins in the cool night. They turned to get the boy once more with caution and moved stealthily towards the stump. Their breaths weighed heavily on the atmosphere, worsening the haze. Their hearts drummed against their rib cage in rebellion to be let out. The haze seemed to thicken again with every step and one of them had his first leg already over the tree stump, where the young boy lay a few meters from.

Like an eagle descending on its prey with such great speed and swiftness, the evergreen forest parted way and judgment took its course.

The other templer stumbled back, shrieking in fear, to see what just transpired.

Another was still.

A frightful sound escaped his lungs again turning him around in flight. His eyes met the unfeeling ones of Kamau and in that cold gaze, he got the message.

If he plunged on, death awaited him, and if he receded, the same. With trembling hands, he embraced the inevitability of his fate. His mouth went dry as he said a prayer.

The templer took his spear, positioned it, and fell on it. He realized for the first time that he'd just made a choice since he came to serve the Laibon, and ironically, it was to end his life.

Kamau sighed to himself. Indeed a notable event had just taken place, which he couldn't deny. The handiwork of a god, it seemed. He walked towards the stump and knew he better not cross it for the safety of his life.

The haze cleared slowly and the lion, majestic in pace and stately in walk, stride out into the moonlight view.

Kamau couldn't move as the lion made a mark with its claws on the ground. It was a line drawn before the stump; a line stained with blood from the fallen Templers.

It denoted a warning.

Kamau understood that he cannot cross if he wanted to live. Nodding in understanding, he slowly turned resignedly from the fierce looking lion and took the path used to track the boy.

Having done its charge, the lion roared into the night with a loud sound that stirred Samuel. His eyelids opened slightly, unable to see clearly. The lion roared again as he thudded back to forgetfulness.

* * *

A twig snapped along a path in another part of the forest. Caleb drew nearer to the clearing that revealed the Osinkira, the Laibon's shrine. His heart raced at the feeling of evil around him. The feeling choked him until he was short of breath. Caleb decided to say a prayer his father taught him in times of helplessness.

> *As a little child relies; on a care beyond its own, knows it's neither strong nor wise, fears to stir a step alone. Let me thus with thee abide with thee on my side—my Father, Guard and Guide.*

Standing before the shrine, he couldn't make anything of it. The shifting shadows replaced strength with fear, and courage with trepidation.

Carried along by the wings of the wind, a message of comfort came to him from memories past.

> *In heavenly love abiding; no change my heart shall fear*
> *And safe is such confounding, for nothing changes here.*
> *The storm may roar around me; my heart may low be laid.*
> *But God is around about me, and can I be dismayed?*

Olanana, the Laibon, emerged from the temple and stood at the entrance. Caleb would have sworn that an ogre hid behind the Laibon's skin. Caleb noticed how the Laibon's eyes etched darkly than the surrounding. On his hand rested the scepter of the gods passed down the priesthood lineage. Olanana's deportment denied the years he'd been alive. The rich red garb was secured by the side and beads, stained in animal's blood wound round his ankles and wrists.

"You know the law that holds this place unseen by any man unless summoned by me, still you dare to trespass this holy grounds."

"No god gave such law." Caleb replied with disregard. "You did and you know orders from cowards do not suffice enough for obedience. Now, where is my brother?"

"You defy me outcast and require your brother from me? You pride yourself."

"You call this play holy? This place holds nothing close to anything sacred. This was created by you. You have always nurtured your will and your heart is turned away from anything. I ask again. Where is my brother?"

Kamau emerged from the east wing and approached the priest. After a few exchanged words, he looked at Caleb coldly, the taste for blood written on his face.

"Ah!" Olanana spoke up after listening to what Kamau said. "You seek the one whose blood the ground has taken; the flesh of whom the king of the pride has devoured. I hold no brother of yours in this place. Seek the beast that fed on its deserved prey, and dig the ground, if you can draw from the wells of sand, your brother's blood." With that Kamau and Olanana laughed in ridicule.

Rage consumed every sense of reason from Caleb. Nothing will feel good now as ending the tyranny Olanana plague their village with but he remembered his father's words. Words so strong that stopped him from blindly attacking these two wretched men who bear no regard for human life.

Samuel, my beloved brother, you cannot be dead, his heart broke in pain. I shouldn't have left you. His eyes well up in tears. Why should he hold back when they claim to have killed his brother? However, his heart held him back. His father's words came back strong with rebuke.

It's sometimes funny how the words of parents make no sense when first heard, only to come handy later in life, especially in times of life and death situations. One could have sworn that it will be lost in oblivion as soon as it leaves their lips but somehow, it really is strung to memory, waiting for the right time to mean the world.

Caleb he recited his father's words to himself, in a whisper:

Peace! Perfect peace! In this dark world of sin? The blood of the Messiah whispers peace within.
Peace! Perfect peace! With sorrows surging round? On Messiah's bosom, nought but calm is found. Peace! Perfect peace! With loved ones far away? In the Messiah's keeping, we are safe, safe, and they.

"You won't live long Olanana. By Sunrise, you shall no longer be alive to see the shining light the Sun gives on both the just and the unjust." Caleb prophesied.

Surprised at the regained calm on Caleb's face, Olanana felt discomfited.

Kamau started towards him who so boldly flout his master but was stopped by Olanana's hand before he even took another step forward. Looking up at Olanana, eyes contact sufficed, for the moment and he stepped back in waiting.

Caleb turned to leave. "Come to the village square without my brother, oh high and priestly one," he declared, "and I'll rob you of the dawn. You should know death, the hasty one, the one you have damned many to, for it draws near. And this time, closer to you." He walked away into the night, knowing in his heart he had to wait. The same peace that kept him when Olanana led his brother away, kept him still even when he just got told that his brother is dead. No one could have survived the Shadow of the forest only to be killed shortly. God has a plan, he thought. Something budded under His sleeves and Caleb just had to wait a little while.

One thing is for sure, Samuel is still alive. He will hold on to that. He must!

No matter how hard it is to dwell on evidence of things unseen.

Imaginary visions kept unfolding before Lydia's eyes. She finally gave up trying to catch a glimpse of his brothers returning to the village. It's been quite a while since Caleb went for Samuel. She was beginning to worry. Looking up one more time, she saw a figure again, not too far away, approaching.

Caleb.

With chin held high, Loiyan ran to him and held onto him. "What of Samuel. Where is he?" she asked.

No response came from Caleb as his eyes roamed about the square.

Loiyan looked up at him. She noticed his gaze view beyond the environs; the mud houses and thatched huts; earthen pots culturally positioned at the right hand side of where the chiefs sit.

Caleb's eyes looked on beyond to the darkness that hold the trees in captivity. The covering, the trees provided, marked the security nature affords for the village. With a sigh, he stared at the tribesmen dancing already. He lowered himself and carried his sister in his arms. When Loiyan shook his shoulder, he realized his sister must have asked the same question many times.

"Caleb, you are scaring me. Where is Samuel? What happened at the shrine?"

"I'm sorry Loiyan". He apologized.

The whole place suddenly looked transient and foreign to him. His eyes wandered again and he couldn't understand why he was so troubled inside. His head went light and his heart slowed in pace. The veins in his hands sank in, though his sister's weight burdened on his arms. Caleb could feel the cold sensation coursing through his vessels down to his feet.

"Lydia, this world is nothing! Vanity is its treasures. Vain are its wisdoms. Loss is its riches; sorrow beyond, its joys. Woe to the man who seeks pleasure in its moments; agony it is to the soul who enslaves his entirety for the search of its gold; mischief it is to the lad who gathers its thorns as friends; and death, to the life that finds contentment in its measures.

"Don't you see how the grave is for the man who bows before its idols? Dishonest weights and measures are evil to the Lord." He let her down slowly. "Don't you see? The end of it all is nothing. Woe be to the man who gains the world and yet losses his soul."

Lydia looked at his brother in awe. Caleb obviously didn't know he had spoken loud enough, for everyone heard him, and with such authority. The dancing slowed to a stop.

They all stared at him, puzzled. Mothers held their young children closely as a black bird flew across the moonlight.

Then, another bird.

The oldest chief got up from where the other chiefs and ilkiliyani, the junior warriors, were seated. His body leaned heavily on the wooden stick that aided his movements.

"An omen!" He whispered. Death, it seemed, will strike not once but twice before the night is gone.

Wails of the grasses mounted at the intrusions of what sounded as probably the smallest of all creatures or rodents, possibly. But a snap was enough to signal the coming of men. Not too far from where Lydia met Caleb, the Laibon and three Templers emerged heading straight for the village square. The last two templers, always stationed by the Osinkira watching the Laibon's dwelling place, and the third warrior, Kamau.

Caleb turned slowly and the moonlight lit up his eyes. Olanana paused for a moment as he gazed into the fury that burned in Caleb's eyes. He surprisingly felt a cold shiver run through his spine, announcing fear to every cell of his tissues; unearthing cowardice under every tissue of his organs and unmasking defeat that cramped every organ of his body.

Kamau sensed hesitation on his master's part and was filled with disgust. He recognized frailty in him. If asked, the man who has the gods' ears must not be afraid of anything but himself.

But no one asked him.

He asked himself.

"It's almost time!" Kamau whispered to himself, "I will soon be the Laibon."

4

Were I to count them, they would outnumber the grains of sand.
But am safe, for when I awake, I am still holding your hand.

Samuel stirred from slumber. He felt a soft nudge at his side.

Arise . . . quickly.

He looked around trying to recall everything. Holding his head that felt queasy, everything came back to him in quick flashes. Thinking he couldn't bear this sudden jolt of memory recovery, Samuel then felt caught up in a trance. He drifted in space in defiance of gravity. His father floated past him, a smile spread across his face. His mother followed. Her beautiful smile made him crave for her embrace.

Then Caleb.

Caleb waved and drifted away into the light that filled everywhere without him knowing.

"Caleb!"

He opened his eyes.

Caleb . . .

Oh . . . no . . .

Getting up quickly, he started towards the village and didn't notice the lion feasting, few feets away from him. Panic drove him all the way; through the trees, he ran as fast as he could. Not because of the scary darkness that loomed all over; neither was it for the lion that declined from pursuit, but for a lingering feeling of being behind time; the urge to stop what is meant to be!

* * *

The village square hummed silence.

All eyes fell on Olanana as he took his seat.

The chiefs stood up in honor of him, though their faces revealed opposite.

Caleb set his sister down on her legs and gently strokes her cheek before turning to face the Laibon. He walked up and stopped in front of Olanana.

The night seemed frozen in time as everything watched in expectation of the unknown. All three Templers stood behind the exalted throne of their priest, ready to protect his life with theirs.

Olanana fondled with the weighty beads around his neck. He lifted his face and stared coldly at Caleb in a battle stance.

"We came here to witness the last age-set initiation of a warrior-chief." Caleb said loud enough for all to hear. "The one who killed the Shadow of the forest."

One of the chiefs stood up to address the priest. "And where is this one?"

Displeased at the chief, Olanana nodded his head to Kamau, and he stepped out from his side.

In one swift move, the chief's back was on the floor holding the spear thrown by kamau that stuck out of his belly. Everyone sighed and parents held their children closer to blind them from seeing.

"You will not be Lord of this land Olanana if you don't bring out my brother this instant." Caleb choked on his words as he fought the rage inside to control himself from launching straight at Kamau for what he just did. Kamau must pay for what he did, striking a defenseless chief. His primary target still remains unchanged.

He'll deal with Kamau later.

"We all thought the menace of these lands was the Shadow but now we know better. The evil force to be contended with here is you. It has always been. And will always be."

Olanana looked at him for a moment before responding. "And what will you do about it? No one can stop me from being Lord. Not even you." His laughter resounded into the night.

"Fight me then, Olanana. If you're sure of your priesthood, then you would know the outcome of our fight wouldn't you? How can the priest of Enkai fall to the hands of a commoner?" Caleb could see his words were taken well as he saw the muscles on Olanana's face cringe.

"A fool must not be answered, or you will be like him."

"Wise words Olanana, but even wiser, answer a fool according to his folly, or he'll be wise in his own conceit."

Kamau saw the best time to carry out his plans. "I will fight you. On my priest's behalf."

"My fight is not with you, Kamau. Though, you will pay for what you did, this is between Olanana and I."

"Why? Are you afraid to fight me, Caleb?" Kamau said derisively.

"No. The best way to kill a tree is to unearth its roots, not to cut off its branches."

An insult it was, yet with such profound truth. Kamau knew he had to find another reason to cause Caleb to fight with him as the priest slowly got up from his seat, a sign that denoted the challenge accepted.

"Well, I understand." Kamau pretended talking to himself. "I gave you the chance to redeem the crying blood of your brother as I took his life in my hands but you threw it away."

Caleb's expression changed instantly.

By the side, Lydia knelt down in tears at the words about his brother's demise.

"You lie." Caleb choked again between words. Tears came unstopped.

"Like you heard back at the shrine, the grounds drunk the very blood of that imp and he has been devoured by the king of the pride."

Olanana himself sat back stunned at the coldness that flowed from his most entrusted templer.

Caleb's left hand shook on his spear as he closed his eyes, reaching for some solace on his inside.

Where was the peace that kept him all day? Why does reason to hold back bear no weight to his grieving heart? He searched his mind to recall the wisely sayings of his father but found none.

"So be it."

Caleb announced the fight with those three words.

Kamau turned to stare briefly into the eyes of the Laibon.

Olanana noticed Kamau's eyes take a characteristic darkness.

Turning away, Kamau stepped right into the middle of the gathering. The heat of fear wasn't the only thing that stifled the night. Death is about to sting one of these men.

With Kamau swinging the spear straight for Caleb's throat, the fight began.

Caleb moved his head back quickly before the spear could draw blood from him, and took two steps back in a defensive stance.

Lydia gasped for breath. She realized she could end up losing her two brothers before the day ended. At such a young age, when many girls are found with their mothers or grandmothers, she bore so much pain that collapsed her shoulders. No one needed to tell her to grow up. She looked around to see if she can catch a glimpse of her grandfather, Kimathi.

Lydia didn't even think, for one second, to see her grandmother after she became bedridden. But there she stood; her grandmother, Esiankiki, a name that means young maiden. She was the most beautiful of the Tabora tribe at one point.

Though it was alright for married maidens to have sexual affairs with any man of the same age set, she was the only one known to have been faithful to her husband. This drove warriors of the same age set, at various points, to try to defile her by forcing their will on her and each time her husband, Kimathi, would always come to save her.

It was a practice for men to wrestle with themselves to get near the bull's skin ritual. This ritual permits warriors to eat, by themselves, meat specially cooked with firewood by the women of their age set. It was done to see if any woman have been unfaithful to the age set and have had sexual relations with another age set warrior. However, many warriors, within the age set, wrestled with Kimathi for the sole reason to lay with his wife, Esiankiki, and no warrior ever defeated him.

The women normally wear jewelry made of beads on their wrists, legs, necks, and ears and sounds could be heard as the beads beat on one another in movement. When it came to Esiankiki, her sound was unique. There was a way in which she moved that generated a sound peculiar to her alone. So whenever a maiden passed by, anyone could tell if it was Esiankiki or not.

The title as the loveliest of the tribe was taken by her only child, Loiyan. The Laibon at the time, Olanana's father, betrothed Loiyan to his son in honor of their god, Enkai.

Esiankiki and her husband, Kimathi, tried numerous times to bear other children but to no avail. When her daughter betrayed her tribe and married the foreigner, she knew it was going to be the beginning of sorrows. The problems that ensued afterwards, coupled with the loss of her daughter, led up to her being bedridden for years.

Now, here she stands, watching her full grown grandson in battle for his life. She opened her arms as Lydia ran into them in sobs. Esiankiki couldn't stop the tears from flowing.

She hasn't seen her grandchildren after Kimathi forbade her.

At the center of the square, a battle raged. Kamau smiled, knowing that earlier move caught Caleb by surprise. Swinging his spear from one hand to another, Kamau stepped closer. He went straight for his opponent's abdomen.

Caleb cracked his spear against Kamau's, to block that move as fast withdrawal saw the spear coming back again for his neck. He moved back in two steps, jerking his head to the right and the left to evade deadly attacks from Kamau.

Kamau went again for his abdomen but Caleb brought his spear down against his, swinging it down and pinning it to the floor.

Kamau quickly made a round turn, kicking Caleb by the side.

The Laibon watched carefully. This time in fear of Kamau and the evil that resonated from him. His most trusted templer moved with such uncharacteristic speed and skill that baffled not only him but everyone watching. Olanana knew that soon enough, Caleb will not be able to hold up to the attacks.

The tribe acknowledged Caleb as a strong wrestler and a skilled spear man. His grandfather, Kimathi, taught him a lot about the art of wrestling and the use of the spear and arrow. This was before the senior warriors' age set forbade him to see them any more. Kimathi did not approve of the union of his daughter and the foreigner but he loved his grandchildren and never held back anything from them.

It all changed at a season when the Emuratare, which is the circumcision initiation for young males, is held. Shortly before Sunrise, young boys that are to be circumcised, stand outside the night and receive a cold shower for purification. They are circumcised by a qualified warrior and at the time it was Kimathi, Caleb's grandfather. When all the boys are circumcised, gifts of cattle are given to them by family members.

During the celebration, Caleb approached his grandfather for circumcision. Circumcision remains the most crucial rite of passage into the tribe. The whole celebration went dead as soon as Caleb came forward. Kimathi hesitated for a while before approaching his grandson in order to circumcise him. The surviving ilingeetani, which are the senior warriors, stopped him halfway before he got to Caleb. They forbade him from ever seeing him or his other grandchildren again if he still wanted to be the part of the age set.

Caleb's life strained with struggles between him and his tribe and it felt like his fight presently with Kamau and the Laibon were also with the whole tribe. His right arm didn't help after suffering the scratch from the Shadow of the forest. He willed his spear with his left hand. Somehow, he had forgotten about the pain until he changed the spear to his right and cracked it against Kamau's.

Caleb rolled away fast before Kamau's spear freed his bowels. The air suddenly felt cold against his skin and the winds, so soothing, came from nowhere, brushing him over in a gentle caress. The moon seemed to claim again the Sun's rays for its own and light up the square in a dawn fashion.

Olanana, the Laibon, noticed the sudden change of the atmosphere. He swore to himself for having seen this happen before.

Somewhere! Not too long ago!

His mind worked fast to recall where exactly. Images of prior events flashed in his mind.

Olanana recalled staring at Samuel as he knelt down in fear but by a sudden rush of wind, Samuel stood up in confidence. When darkness covered the plains and Samuel radiated somehow in a simple light of a somewhat, unknown source, Olanana felt the touch of the supernatural at play.

And now, in this place, the same thing just happened!

Caleb looked at first outwitted and outmatched but now Olanana knew that power had just changed hands. A message had been delivered by the one who walks on the wings of the wind.

Caleb threw his spear down and waited for Kamau to attack.

Everyone stare in disbelief!

The confidence on Kamau's face slowly slipped away. He hesitated to attack and pretended to look calm. He is still at the advantage but couldn't seem to bring himself to take it. While Caleb defended his attack he realized that his right arm was wounded.

But seeing Caleb drop the spear suddenly sent ripples on calm waters.

Kamau remembered when his age set went out into the grasslands to sport and sometimes see Kimathi, the most powerful warrior of the tribe, train Caleb. After a while, word was going round his age set that no one could defeat Caleb.

The ilkiliyani, which are the junior warriors, found reason to hunt and venture on to the grasslands just to witness Kimathi train Caleb. Sometimes, when they spot Caleb training alone, they would surround him and challenge him to a one on one. Each time, Caleb would come out the winner, defeating any one of the ilkiliyani who dared him to a challenge.

Caleb wore his grandfather's skin on his back. Every time one challenged him to a face off, Caleb would decline always and only fought when he was surrounded or without choice. However, Kamau never speared nor wrestled with Caleb until now. The ilkiliyani may have speared him only to see who was stronger but he held on to the cold will in his heart to kill him. It was good he had prepared himself always for this encounter. He watched and studied Caleb close during training.

One thing was certain and undeniable.

The fact that he couldn't defeat Caleb was as real to him then as the head on his shoulders. That's why he sought the spirits. That's why he ended up at the Osinkira: to serve the gods and acquire their powers. The spirits of Enkai lived in him now and he knew it.

His body quivers with the life of divinity. Legions of ancestral spirits thrive in him. It took a while before he opened the gateway into his soul to invite the spirits in and like tonight, he felt possessed with power.

"Caleb." Lydia cried. "What are you doing?"

No answer came!

For a while the village stood transfixed.

Kamau convinced himself to attack but the Laibon knew that to attack Caleb now would be a mistake.

* * *

Kimathi tried numerous times to shoot the flying squirrel down with his arrow, missing every time. The squirrel launched itself to another tree constantly. He should be in the village with his homebound wife, especially now, when it's the purification ceremony.

The purification ceremony!

It skipped his mind completely. "I have to get back to the village." He said to himself. The winds wisped by, beating on the trees. Rainy season is indeed coming. Kimathi looked around in the dark and realized that the surrounding was familiar. He must be close to the village. He must have chased that damn squirrel to this place.

Kimathi watch the squirrel launch onto another tree and quickly checked his loin's cloth only to find two arrows left.

"May Enkai help me." He prayed as he took one out, placing it gently on the middle of the bow. He took his ground and leaned forward slightly to aim well. Kimathi hope to get it this time. The arrow will drop few meters away from him, pinning the squirrel down in the shrubs. Taking a step forward, the squirrel looked back at him before taking another jump to another tree.

"Ah!" he exclaimed. He should have been more observant. Sounds of crickets echoed around him.

Kimathi could hear a certain movement not too far from him.

There was a beast slithering by his legs. Stopping any kind of movement, he knew he had to be still, for the snake to move along. It felt like a small one. *The smallest are the most venomous,* he knows from experience. He waited a little while longer for the serpent to move.

Kimathi let out his long-held breath and looked up to see that the squirrel was no longer on the tree in front of him.

"Now, I have to go home empty handed."

Something fell on the ground beneath another tree close by. He looked up and spied the squirrel on a large branch. Without keeping his cool he pulled out an arrow, aimed and released.

"Gods of my ancestors! How could I miss?" He said, tired. He followed the squirrel as it made way through the trees. He later stopped to catch his breath. The squirrel eased off in flight and stopped on a tree branch. Taking out the last arrow, he said a prayer: "My last arrow. Please don't fail me now. Dear gods, bless me this night with this spoil." He kept on repeating to himself.

Missing again, his belly quivered in protest. He realized he had gone without food all day. The squirrel settled on a lower branch of a tree. He could see the village from here and from the looks, the tribe is gathered at the square, probably dancing and feasting.

"How I'm I going to go home to my wife like this?" he thought to himself. "Dear gods, why do you mock me this way?" His wife would have to do with whatever the feast provided. He looked at the animal that gave him the chase all night for one last time before deciding to head back to the village.

As soon as he turned Kimathi noticed, to his right, glow bugs swarming round the lower region of a tree trunk. He stepped closer and gave a sigh.

"By the gods!" it's an arrow.

He pulled it from the tree trunk and noticed dried blood stains at its tip. "The gods must have provided me with this arrow." He thought loud.

Kimathi held the arrow and glared at it in awe, not knowing the journey this same arrow had gone through all day: from the heart of a lion, to the pursuit of his grandson's life!

Kimathi had no idea that this was the arrow that carried the blood of the Shadow of the forest.

* * *

Samuel was short of breath as he neared the village. He sensed his closeness to the clearing now. The first thing to do was to make sure his brother is alright and then his little sister.

No matter how hard he tried, Samuel couldn't get that image from his head throughout his run to the village; the image of his father, mother and brother waving at him. He noticed scratches across his arms from the shrubs and tree branches he brushed and rushed past on his way.

Something strange happened when he lost consciousness. There was blood around him when he got up and was it a lion he saw when he stirred in slumber? The same lion he saw chasing him in the darkness? Was it a different lion or was it the Shadow? The questions kept coming and he tried to stop himself from insanity. Holding his head, he stopped walking for a while, trying to slow down his breathing. Hands to his sides, he leaned over to calm his heart from reaping his rib cage.

* * *

Not too far away, Kamau circled Samuel's brother, in hesitation. Why did he drop his spear, he thought to himself. He came to stop in front of him and thrust his spear towards Caleb.

Caleb side-stepped to the right, brought forward his left leg to step closer to Kamau and went in for the close line in such a quick fashion Kamau was caught off guard. He stepped back to a waiting stance as Kamau coughed.

Kamau held his neck and sat up on the square ground. He stood up again and watched his opponent in such a relaxed pose. What is all this? He wondered. He moved to Caleb's behind and moved in to strike from behind.

Caleb turned fast enough to evade the back attack and caught Kamau's arm, thrusting him forward. He followed him and used his legs to knock Kamau to the ground. Only this time he caught Kamau's head and trapped it beneath his left biceps before his back hit the ground.

The spear fell from Kamau's hand and he began struggling for breathe. He knew with one quick move, Caleb could snap his head. His head was behind Caleb while his neck downward struggled up front.

"My bone is not with you Kamau." Caleb spoke for only him to hear. "The one responsible for all this is seated over there and that's the person that should be in your position right now."

Kamau tried to struggle but it was no use. The grip was firm and unbreakable. His face paled from insufficient air.

"Do you understand?" Caleb whispered.

Kamau answered with a cough.

"My brother is alive. Yes?"

Kamau confirmed with a cough.

The priest watched Caleb drop Kamau to the floor and grimaced, knowing that Caleb intended not to finish anyone except him. Looking into that face, he held the sacred scepter in his hands and squeezed tightly.

Olanana brought the scepter with him with the intention to will its power when needed. His father, the former Laibon warned him about using the scepter.

It is said that the first Laibon to exist was found as a baby in the forest by two warriors. He was the only one able to use the power found within the scepter, believed to wield the rain to fall, and heal, and see into the future.

Everyone gasped as Olanana raised the scepter. After the first Laibon, the scepter was always kept at the Osinkira. After a while, a larger percentage of the tribe believed it to be a myth and that it never actually existed. But here it was, in the hands of the Laibon. Even after years of the tales being passed down, the scepter still caught the reflection of the moonlight and light briefly travelled down its sides in a sparkle.

Kamau continued coughing. He rubbed his neck readily and noticed the priest stand up to accept Caleb's challenge. Hatred for Caleb coursed through him like punctured bile in his system. While Caleb walked forward to face the Laibon Kamau picked up his fallen spear. With Caleb's back to him, Kamau thrust it right into Caleb's back.

"Nooooo!"

Samuel shouted, appearing from behind a hut only to witness his world end before him.

The priest looked stunned to see Samuel, after been prior informed that the young boy was dead by Kamau.

Lydia cried out loud.

Caleb fell to the ground.

Lydia runs to him, leaving her grandmother, Esiankiki shocked again by another loss.

Samuel followed. He kneels down beside him with Lydia. No time for her to welcome Samuel alive.

Kamau laughed out loud in relish of his slyness.

Tears flowed freely from many as they watched. The chiefs all sighed in anguish, knowing that there isn't anyone bold enough to challenge the Laibon the way Caleb did.

Lydia stopped crying and held his fallen brother by the red tunic, rocking him back and forth with silent whispers of prayer escaping her mouth. She brought out the parchment.

Caleb looked up at both of them, smiling stiffly. He raised his hands to touch Samuel's cheek and instructed him to come back for their sister.

Samuel didn't understand what he meant but was more taken aback by the peace in his brother's eyes.

Caleb's lungs collapsed slowly out of blood loss and in one brief instant, Samuel knew his brother had gone to join his parents.

Just like in his vision.

Olanana, the Laibon, knew that there was one more killing needed to be done. He stared right into the face of the boy he wanted dead more than anything. As the priest, he knew he was meant to bless the initiation of this lad as the head of the ilingeetani.

Samuel stood up and looked down at his blood stained hands.

The priest took a step closer to him.

* * *

At the same time, Kimathi pulled at the bow with all his strength. His utmost intention is to go home with the squirrel that evaded him all night. He pulled the bow with so much force, stretching it to its limit. The squirrel sat on the lowest branch of a tree, watching and waiting.

He released the arrow with such force. The squirrel takes a dive to the nearby bushes. The arrow came alive again, for the second time today.

This time the arrow cut through the air for one destination: the village square.

The Laibon stood right before Samuel with the murdering intent all written in his face. He would have to strike the child down in front of everyone.

The arrow descended and struck him from behind, straight to the heart and the scepter went up from his hands into the air.

Shadows of evil came from nowhere and went straight for Kamau as he caught the scepter in his hands. It seemed he'd just been possessed ten times more by evil than his master was. The legend behind the scepter is that anyone who wielded the scepter will receive double portion of the ancestral spirits from Enkai.

Time lost its essence.

Everyone watched Olanana go down in death by one swift arrow plunge, and Kamau take control by one quick catch of the scepter.

After a few jerks, Olanana's body went silent on the ground. The ilingeetani watched with a stern look on their faces in awe of what just transpired.

Kamau pointed the scepter towards the other Templers and they knelt down to him in fear. With that act, the ilingeetani all knew that darker days are yet to come if Kamau reigns as the new Laibon.

One of the chiefs looked at the boy standing beside his brother's body, wondering to himself. There must be something about this boy that made Olanana want him dead so badly. Without thinking, he ran towards Samuel, took his hands and ran away with him.

A templer threw his spear for Kamau, the new Laibon. Kamau caught it and turned immediately. He took two steps forward and threw the spear in his hands at Samuel.

Lydia cried out for Samuel. The chief turned around and placed himself in the path of the spear.

Samuel watched him fall to the ground. He looked at his sister in tears.

"Go, Samuel. Go." Lydia whispered.

Samuel turned and ran into the forest.

"Keep on running boy." Kamau's voice echoed like the voice of a legion. "I'll let you live for now. Gather the years and strength you need for your sister's sake."

Samuel stopped at the sound of that.

"You know what will happen if you don't return for her at the turn of a decade?"

Samuel knew exactly!

The laws of the tribe commands a girl be circumcised and then she is declared engaged or free to marry. Her hand can be taken by her betrothed or the best suitor afterwards. He realized that Kamau intended to have her sister and if she refused, Kamau will not hesitate to make her a sacrificial example to anyone who disobeyed him, an act Kamau will take joy in doing.

He knew Kamau just gave him ten years to return and Lydia was six years already. Samuel knelt down in the bushes and made a vow saying:

"Oh god of my father! If you will be with me, and keep me in this way that I go, and will give me meat to eat and the strength that I need to bind this strongman, so that I come again to this land in peace; then shall the lord be my god; and this land shall be the lord's land and my whole life shall be in service of thee."

And so began Samuel to journey through the forest to find all the strength he needed to return and deliver his sister. The clouds heard his tears running down his cheeks as he made way through the bushes and the heavens opened in weeping. The waters from above came pouring down heavily.

His heart felt marked with scars of unbearable pain. What will he do? How will he return back for his sister? He had nothing with him. It was hard to find meat when his brother was around. Now, he had no idea of how to feed.

Life is full of sorrows, he thought to himself. Now he has to take his place among the animals. He could still hear Kamau's laughter ringing in his ears. It played in his heart and mind like a resounding echo reverberating from the mountains. At one point, he held his pounding head to ease out the noise within. Hatred burned his eyes and dried up the uncontrollable tears.

Samuel stopped beneath a tree to rest. He couldn't see the skies clearly from his resting place, because the trees formed coverings all over. Kamau's face remained carved onto his heart at the robbing of his blood-stained hands. He had been hunted by the face of Olanana, the former Laibon, but now it was totally replaced by Kamau's.

He found a small clearing beneath a tree a few hours later and there he slumbered.

5

When I say, my bed shall comfort me;
my couch shall ease my complaints;
Then thou scarest me with dreams, and terrifest me through visions

Samuel was seriously troubled when he saw an arrow piercing a lion and immediately the same arrow flying past him.

Then, there was darkness.

He couldn't see anything for a while. It was like he was lost in a never-ending vacuum incapable of darkness. Suddenly, he was standing in front of Olanana. From nowhere, the same arrow flew straight for Olanana and pierced him from behind. Kamau's laughter echoed all around him and he held his head to block out the sound.

"I swear, I'll kill you Kamau," he shouted, at the point of hysteria.

You will kill no one.

He looked around to see who said that. There was nothing, only a small light shining. He thought it to be a glow bug but the light started coming closer and brighter. The light came to stop in front of him. The hairs on his bare skin stood up trembles.

Don't be afraid.

The light engulfed everywhere around him until his eyes hurt from its brilliance. Nothing on earth could be as white as this, he thought to himself. His mind couldn't fathom what could bear so much brightness. No words could describe it.

Its intensity felt more than the Sun but somehow, it didn't hurt his frail body as the Sun would.

In an instant, he was in a cave nurtured by the same light he couldn't point its source. There was a burial chamber and in it a body rapped in a clean linen cloth. Inexplicably, he could see through the cloth, the closed eyes of a man. The eyes opened and shone brightly.

It was the source!

The light was coming from the man.

He couldn't explain it.

Before his very eyes, the linen cloth went limp!

The body was no longer there!

He jumped back with a shout and woke up suddenly.

Breathing heavily, he realized he must have been dreaming. He turned his eyes to the right, and then to the left to check his surroundings. Samuel could feel his red tunic drenched with sweat.

The songbird sang so sweetly in the distance and the sound alone eased fear out of him as the Sun rose in the east.

A frog croaked nearby. A stream must be close by. He got up and kept on walking closer to where the croaking sound came from. Samuel soon stood before a stream mostly covered with fanciful shrubs growing on it. The Sun rise caused the water surface to glow in a display of colors.

His legs had already collected dew droplets from the bushes as he walked. He stepped into the stream and splashed water on his face. Samuel lowered his hands and still noticed traces of his brother's blood.

Burying his face in his hands, he left it there for a moment, weeping. He recalled the shining brilliance of the man's eyes in his dreams, piercing into his very soul.

Who was he? He wondered.

How did the cloths get to go limp all of a sudden?

Definitely, the man's body was no longer beneath it. The longing for a greater light stirred within him, even as the Sun rose brightly, with its rays cutting through the covering the trees provided. He could feel the Sun's warmth against the back of his hands but his inside felt dark like a moonless night.

Something blocked the Sun's rays for a brief instant and then moved away. He could hear the flapping of wings in a distance. A large bird must have flown past. Lowering down his hands from his face, he looked up and saw a large black bird above him. It circled a couple of times and descended towards him. Trapped within its claws was some thing he couldn't identify. Alighting gently in the bushes, it stole a moment before lifting up back into the air. Heading back the way it came, Samuel noticed that there was nothing beneath its claws anymore. It must have dropped it where it landed. He watched it drift away in the air and waited for a while before stepping out of the brook towards the place the bird had just landed.

He got to the small clearing and found meat. He looked up to check if the raven intended coming back for its kill but it was nowhere in sight. Staring for a moment at the meat, it looked dried from the scorching Sun, ready to eat. Hesitating for a moment, he tried to pass it off as a coincidence but his gut told him otherwise: his father's god was living up to the vow he made before leaving his tribe. Samuel made his way back to a tree covering with the meat in his hands. He found comfortable position, started to eat, and later quenched his thirst by the stream.

Samuel's body relaxed on the thick roots of the tree but his mind was far from rest. Rubbing his palms on his cloth, he felt something beneath his tunic. He couldn't recall putting anything in it, and besides, it should have fallen from all the running he did in the night.

It was the parchment.

His sister must have slipped it in when they held their dying brother. Holding back tears, he began to read, noticing, for the first time, that it must have been made from sheepskins. His heart bore gratitude to his brother for teaching him how to read.

"*I will raise them up a prophet from among their brethren, like unto thee.*" He began to read slowly, fumbling on the words.

"*Like a sheep he was led to the slaughter, and like a lamb silent before his Shearer, so he does not open his mouth. In his humiliation justice was denied him. Who can describe his generation? For his life is taken away from the earth.*"

Who was this prophet? He wondered. And where did all this take place? Why would a prophet be slaughtered like an animal?

Midday will be here soon and he instinctively felt the urge to move on. Putting the parchment back into his cloth, he started walking, obviously not knowing where he where to go. Anywhere far from Kamau will do, at least till he finds power enough to challenge him, he reasoned.

Walking for hours robbed his system of fluid. He looked around and spotted a palm tree. Finding a rough stick, he bruised the lower frond and pulled it down so that the tree bled water at its injury. The content was enough to quench his thirst.

He continued walking until the Sun began its descent. Samuel noticed, as he robbed his abdomen, how hungry he was. A twig snapped not too far behind him. He turned to look at what was coming but saw nothing. Fear to look away kept him from moving away. Rather, he moved closer to where the sound came from. He had seen hyenas around midday and felt at ease because hyenas most times never attack animals they are not taller than.

Suddenly, a bird flew up into the air; he fell back with a cry, startled at its largeness. It was the same black bird he encountered in the morning. Running with happiness to the spot where it just took up from, he knew fresh meat was waiting for him.

"Oh! Ashi naling, thank you, thank you very much." He exclaimed as he starting feasting on the fresh meat.

He found a cozy spot to rest for the night. Samuel knew he would soon be approaching sandy plains, because the wind that blew that afternoon was hot and full of dust particles. The forest faded in density as he traveled daily.

He sometimes remembered his family: his father, roughening his head as he told them stories of where he came from, his mom nursing Lydia and Caleb fetching more firewood for the night.

His father's tales were of how his forefathers were taken to a foreign land as slaves, the years of endless inhumanity and maltreatment inflicted on them. It was all still fresh in his mind.

"We were seen as different," Lusala continued with the story of his origin, "Sun burnt and evil. Yet not all accepted the Egyptian's values. Some said there would never be equality with another race and that we must reclaim our native lands. After a war that took thousands of lives, my forefathers got their heart's desires. They were able to reclaim their lands and have since built a kingdom beside a great blue river." Lusala added more firewood. "While the rest settled far north, God called me out to travel south."

"Is that how you came here?" asked Caleb as they sat around the fire in front of their house.

"Not at first." Lusala replied. "I met a man on the way. He was an official of Kandake, the great queen of our land-Nubia. He was in charge of all her treasures. It was through him that I got saved." He looked up and smiled at his wife. "I've never seen anyone full of light and happiness before in my life. He helped me find hope when I was weary of living."

"He told me how he met a man on his way back from the land of the Jews, who explained to him the parchments he carried."

Samuel remembered watching his face light up as he recalled the memories of his encounter with the eunuch. Peace welled in his eyes with words unspoken, so overwhelming and outpouring.

"He called me second born," Lusala had continued, "and gave one of the parchments he carried. The one I have is the same one the man he met on his way explained to him." Lusala brought out the parchment and showed it to them. "I have traveled far and have been in situations where I thought I would never survive but somehow, the lord has preserved me."

"You will be surprised when I tell you this."

"What? Tell us please." His listeners begged.

Lusala stared into the fire for a while knowing he kept them in suspense.

"Well, the eunuch said that while he spoke to the man who explained what was written in the parchment, they came by certain water settlement on the road.

"The eunuch ordered the chariot to stop and pleaded that he must be immersed into the water."

"Immersed? You mean like bathing?" Caleb asked.

"Not exactly."

"So what does it mean?"

"It's like being dipped into the stream and brought out like a ritual."

"Why not bath in it and fetch some to drink while he's there? Wasn't he tired from the journey? What does a chariot look like, father?"

"Mother, I'm thirsty." Samuel walked to his mother and rested his head on her shoulder.

"Go inside and get some water from the vessel."

"Sit down child and listen. I will soon be done with the story." Lusala interjected solemnly.

Samuel grumbled under his breath and took his seat again.

"The dipping into the water signifies a pledge of a good conscience towards God. It is a declaration that you swear allegiance to no other god but the One declared in the parchment; the Messiah that has come."

"A Messiah? You mean someone who will save us from the Laibon?" Caleb asked.

Samuel was moving his leg front and back in silent protest. He wanted a drink and wasn't listening to the story enough to ask any question. Besides, he never understood many of the stories his father told. His father once scolded him to ask questions when there is reason to but he never did.

"Caleb, sometimes we need to be saved from a greater evil within than the one we see or witness." Lusala explained.

He spoke to them in so many words afterwards about the eunuch and himself.

"Do you know what we stand for?" Lusala now intended to speak to them about their race. He waited for the obvious response and then continued. "I have been privileged to see different people of different skin colors and I tell you, we stand out in the crowd.

"We are kimitians-the black race. Our name means strength and perseverance. We never give up when we set our will to achieve something, or at least we are not meant to. Remember my sons. No matter the obstacle that lies in your path, to fail to persevere, is to deny the very essence of your existence!"

The very essence of our existence!

Those words echoed in Samuel's mind. Slowly, he drifted to sleep in the forest.

In his dream, he found himself in a garden, and in the garden was a burial place. There was an earthquake that shook the whole place and suddenly he saw some celestial being descending from the heavens. This being, rolled away the stone and sat upon it with a countenance that shone like lightning with raiment as white as snow.

Samuel knelt down and quivered in fear. It was like the stone was rolled away for someone to come out but no one did. He was sure it must have been only for a moment that he waited for someone to come out but it felt like forever.

"***Come; see the place the lord laid.***" The creature said. The truth dawned on him and the strange feeling coursing through his essence felt soothing. The magnificent creature rolled the stone not for anyone to come out but for him to go in.

Samuel felt himself trembling as he obeyed and entered the burial-resting place. He saw a napkin wrapped together in a place by itself, aside from the linen clothes. How could someone defeat death? He couldn't fathom it. It was one thing to be terrorized by the Shadow of the forest but even the Shadow couldn't defy death, he reasoned. Turning away, he suddenly felt he had seen what was not meant for him to see. He ran out of the cave and felt darkness coming unto him the farther he ran.

He was getting tired and was about to stop when a twig snapped behind him. Samuel glanced back and saw a lion coming after him.

He willed himself to wake up but couldn't. This couldn't be happening again, he wondered. The Shadow was dead so this couldn't be it.

He could hear the lion's grunting sound getting closer. Samuel made a sharp left turn and brought his hands up as he moved through the trees. He felt the trees lash him with their lower branches for disturbing their night's rest. Breathing heavily with tears, toppling down his cheeks, it was time to give up to what pursued for his strength slowly failed him.

Samuel saw a small clearing and a hollow cave that would fit him perfectly. As he came to it, the lion came from the left side and leaped at him with such fierce that would have ended his life if he hadn't dived lower and turned. He felt the wind driven by the lion's fierceness bruise his left shoulder. Samuel landed on his back and crawled fast into the cave with his back. He could hear the lion scratch the cave floor, grunting as loud as it struggled, trying to get in.

Samuel crawled deeper into it and felt pain on his left shoulder. He touched it and realized that the lion must have scratched him before he crawled in. Pain shot through him when he tried to lift his left hand and he woke up suddenly, almost screaming.

He held his left shoulder and surprisingly felt pain. It was just a dream but somehow his left shoulder seemed to hurt for real. His mind must be playing tricks on him.

Samuel tried to slow his breathing. Fear gripped him in the darkness. He heard footsteps in the distance and stilled himself. Normally animals had begun migrating into the region in large numbers again. The sense is the season is changing.

The footsteps were getting closer. He had seen some pretty large animals the day before, when he strayed to an overgrazed area. It was a muscular one that had an unusual, robust snout. It must have stridden gracefully without his knowing. Samuel remembered how much of a fright it caused him and the animal when he turned suddenly and screamed.

But this sound was different. Someone or something seemed to be approaching him.

Without thinking, he got up and ran. It felt like his dream was happening in real life. His mind must be playing tricks on him as he found himself feeling the lower tree branches and making the same sharp turning. He looked back and was glad nothing seemed to chase him.

He stopped and rested his hands on his hips in akimbo.

"Child, why do you run so?"

Samuel turned suddenly to see a man standing beside a tree, his face so serene and comforting. The man was draped in red like an ilingeetani. However, his face evoked reverence and calm at the same time. He didn't know what to say and just started blabbing.

"There was a lion chasing me and also a man there," he said gasping for breath, "he died but his body disappeared. How could that be?"

"Didn't your father speak to you about who that man is?"

"Yes." Samuel replied. "I never understood his stories and I never questioned him." He said ashamed.

"My son, whom do you seek?"

"The large creature that rolled the stone, he said the lord laid there. Who is the lord?"

"Samuel!"

The man called his name!
Samuel looked into the man's face and he felt scale fall from his eyes. He stared into the man's eyes. It was the same eyes that pierced his soul.

There seemed to be light originating from his eyes and lighting up the whole place.

This was the man that was buried!

His legs grew weak and knelt down.

"Help me. Please." He began to cry and it seemed his inside opened up in crashing pain. Are you the one my father spoke of?"

"I am as you say."

Samuel felt himself shrink under the radiance of light slowly emanating from the One who stood in front of him.

"The parchments you hold read it and live. All the power you seek lies in your hands. Fear not, my beloved.

"Arise now and wake up from your slumber. The world awaits."

As Samuel rose from where he knelt, he woke up in the forest all drenched in sweat.

He must have been dreaming the whole time. He thought he woke up before but now knew that he was still dreaming.

The dawn had made its way from the east. He brought out the parchment in obedience and began to read, thirsty for its knowledge, more than ever. His eyes searched through it to know the One who defied the sting of death.

. . . that was seven years ago . . .

6

When I was a child, I talked as a child;
I thought like a child, I reasoned like a child.
When I became a man, I put childish ways behind me.

There once lived a man a very long time ago.

His name was Kumpash and he had two daughters and a son. There was a war in those days with a neighboring tribe that hindered anyone from taking their cattle to the salt lick, as the norm was. A salt lick is like a natural chunk of salt deposit. Animals love it because it contains loads of minerals and nutrients the body needs for strong bones, muscles and general growth. It is tradition that animals be taken to the salt lick deposit or else the cattle suffers and produce no milk.

Kumpash's only son decided to take the cattle to the salt lick; an act that jeopardizes his life. His elder sister accompanied him on the way and when they got there, he built a kraal, a circular enclosure for cattle or livestock with a hedge of thorns. While he was away, the enemies from the neighboring tribe showed up at the kraal and met his sister.

One of the enemies discovered the kraal when Kumpash's son went out to feed the cattle. The enemy discovered the girl and loved her. The enemy visited again and again and bonded with her.

The enemy brought others to see her without Kumpash's son knowing. The grounds, unable to conceal secrets of intrusion for long, gave in to Kumpash's son's inquisition as he came back later in the evening. He noticed the footmarks. When the sister said nothing he came up with a plan. The very next day he went out again with the cattle for a while and then came back to hide beside the kraal.

The enemies came again.

When he heard his sister telling the enemies to come back that night to fetch her, he realized that his sister had betrayed him for good.

That night, he acted like nothing was wrong till the enemies showed up. He then surprised them and killed some of them, setting the others running behind their heels. Kumpash's son later returned back home with his sister and the cattle and told his father about the defeat of their enemies and the betrayal of her daughter. The whole village was torn in disarray and decided that in order to curb the lust of young maidens; they will be circumcised as a rite of passage. Also, the respect held when maidens wear anklets, symbolic of preventing early pregnancy, was lost afterwards.

That was how female circumcision came to be.

And who told you this?

"My grandfather did."

Samuel replied the One who came to see him from time to time. Whenever he heard the voice of the One walking in the forest, he would move closer and then sit down to talk. It took him a while to get used to it because he thought he was losing his mind talking to someone he didn't see.

After years of wandering and keeping a safe distance from animals and tribal settlements, he'd come to find peace whenever he hears the Lord's voice. He remembered the first few times he heard it. He would run away in fear and when he stopped to rest, he would hear it again.

Here he was talking about circumcision. The One had said that the circumcision that he commanded was a seal of the righteousness of faith. Samuel then tried to unlock the mystery by recollecting the story about how circumcision began in his tribe.

"Our circumcision could also be based on belief. It is done to prevent misconduct by young girls while for the men it is our pride and joy that ushers us through to adulthood."

Do you feel less of yourself since your family wasn't accepted and you haven't been circumcised?"

Samuel kept quiet as his sputum was too big for him to swallow. Though he had never felt any connection to his tribe, it was still a pain that he still never belonged. The years of loneliness may have robbed him of his identity but still stirred a deep hunger within him to return and gain acceptance from his tribe.

There is drainage of strength to become all you can be when there's no one to acknowledge you or your work. How lonesome it is to stir from slumber everyday and hold your conversations with the passing winds, swooshing trees that shade from the Sun, and even try the animals in the distance. What is the purpose of a man when he holds no close ties to anything? His mind wondered.

You hold close ties with me.

"Then circumcise me." Samuel answered. He was used to the One reading his thoughts without having voiced it.

The circumcision I require is of the heart, not of the flesh. Without faith, it is impossible to please God. He that cometh must believe that He is and that He is the rewarder of them that diligently seek Him.

Another mystery! How was he ever to comprehend anything when the One always spoke in proverbs?

He took refuge in the forest, never crossing onto the sandy plains all these years. His food came from hunting and in times of lack, the ravens brought him meat. He usually went with the large muscular animals, which stride with relatively slender legs, to drink from the river. It felt like a ritual to see these animals drink high quantities of water at least every three days. Samuel usually went with them and was always mindful of the large horns these animals bear while he drank. Their horns extended to the side then bent up and inward, used as a major weapon of attack or defense. Now he drinks mostly from the bottlelike trunks of baobab trees, lower fronds of palms, and green bamboos, which seemed more than enough after he almost lost his head to a reptile in the river with a skin covered in hard scales.

One time, the weather took on a severe toll on its dependents and the animals moved far away in search of food and water. Samuel found a small water settlement and had only taken a sip or two to quench his three-days old of thirst when the large reptile emerged from the water suddenly. He narrowly escaped the attack and had since moved away from quiet waters to drinking the early morning dews that settled on leaves and also sap of certain trees when the waters receded and dried off.

There was a river that flowed from up north. It gathered together to at a point safe enough for him to wash on its banks. Samuel read the parchment over and over again, the voice of the One from his dreams and visits, he kept with him always.

His slim chances of survival in such terrible terrains never troubled him as much as the mysteries the One shared with him. However, all the mysteries became plain when he met the Messiah. There was a sudden rush of life that filled him in a quick overflowing, spiritual sensation.

Each troubling question that had wounded him for years were gradually straightened by a new understanding; an understanding so profound and yet so simple, his mind was exhausted in reasoning but his heart leapt every single moment of it.

One day, he climbed a tree and had slumbered at noon when he felt nudged on the side. He looked down and there was roasted meat on the coals, and a palm leaf with water inside. He rose up to eat and drink, and climbed the tree again. He watched as an animal strayed from its group. The animal wore a deep colored upper coat, separated by a light flank stripe from its white belly. Not too far away a predator closed in stealthily. Samuel knew how sudden silence sometimes could mean imminent danger, especially after his encounter with the Shadow of the forest. He closed his eyes to rest.

At another time again, he felt a touch and a still small voice saying, *arise and eat for the journey is great.* He rose up to eat and drink. Samuel knew it was time for him to pass the sandy plains to the long pile of endless sand dunes.

Now a young man, he wore the coat of skin his Lord made for him and began to venture through the hot plains in obedience. The journey under the scorching Sun was suicidal if not for the same One who watched over him all those years in the forest. By divine providence, he spotted trees along the way with moist pulpy centers. Sometimes he would dig or pry the roots out of the hot sand, cut them into short pieces and smash the pulp so that the moisture ran out. That took care of his thirst.

He remembered in one of his dreams how he was instructed to get into the lands up north and there he would find a city on the sands.

Samuel went in the strength of that meat for forty days and forty nights. The days were hot as ever while the night unveiled a wicked cold that chilled his blood. The sands would sometimes come alive and take forms when the winds blew strongly. On the midday of the fortieth day, he spotted something shining in the distance. Thinking it was a mirage; he shrugged it off. He had been traveling for a day without water and prayed the mirage to reality. As he came closer, it looked more real.

With the last ounce of strength he reached higher grounds that revealed the landscapes. It was a large city not too far from the flowing river that cut across the land from the north to the south, its gates reflected the Sun's rays. He ran towards the river and sunk his dark skin into it. Such a sweet drink it is to quench a long thirst. It felt like the wait was worth the take. Though the water was tasteless nothing could enrich more than what truly satisfies. The washing sensation that tickled and trickled down his throat left him light and ethereal.

Samuel later walked up to the magnificent kingdom of Meroe, situated at the junction of several main rivers and caravan routes. These routes connected the central part of Africa through the blue and white Niles with Egypt and the Ethiopian islands. He could see caravans carrying grain into the city and another carrying ivory, incense, animal hides, stones prized as jewelry and arrowheads from shipment downriver. The great black kingdom was in trade with Egypt and the Greco-Roman world by barter and not coinage.

Dust rose up into the air as convoys entered the golden city. Breathing heavily, he entered the city pulling up his coat of skin to cover his nose. He was surprised to see so much activity, even by the city entrance: buying and selling was on with shouts coming from the throats of eager men wanting to do away with their merchandise, professing claims of lesser priced goods. Samuel stopped for a moment to touch the golden city gates and marveled at the architecture. Several well-armed bands of horse warriors and camel-borne warriors rode in, almost trampling a man beneath their horses. The man ran back and was almost struck by an incoming caravan. The man then tripped and fell over a man's merchandise.

Samuel stepped closer to help the man up but got bathed with obscure words from the man who looked at him in obvious disgust. The words sounded like curses from the expression on his face. Samuel moved away from him. He could feel the perusal of merchants and sellers who obviously didn't have any customer in attendance, enough to let him know how alien he must seem to them. He ventured further and could see ahead of him. To his left a line of wretched-looking people who were captives ready to be sold as domestic slaves and soldiers. A man in jalabia, a traditional long white robe, walked away after purchasing some female captives.

He could hear shouts of men coming from his right. He turned to see a man, with dirty short kilts of animal skin that reached his knees, run to help some men carry something. He watched them with interest and saw them carrying something heavy. The man's imma, the turban on his head, fell off. Smoke rose from the iron smeltery to which they went in.

Another world!

Everyone seemed to be on the move and there was a lot of noise hanging in the atmosphere. Samuel had never seen so many people before in his life.

He heard a female voice from where slaves were sold and turned around to see what was going on. The woman wore long colorful skirt with her torsos bare and had on attractive earrings and beads that announced affluence.

She stared at Samuel. So also the man in charge of the selling of slaves. Things slowed to a stop around him as they waited, obviously for something. He realized from their stare that the woman must have demanded for something that had to do with him. Some people began to stop whatever they were doing and started looking at him. He was expected to do something but didn't know what to do. The slave seller addressed him this time but Samuel didn't understand the language spoken in this kingdom.

He remembered that Caleb once told him that it isn't the differences of languages that solely determines understanding and co-habitation of the human race. There are some who are born from the same womb and ate from the same place but still don't understand, neither can they relate with one another. Unfortunately, Caleb was wrong this time and he couldn't tell what they wanted with him.

Closing his eyes, he prayed to God to help him. More people stopped what they were doing and looked at him with an expression that denoted expectation or some kind of action from him.

"I want him."

The woman said again in Nubian and Samuel was surprised that he now understood her.

"I said come here slave." The slave dealer's voice rose by a pitch. He was bare-chested and well built. The slave dealer had on shorts that tightened around the waist and knees. The stench that seeped from him revealed many years the slave dealings and overcrowded decks of sails in transport of both material and immaterial goods. His dark skin honed from the cold-hearted Sun. He wore a mean look on his face with one golden earring on his left ear.

"He's a fine purchase isn't he?"

Samuel walked towards them. Slaves stood with ropes over their shoulders, waiting to be purchased. Some were half-naked and tried to cover themselves with hands held down by gold chains while others had more than their faces downcast. Some of the captives' eyes blazed fighting spirits. In the despair that whelmed over their unfortunate lives, there still glimmered hope.

The auctioneer gripped Samuel's arms, walked around him and sniffed. "He is strong and handy. It will cost you."

"Name your price." The woman said.

As they bargained, Samuel couldn't help but notice that those slaves whose spirit had been waned by unbearable loss wore pain on their faces. They must have traveled far and were obviously separated from their loved ones, wondering if they were alive or dead. The gentle whisper that carries insurmountable weights of value of what is most important fleetingly passes until loss embraces actuality. So delicate it is that we must hold dear to heart the ones that have grown too familiar less they join the carriage that's destined for everyone to pass on, from this world to the next. Samuel looked into their eyes and their pain matched his with equality and depth.

"Follow me." The woman said.

Samuel wanted to let her know that he wasn't a slave but felt the nudge to keep his peace and so he did. He walked behind her as they walked past a few gold houses. It seemed like gold was viewed as a normal resource material for everyday use here. Everywhere he turned there was something made or covered in gold. Even slaves where chained with gold chains.

The houses they passed looked small but each one caught the rays of the Sun by its edge and sparkled. The poorest looking houses were covered in shades of hard fire bricks. Samuel had never seen anything like it before in his life. They stopped briefly for a herd of camels to pass. He glanced briefly at the other slaves behind him that the woman had purchased. Her two guards were at the rear in escort.

They passed by a crowd of men cheering as men wrestled at the center. He stopped to watch one mock the other before closing in to grab his left leg. One of the woman's guards pushed him ahead as one of the wrestlers was flipped over. The crowd cheered as the wrestler landed with a thud as his back hit the ground.

After walking for a while, they approached a large building with a well laid out façade. It was the most beautiful house Samuel had ever seen. Even the other newly-bought slaves looked up in awe at the house that demanded their services. You could almost read the expression on their faces that at least they would be working for a rich master, and for a slave, that meant more than anything else in these desert areas.

The gold house stood with pride above others made of fire bricks from Sun-baked mud, the norm in this side of Africa. The three-storey west side mirrored the east side in architecture and style, both holding four windows on each floor. The central championed the others with five floors, the top most floor extending a balcony. All three sections were crowned with flat cemented roofs and the heavily weighted house rested on gold-plated Lebanese cedars.

There was a beam of palm tree on the right and a dried acacia tree on the left, tall enough to the second floor of the beautiful home. They were all ushered to the courtyard on the east side. Servants came to meet them and one by one, the newly-bought slaves were instructed on where their services will be needed by the woman.

Samuel struggled between rage and grief at what had become heartless, racial inhumanity when slave children also came to meet them. He felt the urge to find a way to save them but discarded the foolish idea. The languor to laze around while another carried out ones duties have driven mankind to acquire no more the services of animals but now of other fellow men. Innocence had already been driven away from the children as they drink from the dregs of cruelty that describes humanity.

However, the truth still declares itself. Just like there won't be a Master without an Apprentice, so also there won't be any Rich without the Poor, neither the Served without the Servant. As long as the callous, bitter fingers of time guide this earth with its limits and changes, so also must this order continue unfortunately. Besides, all he had to do was to minister to what resides within and try to reach that which longs to reside and recede from sin. One of the guards grabbed him by the arm and shoved him forward as he noticed right by the left side of the house, the small gilded statuette of the lion-headed goddess Sekhmet, whose flaming breath he later learnt was the cause of the scorching heat of the Sun.

Rhesa looked at the young man she purchased at the marketplace with obvious interest, admiring his build and stance. She told him to follow her and approached the western entrance to the building, hoping her husband would approve. Her Egyptian husband was expecting someone dark skinned and native, not a foreigner to work around the parchments of his business holdings.

The other slaves had been led along a pathway to the back of the house while the woman told him to come with her. After a long flight of stairs beautified by gold banisters, they later stood behind a man, clad in luxurious linen robe with colorful long sashes. Common sense declared him the master of the house.

"Wait here while I speak with the master." Rhesa said to Samuel. "Pray he accepts you, slave, for if he agrees to your purchase, you'll be well treated. May your god favor you."

Sahid was at his private chambers, rising from prayers. It's been three years since there had been deng, the local name for rain, and he tirelessly sought the face of the gods to bring rain. The death toll had increased as people died out of poverty and drought. The full extent of the ensuing devastation hid behind by the vibrant life of the marketplace. Buying and selling went on Meroe's backyard. The Nile retrieved further away from its banks with every lick of the Sun.

The city had always enjoyed a rain bath from the heavens when the usually dry hills and plains greened with grasses, and the waters flowed down the wadis, a local name for the valleys. The drought had dried up the wadis and then turned to the Nile to inflict its wrath. What wonder it is that one's striving is to attain and obtain some resource that doesn't necessarily constitute life's basic necessities.

Sahid stood up. His mind traveled back in time to when he slept on dusty roads that led to affluent tree-lined avenues. Many times he'd slumbered beside the stone wall that surrounded the residences of royalty. Members of the royal court passed him by and scorned him so much he vowed to someday be someone of great importance and recognition. Someday, he'd have his place among court members and dine with royalty. He'd lived the dream. He'd attained it all. The pursuit had been tasking and draining but now he stood at the pinnacle of wealth and importance and didn't like the taste of it in his mouth.

He touched the golden rings he wore and felt the beat of rare jewelry around his neck as it weighed on his skin. The foreign linen robes that always got people's admiration when he walked by or even sat with the court members now felt like rags on him. He wondered why he had to have gone so far before realizing the truth. Whenever he went to Rhesa's chambers to spend the night, he'd see her going through jewelry box and the sparkling brilliance of it all now resembled mere rubbles from quarried stones.

Rhesa thought her husband looked drawn and in poor humor; a sign that disapproved of any interaction. With a deep breath she gathered her courage and she approached him. She waited for her husband to acknowledge her presence and nod in permission for her to speak.

"My lord," she said, "I've returned with the slaves and I brought the one intended to be your personal aide. He awaits your inspection."

"Native?"

"No, my lord. None were available." He hoped the lie wouldn't show on her face. "He doesn't look like someone from around these regions. Probably from the south." She said and saw his husband's mouth tighten into a hard line.

"He looks? You bring a stranger without knowing where he's from?" Sahid said angry with his wife. "And you bring him into my house?"

"Sahid walked with her to the chamber entrance to see the slave.

Samuel stared at his surroundings, taken by its beauty. He never thought such elegance existed when it came to homes. He was accustomed to a shelter made of artistic cow dung.

A copy of the portrait of Meritamun, daughter-wife of king Ramses II lie beside the air opening; iron wares shone brightly from cleaning on the wall and a gold seat amidst others located by the entrance indicated the master's seat. Unknown to him, the master stood observing him for a moment. Samuel turned to see his new master and her wife in front of him.

"So this is the one you speak of," asked Sahid, "the one to serve as my aide."

"Yes, my lord." Rhesa replied.

"You presume he's suited for hard labor?"

"Yes. With good food and rest, he'll serve you well." How could she tell her husband that she somehow felt the urge to buy this young lad the moment he saw him.

"With the rain crisis, you know I don't have the time or the inclination to pamper slaves." Sahid looked at the young man again, studying him more closely and wondering what it was about him that could have made his wife buy him. After a while, he approved with a wave of his hands. "I guess he'll do. He does understand Nubian?"

"Speak up slave." Rhesa said.

"Yes my lord." Samuel answered, faced down. He admired the leather straps of his master's expensive sandals, woven securely around strongly muscled claves. His eyes caught the floor on which he stood and he could see his reflection from the polished, marble floor.

"What is your name slave?"

"Samuel."

"Samuel, then. Come with me." Sahid said imperiously.

Samuel followed obediently, taking in the wonders of the great house. They crossed the open court. The delicate smell of roasted meat made his belly churn in hunger. His master led him into a chamber strewn with merchandise.

"All those things need to be arranged." Sahid said as he reclined on a seat.

Samuel set to work, carrying vessels of grain to be stored and animal hides to one end of the chamber. He felt his master watching him work, and he carefully placed the vessels away.

"The deep south is said to be enriched with rainfall and trees." Sahid said.

"Yes, my lord."

"How is it like? I mean living in the south?"

Samuel straightened slowly and wiped the sweat from his face. "It's beautiful." He said quietly.

Sahid looked into the young man's brown eyes. Slaves didn't usually look at their masters in the face, but he didn't feel any offense at this lad. "I intend to travel south someday."

Samuel turned away to continue his work.

"What about your family, Samuel?"

"They're all asleep except one, my lord."

Sahid found Samuel's referral to his dead family as asleep fascinating. "Go on."

"My sister lives. My parents were killed during the purification ceremony."

"What is the purification ceremony?"

Samuel told him about how the spiritual leader would come as instructed by the gods to cleanse the tribe from evil and prepare them for blessing and how his parents didn't believe in the gods of the land but in the supreme God.

"We sometimes attribute remarkable occurrences to the direct influence of the gods and sometimes make rituals." Sahid declared. "There are many gods served in this region. Some view humans as ants to the gods, whose actions can't be questioned while others use their cattle shed as a shrine." He robbed slowly on his expensive long robe. "Most importantly, the rain is of major concern to us here. It's been associated with the spirits of the ancestors."

Sahid noticed how tired and hungry Samuel must be as his breathing became burdened. After finishing with the arrangements, he would get some meal and rest for the day, he thought to himself.

"The rain hasn't fallen for three years now." Samuel said as he continued working.

"How did you know that?" Sahid asked, surprised. He waited for an answer but didn't get one. He must have heard at the marketplace. "Why didn't your god intervene and save your family?"

"Because His ways are different from ours."

A frown crossed Sahid's face as he mused on what the slave said. He couldn't understand why a god wouldn't come through for his subjects. His own god hadn't done anything about the rain so why would he expect less from any other god.

"Then why do you serve him?"

The question seemed to be not only for the slave boy but also for himself. He didn't want to admit it but Sahid was beginning to lose faith in the gods. You would think that since the gods are so many, one of them would get up and do something about the drought crisis.

"I spent seven years in the wilderness and found my resting place amidst lions, wild dogs, reptiles and many other dangerous animals and outlived them. I then journeyed for forty days without food and only feel hungry right about now, Master."

"Is that why you serve your god? How do you define intervention from a whim of coincidence? How do you place a line between hands of skill and a twitch of luck? Do you claim to say that you are the only one to have gone for forty days without food?"

"Master, there's nothing new under the Sun. I believe we try too hard to seek the face of God in the abundance of complexities that surrounds us yet He stares at us in the very simple things of life. If I may ask, how do you explain how life stems from a seed?"

"You haven't answered my question slave?"

"Exactly, master. I don't claim to have all the answers to life's questions. I know I felt empty once. My inside felt like a hollow place with unknown depth. It took me a while to realize that even the works of our hands, rooted in years of hard labor feel vain sometimes when you receive the rewards. We all have attributes of godliness in us and so we judge divinity and humanity based on it."

"Why do you know claim a god who left you when you needed him and why is your god the true one?" Sahid couldn't have more described how vain it was he felt about all he'd acquired the way Samuel just did.

"When you have tried all you can to reach Him and he turns around and reach you, wouldn't anyone respond naturally? If I may, wouldn't you serve your god more so if he poured down the rain you need? What if your god bestows more and save you from what ails our soul? Sin!"

"And what sin did your family commit?"

Samuel gave no answer.

Sahid got up from his seat, tired and hungry. He figured the slave boy didn't answer because he hadn't come to peace with that part of his life. "It's ridiculous to believe in something you cannot see. That's what I believe." He went through some of the merchandise he just purchased and picked up a hide from one of the vessels.

"You can't see the wind but you know and sense its presence all around you." Samuel said with his back to his master as he worked. "And it is. No one knows where it goes or where it comes from but it's of great essence that it is. We breathe in air and yet can't touch it and can't live without it" He straightened for a while. "This is the same with God."

Sahid blinked, surprised at such comparison. He glanced at the wretched slave, noticing that with such build, a little food and work and he would make a fine price for a wrestler. It will be good to see how a foreigner fights in the arena for a change, but he shrugged the idea off immediately it came to his mind. Somehow he knew this young man would serve him well. But he needs to be taught that a master isn't addressed by a slave the way he addressed him boldly all afternoon.

"What would you have me do now, master?"

"Enough for the day! Go! Get something to eat. Instruct the cook to bring water to wash my hands and food also."

"Yes master." Samuel turned to leave but then realized he didn't know his way around the home yet. Sahid realized that and gave him instructions.

Sahid watched the lad as he left his presence. Although the discussion was more than ordinary he knew he may find a friend in him. There aren't good friends or bad friends. Well, at least that's what he believed. To qualify a friend by good or bad would be to weaken the essence found in its meaning. Friends do not need to be qualified or stressed. You are either one or not. Good cannot be found in bed with evil. Friends are found in those who most times have walked the lonely places, and still have their spirits unblemished.

7

Hear O people and I will testify unto thee;
Give ears to what I say and hearken unto me.

Over the next few weeks, Samuel worked in the storehouse and ran errands for his master. He was placed on the fields to farm and help out as much as he can. He was handed a large rough hand axe with one end pointed and another rounded end, which was used for hammering. He learnt things quickly, grateful to God for understanding the local tongue. He was the one who was later summoned to replenish his master's cup with wine when he dined with his sons and afterwards stand by the side with a bowl of water and a soft cloth for Sahid to rinse and dry his hands. May not sound as much but it was an elevation in servant hood sought by many slaves.

Roman oil lamps, with handle in the shape of a galloping centaur, usually lit up the rooms at night. Sahid usually spoke about his concerns for the kingdom with his sons, Raja and Calil, while his only daughter, Makarasa, dined with his wife alone in their chambers as the custom was. The discussions usually fascinated Samuel as he would stand silent and listen with avid interest while at times, he found himself caught up in admiration of the varied art pieces that adorned the home.

There were carvings and drawings of people involved in different events on the walls. One he always took note of was that of a man attacking his enemies with a lion on its lower right corner. He asked the cook about it and she told him it was the Kushite Prince Arikankharer, and the lion of the stone plaque symbolized the Kushite warrior god, Apedemak.

"What do you know about lions, slave?" Raja, Sahid's first born son, broke the silence. He was the same age with Samuel. He took a small vessel to drink from and the hump between his arms announced his heavily built body. He noticed Samuel stirring at the carvings of the lion and decided to prey on him.

"Lions haunt my dreams master."

"What could you have possibly done to make Apedemak mad?"

"I'm afraid it has to do with my encounter with one when I was a child." Samuel touched his left shoulder as he reminisced when a lion scratched him deeply in one of his dreams.

"Is that why you rub your shoulders? Is that where it struck you?"

"No. I got scratched by one in my dreams once."

"Father, why would you bring an offender of Apedemak to stay here? For all we know he may be cursed by the gods."

"He's not from these lands as you well sense from his accent neither does he believe in our gods." Sahid answered his son.

"Maybe that's the problem. Unbelief! From now on I command you to renounce your gods and worship with the other slaves."

"Need I remind you that he's my slave and not yours Raja? He will worship whomever he pleases. Besides, we need all the help we need from any god who answers our cry for water or else I may have to order all of you to move to Alexandria."

"Father, I think it's time you let me run the family business. I can go, as soon as you command, to Alexandria and look over your business holdings over there while you do what you do best here in Meroe."

Sahid returned to his meal and didn't answer Raja.

"Father, did you hear me?"

"I'm not deaf, child. I'm not that far gone in age."

"I'm not a child, father and you know that!"

Calil excused himself from the table without anyone noticing. Samuel watched the boy leave the room and wondered if he should leave too. He could see from the boy's countenance that this must be a usual occurrence.

"Then stop behaving as one!" Sahid shouted.

"What task have you given me that I have failed you, and yet you demand from me morals irrelevant to achieving success in any vocation?" There was pain revealed in Raja's eyes.

"You're wrong, son. Morals have everything to do with it. The evil you perpetrate have not only reached my doorsteps but like an infectious, incurable disease, sucks the life out of this family. If you cannot rule your own soul, how can you rule an empire?"

"Well, it's not like you have been around to show me. Besides, your riches would have been more if you could just hold back from giving away so much. It stifles me to hear the reports tumble in. I think you would rather leave nothing for your children and give it away to squanderers."

"Leave my presence!" Sahid stood up in anger.

"I would wish for nothing more. Slave, take my place." Raja stood up from the leather-strung wooden chair decorated with ivory inlays and strode out.

Raja couldn't reason with his father's decisions when it came to his investments. His father owned many ships used for conveying goods from other nations to Nubia. His father also owned a very large farmland where he grew crops of cotton, dates, and millets. Normally, there wouldn't have been the use of oxen to drive waterwheels but the absence of rain had hampered situations so badly.

What made him angry was his father's charity. He had awarded most of his merchants, freedom to start their own trade but failed to realize that he was being stolen from. Raja stormed out of the house and left for his best friend's place. He hated his father with a passion. He closed his brown eyes and tried to shut in the pain. Only one thing will spare him the agony: vanities at Manute's place.

There was always some celebration going on at Manute's home. He might as well drown his anger with the offerings of the night. It did him no good in the morning but he longed to be spared another torturous night of weariness and insomnia.

Once the slave by the door saw him, he let him in and greeted him with his head bowed. Raja didn't even pay attention to how he shoved the slave aside. He pushed himself in and walked straight through the well lit passage to the living room. Two female slaves played the harp and the flute for amusement.

"Ah! My friend! Glad you could join us, eh?" Manute rose up when he saw him and approached him with a rueful smile.

Raja grinned and took his seat beside Atlanersa without saying a word.

"You look like you just got up from a rhino's horn. I'm afraid turmoil seems to have found a companion in you, my friend.

"A zebra takes its stripes wherever it goes, I guess." Atlanersa suggested. He was definitely losing control to the strong drink Manute had offered him.

"Don't tell me! Your father?" Manute snapped his fingers for a slave to pour his friend a drink.

"How can I appease your spirit tonight then? What will it cost me to wipe off the horror of hate I see on your face?"

"Raja couldn't bring himself to say a word. There was so much bottled up inside that he felt he was going to explode if he opened his mouth. He watched as the cup Atlanersa held fall from his hands. Also the son of a prestigious court member and of the same age and build as he is, Atlanersa had no brains at all. He most times mistook his rambling words for wits. He would always talk about how useless it is to be a soldier if you don't engage in a real combat. Everyone knew Atlanersa always had more of the mouth than guts. It was the same mouth that could never get satisfied by inestimable quantities of strong drinks. From the way the Roman lamp lit his skin, he must have been robed in darkness when he was born, Raja thought to himself.

"Atlanersa, you're drunk again." Manute cried out.

A female slave poured a drink into a silver cup and knelt down to give it to Raja. He took the cup from her and looked at her. She kept her face down as she got up and Raja violated her with his eyes.

"Ah! She's a new one." Manute interjected. He rested his back on the chair and placed his left hand on his pot belly. His eyes looked like it rested deeper than normal. "Maybe she can ease your spirit and calm your nerves."

"How many have you had now, Raja? Or have you lost count of the maidens we've robbed of their innocence?"

Raja looked at Manute that instant and for the first time he felt like a scum. How did he end up doing this? How did he come to bear the company of such vile creatures for a human? There will always be a limit to which one can blame another for their actions. You can force your will on another but you cannot change the will of others. His father always said that if a slave realizes that, he or she has attained freedom already, even in bondage. Now here he was contemplating about having his fill of lust when it dawned on him that his father must have referred to this same setting: the disgrace of a court member's son who belittles himself to gain pleasure when all he could ever need was at his beck and call.

Manute smiled at him and Raja looked back wondering how he got to be friends with such lowlifes.

Atlanersa began ranting his gibberish about war and his lust for blood spill. "May the gods bring division amidst the neighboring tribes and cities. May the god of war reign in these lands once more and give me one chance to know what it is to live." He belched loudly and swayed his hands as he got up.

"You don't know what it is to have all your nerves on edge; and your heart cracking its rib cage when your life is on the line."

"Oh! I see! So, you're going to tell us Atlanersa? You can't even hold your drink let alone a sword." Manute burst out laughing. His belly rippled in resonance.

The young maiden sat on Raja's laps at Manute's bid and ventured to please him. For a moment, he entertained it. His sense of reason faded as the beast in him stirred. Every night he would return to his chambers amazed at how he wore different identities. In the comfort of his leather-strung wooden bed, he could swear it wasn't him that perpetrated the evil the lips of people testified about him. How strange it is that you do the unthinkable when cheered by your peers and never would have thought about it if alone. Raja had lost count of the many times he vowed never to see his friends again. He tried it once for a few days but felt so lost that when he returned, the evil he resumed defied humanity.

He might as well go on and have her. Stolen waters are sweet and bread eaten in secret is indeed very pleasant. He had never taken responsibility for any of his actions before. Why start now? Even when he saw in his mother's eyes the pain he'd caused her of finding out about the female slaves he abused and molested, there was always a great struggle within her as she let it lie without confronting him. Unfortunately, he couldn't change the past and besides, he was far too gone now to seek penance. There was a smear on his inside that nothing could cleanse. All he'll ever be is clearly written in the eyes of his father.

"I see you have come again with your tails between your legs." Atlanersa intruded his thoughts.

"You bear no ounce of manhood with the way you crumble at your father's knees."

Manute stood up and tried to stop Atlanersa. He was obviously saying too much now. Raja's face hardened even more than when he came in and Atlanersa was way too drunk to curb his mouth.

"Leave me alone and let me speak to this coward." Atlanersa pointed to Raja.

"You wimp in his eyes and suckle like a new born in his presence. Yet you parade yourself with muscles that fail to fulfill the purpose you have it for."

"Atlanersa, it's enough." Manute's raised voice stopped the two slave from playing the harp and flute in the room.

"Manute, leave me alone. We spoke about this before right?"

And there it was!

Raja's blindness lifted at that statement.

A few seconds later, Manute's voice trailed behind Raja as he stormed off in anger. He had shoved the girl away from his lap, punched Manute as he tried to explain and took his leave, vowing never to return again.

Raja was almost running home damning himself for caring what anyone thought about him, especially his father. One truth followed him as he embraced the cold night: he may never be able to redeem his image anymore but in his heart he longed to find father with his father!

A fortnight later, Sahid rose from his bed restless and took a stroll around the house. Listening to the sound of the winds in the moonlight, he ran his hands over his growing beard. He couldn't sleep and could put no stop to his disquiet. The fields weren't doing well although his wealth still grew despite it all. Water used by the city was taken from the Nile as wadis lay dry, with no rain for three years now but the Nile thrived due to an uncharacteristic wealth of rainfall in Egypt. Rhesa had come to him in the night, soothing him of his unrest for a while. He'd spent an evening with the Kandake, who ruled as Queen of Meroe and her court members, discussing growing concerns about the weather, enjoying light conversation about the growing Roman Empire and closing the night with amusing dances from beautiful, foreign entertainers.

Still, the headache remained burdensome, and the gods were not helping. The gnawing restlessness and vague discomfort he carried on the inside was eating him alive. The lion god had been consulted numerous times and he knew he would visit the temple very soon himself. Sahid wandered the passage and came down the stairs, his mind leaping from one thing to another: his shipments unable to reach here in order to avoid the danger of cataracts, the concerns about reaching another treaty with the Romans, and then back to the weather. His nerves were stretched taut in weariness.

Pausing beneath the dust-covered fence, he could almost taste the drought in his mouth. Maybe he was overworking himself, and that was why he was so on edge. He hadn't had a descent night rest for a while now.

The wind suddenly blew strongly on his face from nowhere and movement beside him caught his ears as he got to the main entrance and turned to the side suddenly.

"It is a beautiful night, master." Samuel said as he sat by the entrance to the house.

"What are you doing up so late, Samuel?" Sahid relaxed as he realized it was his personal aide. He had come to feel peace whenever he conversed with the young man over the weeks.

"I couldn't sleep as well, my lord."

Sahid studied him for a moment and in the moonlight he could still see peace edged on his face. He moved closer and rested his back on Lebanon cedars that stood as pillars, wanting that kind of peace.

"Master, you look worried. What bothers you so?"

Sahid kept his silence for a while and didn't say anything. Samuel didn't ask him again and he was grateful he didn't. He knew he could confide in this slave. "Samuel," he said, in a familiar way. "Samuel, tell me about your dreams."

Samuel looked away, transiting into the world his dreams shaped.

"In my last dream, I crawled into a cave. There was a lion trying to get in through the small crevice so I moved deeper into the unknown. The cave expanded into a small space and I stood up straight in it without needing to crouch in its shadows. My heart beat slowed from the chase I endured by the lion. I was young again. About ten years of age. I may not have been able to identify my immediate surroundings but I could see myself. Or should I say feel it.

"I stretched my hands to feel the wall and then whimpered in pain as a stinging sensation went through my left arm. The air, though oppressive, still brought the news of the lion's restless efforts to get in.

"And then, there was silence!

"It was like for an instant, the whole universe paused in motion and I alone lived it. Such a silence it was that my thoughts found the vocals to voice out at last and it voiced panic and silence so great I could hear blood flow in and out of my heart like a crashing cymbal.

"Not too far, from nowhere, evolved a light bug. So tiny and yet its littlest of lights derided the gloom and lit up the cave. Naturally, I followed it as it riveted in the air, dancing to a tune it alone knew.

Then it seemed to descend a little and landed on a small rock. I moved closer as the light began to grow."

"What do you mean grow?"

"I mean literally. Exactly the same way before."

"What do you mean? So it wasn't the first time you saw it?"

When Samuel didn't respond, Sahid took it as a yes. How strange it is to have a dream and then continue it again. He could understand if it was a fantasy but what he got from Samuel denoted something else. It seemed this lad had lived a rough life already, asleep and awake.

"I stopped at some point and couldn't go closer. The light had seeped into my skin so much that I felt burnt all over and filled in all fullness, at the same time. When I opened my eyes I saw, right where the light bug had landed, a blazing sword. No one needed to tell me what the sword was for."

"To kill the lion right?" Sahid asked.

Samuel nodded and continued. "I walked closer and for a moment looked at the two-edged sword in awe and esteem. I stretched my hands and grabbed the hilt and it immediately became a parchment in my hands."

"A parchment?" Sahid watched him for a while trying to comprehend. You mean like a document made from sheep's skins? The same one foreigners to Meroe sometimes use for treaties, declarations, and possessions?"

"Yes."

The story fascinated him. Sahid wanted to know how it ended but it all sounded like Samuel was out of his mind.

Samuel looked into his eyes and saw the doubt that found its home there. He brought out the parchment from his side and showed it to Sahid.

Sahid face in the moonlight twitched in surprise. There truly was a parchment.

"Where did you get this?" Sahid tried to mask his surprised tone.

"It belonged to my father."

Said didn't know what to think at this point. He looked at the young lad and felt like the next question might be the turning point in his life. He looked away and sighed heavily.

All he wanted was some answers. Why had the lips of the soothsayers and palm readers being filled with emptiness from the gods? He wouldn't be here desperate enough to care to know about another god. Besides, it wouldn't hurt to know what this god can do.

"What does it say?"

Surprised by his question, Samuel stared at him. He was glad that he could now share his faith with him. Sahid sat beside him by the entrance.

"I'm waiting."

"My God measures the oceans in the palm of his hand," Samuel began, "and uses his hand to measure the sky. The dust of all the earth he measures in a bowl and weigh in scales the mountains and the hills!" he declared.

Sahid looked at him puzzled. "If your god is this strong and mighty, why has he deserted you?"

"He hasn't deserted me, master. He's kept me alive up till now. I have food, shelter, and a good owner."

Sahid was taken at his words. "What use is it to serve a god that doesn't come through for you?"

"His ways are different from ours!" He answered simply.

"Tell me something. Doesn't it matter to you that you don't have your freedom?"

"We all are slaves one way or another, my lord."

"What do you mean? I serve Apedemak, the lion god, and other gods of my ancestors." He answered defensively. He wondered why he admitted this to a slave. "It is of utmost importance that I find my reason to serve my gods, as you do yours." He said resignedly. "We all need the peace of the mind, something I've searched to have, for years."

"But we are driven by what enslaves us. It may be good or bad, right or wrong. I believe to attain peace, something else matters more."

"What?"

"A self-realization of the soul in admission to its misery and wretchedness, and the need to heed the utter cry of its Savior and Creator—God himself, through the sacrifice of the Messiah."

"A Messiah? Of what?"

"If I may ask you master, why do you seek to save your family from the drought's onslaught?"

"Because they are mine. It's my responsibility to watch after what is mine."

"If I may, your face veils the true reason why you would do this as of duty when in truth it's out of love."

Sahid kept quiet and looked away. He considered it a weakness in a man who confesses to the love he has for his own. Although his life-long work was to secure his family but to confess love would bruise his pride.

"Wouldn't you deem it the true act of God if He would do more than we mortals and consider it nothing to lay down His life for his own also?"

"You embrace your religion well, Samuel." Sahid felt weary. The weariness of the mind took toll on his bones. Sahid robbed his thighs with his hands and willed himself not to dwell on what Samuel had said.

"Master, we all have been looking for God from generations gone, unable to find him. The truth is He found us." Samuel suddenly felt the need to tread softly. His master was a man devoted to his beliefs and could end his life by mere whim if he ever thought he spoke less of his gods. No one after drinking old wine wants new wine, because he says, the old wine is better.

"How?" Sahid asked as he stared at those dark brown eyes, unable to calm his curiosity.

"He sent a Savior to come for us and to take our place. One born to die that we, destined for death might through His own sufferings, live."

"Is this the same beliefs that got your parents killed? The same beliefs you now hold on to?"

His words stung Samuel. "Yes." He said quietly.

"And this savior, who came to set us free from death, let them die?"

It was more of a statement than a question.

"The death I speak of is different . . ."

"No." Sahid interrupted him, "The death you speak of will soon be yours. You may retire for the night Samuel." Sahid looked bereft; knowing that such words could get anyone killed especially when it claimed a greater god than the lion god. He was more afflicted internally by Samuel's words than he let on. Sahid had come to trust the slave more than the others now but he knew the young man burned with zeal for his beliefs, and that could mean trouble for him one day.

"Would a god be godly even in death?" One final question.

Samuel stood up and looked at his master. "Would you think different if you realize that if a god cannot overcome death then death is the true god? But He defeated death by rising up from it."

Surprised, Sahid glanced at him as Samuel walked away. Those words went deeper than it should. What scared him more was realizing that if all men are subject to death, a true god wouldn't.

8

I find enmity in those around me, yet my trust rests in thee;
The road may be hard but one day, it's your face alone I'll see

Rhesa found herself watching the young man who served as her husband's aide every time he was around. She wondered what it was about him that fascinated her so much. He was devoted to his husband and seemed to sense his husband's every mood and need, seeing to him with gentle humility. Many had served Sahid but not like this foreigner did. Sahid was high-strung and difficult. She knew. She is his wife. Others slaves obeyed for themselves. This one served wholeheartedly.

Rhesa could see it in the way he helped Sahid out when he was writing in hieroglyphs, a devised way of communication which was entirely different from the Egyptians-cursive alphabets of twenty-three characters. What was most amazing was that she could see that her husband trusted this man like no one before.

It took a while before she realized that she was always trying to see Samuel every day and making sure he acknowledged her presence; only a matter of time before envy overtook her when Samuel spoke to any female, including the slave maidens and her very own daughter, Makarasa.

There was no one as plain looking as Makarasa in the entire kingdom. No one seemed to give her audience, not even her family. At the age of ten and five years, she already longed for anyone to speak to her. Her father always told her how beautiful she looked but she knew different. It was no use to struggle with what others perceive of you, she thought to herself; how fruitless to claim difference to views multitude assume. That was why no one could understand how she felt when Atlanersa, her brother's friend, looked at her like he'd never seen a maiden before in his life.

It was a few fortnights ago, when Raja entertained his friends with a feast while their father was away at the castle to see the Queen. Rome was expanding its empire and the sea held no boundaries to its campaign. If there were to be any attack at such a time when their countrymen were slain by the invisible hands of the drought, the outcome would be disastrous. Egypt was already conquered and they knew the Romans wanted the golden kingdom of Meroe.

Makarasa had been warned by Raja never to show her face when he was with his friends but Makarasa would steal out and watch as they drank themselves to stupor in the same place their father dined with his sons. Atlanersa, Arakakamani, Kashta, Raja, and Manute were known to have grown up together. The only one that never joined the powerful legion of Meroitic warriors from childhood was Manute which explained why he was seriously out of shape. It was with great pride that all the males embraced their drafting into the warrior hood but not Manute. Looking at him confirmed exaggerations that his belly makes a swooshing sound when he walked. Makarasa witnessed sometimes how some of the young female slaves flirted with them when they served.

Raja had invited the gang to feast while his father was away. They had only settled down for a while before Atlanersa was infuriated by the others. Everyone was tired of his consistent jabbering about war and his thirst for one.

"Please spare us the night Atlanersa. We're here to have a great time and on you go again." Kashta took the golden seat, the Master's chair, and watched Raja briefly if he was going to object. He saw a frown cross Raja's face but it quickly disappeared.

"By the way, everyone knows you are the weakest in practice." Arakakamani broke out in laughter and others joined in.

"So is this what you think of me?"

"Think? You talk as if you're offended when all we say is the truth."

"I might be the weakest of all but you sure aren't the strongest in the legion, Kashta."

"Then who is?" There was silence in the room as all eyes were fixed on Atlanersa.

"Akinidad! He is the strongest of us all."

"Well, we can settle who is the strongest between us can't we Atlanersa?"

Kashta got up, obviously offended by Atlanersa's remarks. His ugly cold face soiled the air with silence.

"You will not turn my father's home to the practice grounds."

"I say we settle it. Right here! Right now!" Arakakamani infuriated Kashta and blew more air to the fire that stirred in the room.

All the doors to every room was made from cedar wood imported from Lebanon and the one that led to the room was wide open as slaves brought in strong local drinks. Makarasa concealed herself behind roman silk drapes in the adjoining room that normally shielded the angry Sun. The adjoining room was where visitors were refreshed and most of the casual meetings related to their father's trading were held.

"There is another way of settling this dispute." Manute tapped his belly without looking up.

"How?" The question came in a chorus.

"A contest of horseback riding and archery. No one needs to know aside from us. We can all find out who is the strongest amongst us."

The anger on Kashta's face disappeared as laughter roared out of his mouth.

"What's so funny Kashta?" Manute asked.

"When we argue about who is strongest of us, we actually didn't include you Manute. Your looks defy your words."

Manute stopped robbing his belly and looked up as his friends started laughing. Atlanersa was the only one who kept a strong face as he looked at him.

"Thank you Raja for inviting us but I think I'm going to go now." Atlanersa announced.

"Why? We were just playing." Raja answered.

"The more reason why I want to go. If it's alright with you all we can start the contest at dawn."

Manute looked at Atlanersa and admired him for not joining the others to laugh.

"So be it, then. Tomorrow we begin." Arakakamani declared by hitting the table before them with his strong fists.

Makarasa hurried to get out of sight as Atlanersa turned to take his leave. Manute decided to follow but was having problems getting up as his legs briefly rebelled against supporting his weight.

Atlanersa walked out exasperated by those he called his friends. He couldn't fathom how they'd gone on so long in friendship when they never liked one another or said things to hurt one another. He always regretted being with them and yet he found himself in their midst. What is it about change that stirs fear in man, he wondered. What keeps a victim within range of his or her attacker after history states otherwise? Why would pretense be lived by an individual in more hours of the day than the true self in order to please those who obviously cared less? The questions were coming to him so fast that his mouth turned bitter from the inquisition.

They had all done terrible things when they were together. It seemed they all looked for means to assert strength on the weak when they came together than any other thing else. The painful truth was they were the ones weak. Not in valor or physical strength but in mind and spirit.

He was about to get to the entrance when he noticed someone move by the pillars close to the entrance. Atlanersa moved so fast and pulled out the maiden that was trying to get away.

A small cry escaped Makarasa at Atlanersa's strong grip of her left arm.

"Please don't hurt me?" She let out.

"What are you doing here?"

"Please, I'm sorry. I'm sorry. Please . . . you're hurting me."

Atlanersa brought her to the moonlight and saw her face for the first time. He looked into her eyes and he softened his grip.

"I'm Raja's sister."

"Sister? Raja never speaks of you."

"I know. I don't exist to him." Makarasa looked down in fear. She had never been so close to a man other than her brothers and her father like this before.

"Atlanersa tipped her chin up and looked again into her eyes. He could see how vulnerable she was and how terribly innocent.

"If you have been up all this while you must have heard our conversation right?"

"Yes. Please let me go."

Atlanersa didn't know he was still holding her.

"Sorry I came after you like that. Warrior's instinct I suppose."

When Atlanersa left her and took a step away from her she felt so alone and chided herself within for reacting this way to the mere touch of a man.

"What's your name?"

"Makarasa."

"So what do you think?"

"About what?"

"Our contest tomorrow."

"Just another endless display of men who have no constraint on their egos."

"I presume this is not the first time you've witnessed such unbearable display from such selfish creatures."

"The whole kingdom is swallowed in it." Makarasa turned fully to face him."

Atlanersa abused her briefly from head to toes with his eyes.

There was silence between them for eternity that Makarasa looked away before turning away to go to her chambers.

"So will you come?"

"Come? You mean with you?"

"No, Makarasa. I mean come to the contest tomorrow." Atlanersa noticed her surprised tone and couldn't find the reason why she looked so nervous.

Atlanersa recalled the proverb of how the moonlight revealed the true self within a person. He slowly stepped aside for the night light to embrace her completely. The moon, in agreement, cast a glimpse into her soul and she emanated so much confidence with so much femininity that it took his breath away. She was very beautiful but he knew better than to make a pass on his friend's sister.

"Why should I?"

"Because I want you to."

Atlanersa saw as her eyes lit up in astonishment as he took his leave.

Makarasa watched him approach the guards by the entrance and then disappear into the night. Her dark skin came alive at his words. She had never been spoken to like that before. Though she knew what Atlanersa was capable of. His brother and his friends were known to do only two things: train as warriors and take their fill of maidens. Nevertheless, it felt wonderful to be wanted or at least told so when it most probably was a lie, as far as Atlanersa was concerned. It wouldn't hurt for her to show up for the contest. Raja would definitely be angry but he wouldn't tell their parents.

Makarasa turned in for the night as Hammed, her father's most trusted servant, stepped out behind a pillar with a wicked smile on his face. He was the one in charge of Sahid's dealings outside of Meroe, and also of everything that happened in the house. From the expression on Makarasa's face, Hammed knew she was definitely going to go to the contest to see her new obsession. He turned and walked away knowing the master wouldn't want to hear this about his only daughter.

And that was exactly what he intended.

Sahid had made plans about his daughter's future. The plan was to marry her to a very rich man who lived in Alexandria, a very great city at the borders of a great Sea, to the North of Egypt. If it were left to Makarasa, Hammed knew she would go in the carriage of her first lust: Atlanersa, her brother's warrior companion.

He walked back to the slaves' quarters making sounds that matched the air's stillness. If there was anyone skilled with the arts of hearing when the very air he or she breathes sneak up on the individual, then that individual can know when Hammed is present in a place or not. His silhouette matched his shadow and camouflaged whenever he wanted.

An evil thought came to his mind: he would allow everything to play out for a while. Makarasa would get involved with Atlanersa then he would tell Sahid about it. Hammed didn't need any motive. The sorrow he would cause was enough joy for him to relish in his plot.

All of this happened before Samuel was purchased from the market.

Sahid's announcement of his daughter's marriage engulfed the home in celebration. Preparations followed immediately. The party would be filled with dignitaries: men and women of royalty and high social class and it will even be graced by the majesty, Kandake herself. While he set his servants at work, his daughter, Makarasa, settled into despair. She went to her mother's chambers, deeply sorrowful.

Rhesa noticed the grim line on her daughter's face as she entered. She must be worried about marital life, she thought. Rhesa remembered when she was to marry Sahid. At first, out of duty; duty to her parents and to her husband-to-be that made her comply. But after a while, the duty grew to love. Sahid was a good man and still is, she thought to herself. The only problem is after all this years; she had failed in one thing and one thing only: she had failed to soothe his inner troubles; something she, herself, suffered from.

How can you give what you don't have to another? How can you administer treatment for another's ailment if you suffer from the same? You can claim to be all you can, and to do all you are capable of, but to offer what you don't possess would be to open a treasure chest with nothing in it. Her mind dwelt on the issue every time she tried to speak with her husband.

She remembered the last time she squeezed out an answer from Sahid after years of trying. He admitted to the fact that something ailed him within but he just couldn't put it to words.

Rhesa now watched her only daughter briefly and was thankful she was getting married at last. She tried to convince herself it was the best thing for Makarasa. Any mother would wish the same for her daughter. Her daughter's future was certain of no lack at all. Of course she knew she didn't love her husband to be but that's only a matter of time.

Like hers was.

When Sahid told her about the arrangements for their daughter, Rhesa was shaken about the thought that slipped into her mind. If it were the reason of her daughter lacking no good thing, everything would be fine. But she was happy that Makarasa would now stay away from Samuel. Her daughter seemed to be taken by the slave boy and that she didn't want to happen. Besides, she was the one who purchased him so if there were to be anyone that should have long conversations with the slave lad it should be herself and no one else. This reason why she felt this way was still locked up in self-denial.

Rhesa raised her hands in invitation towards her daughter to comfort and talk to her about what ailed her.

"What is expected of me in marriage, mother?" she wept as she came to her mother's arms.

"Love and faithfulness, my child." She noticed her daughter's eyes fill with tears as she withdrew from her embrace. "It will turn out well. You'll see." Rhesa comforted. "He is a well respected man and holds considerable wealth both in Meroe and Alexandria."

"With the present drought, is it right to even celebrate and marry when thousands are dying?"

"You don't have to worry about others. It's time for you to think about your future family, and besides the gods will bring rain."

"I doubt it."

"Be careful what you say about the gods, child."

Makarasa folded her hands and looked up at her mother. "I spoke to Samuel the other day." She confessed. "He told me something very strange about his god and his homeland."

It sounded more like her daughter had feelings for the slave. She had to admit, there was something quite charming about the young lad. "Well, the small talks with the slave boy will end soon since you are getting married."

"Mother, you should hear it. It doesn't make sense, yet it would be wonderful if it were true."

Rhesa's mind flashed to the marketplace where he bought Samuel. She remembered just seeing him stand there, in the distance, without the other slaves. She couldn't explain why she so much felt the nudge to get him into her household, but she did. Her feelings for the slave boy felt both complicated and surreal. "I have to say there is something peculiar about him."

"I agree too, mother."

"Mother, what I'm I going to do? I don't even love the man I'm going to marry. I don't even know him." Makarasa sounded strained.

"Your feeling for this slave is hindering you from thinking straight. You can't possibly think you love him."

"It's not him."

"What do you mean? There's someone else?" The question came out in a whisper.

Makarasa didn't answer.

"Who is it?"

"Atlanersa."

"Atlanersa? You mean your brother's friend?"

Makarasa didn't answer and slowly lowered her head. She fiddled with an intricately hinged bracelet made of gold on her left hand. She doubted if she would be able to pull the bracelet out now after her mother had been making sure she ate a lot for a while now. The culture of the lands considered a plump woman beautiful and the cook made sure every morning she had milk in a Karanog bowl, a somewhat large container for drinking.

She asked the master cook at one point to tell her what she needed to apply to her lips to make them full. When the cook asked why she needed it she made up a story of how her friends mocked her for having small lips. The truth was the contest her brother and his friends had wasn't the last time she saw Atlanersa. Makarasa recalled how he looked at her before the warrior friends began their challenge. It felt so strangely new to her to be wanted.

After Atlanersa lost the horseback riding and didn't do well in the archery he still had the nerve to say he'd win the next time.

The very next day afterwards, she was the one competing with Atlanersa in horseback riding. Only this time they were alone. Few months went by and they competed in practically everything, especially in *wari*. It was a game where pebbles were moved through a series of holes on a well carved wood with equal round disks on each side.

At first, Makarasa thought Atlanersa was making her win every game they played. It was later it dawned on her that Atlanersa was actually never the best at anything. The more he lost the more his mouth would rake about the next time guaranteed of his victory.

Maidens gathered at many Sunsets beneath the moon to dance to the drums played in honor of the gods.

Skilled men and women would usually beat drums hung around their necks while many others would dance about waving palm fronds. It was quite unbelievable to see many poor people find comfort in such ceremonies. It was said that sorrows were temporarily forgotten while the dance lasted, and long-forgotten hope revived in the twilight.

Atlanersa and Makarasa danced to the drums one night. She realized that Atlanersa hadn't made a pass at her like it was normally said of him. She looked into his eyes and knew that she truly loved him for the man he was within and not for what people said about him. He seemed to have a genuine interest in her. Who would have thought that a man of evil could turn good? Who would have imagined that it didn't take the most beautiful of maidens but the plainest of all to cause him to change?

Her mother would never understand the pain she felt now that their fates wouldn't end like she'd dreamt. Atlanersa turned furious when she told him about her father's arrangements to marry her off to a stranger. He left her in anger and swore to never see her again.

Tears came to her eyes as she looked at her mother again. How was she to begin telling her the gulf of pain she felt within?

"You couldn't be in love with that warrior?" Rhesa interrupted her thoughts.

"You know what is being said of your brother and his friends. How could you take any word that comes from him seriously when it's second nature to him to toy with the hearts of maidens?"

"Mother, he's never tried to lay with me?"

"I don't know why but I do know you must never see him again."

Rhesa made sure she got a nod from her daughter before embracing her again. Tears blurred Makarasa's vision.

"Don't worry. You will grow up some day and come to see that this arrangement is the best for you."

While Rhesa felt relief that her daughter felt nothing for the slave boy, Makarasa wept all the more. When she left her mother's comfort her mind was made up. The two ladies of the house had reached new conclusions:

Rhesa was happy the slave boy was all hers now.

Makarasa would see Atlanersa one last time.

* * *

Bulahau and Makarasa were married before the watchful eyes of the priests at the great temple of Apedemak. The temple was located in Naga, an important religious site, east of Meroe. The temple looked outstanding from afar and once you come up close you would really see the very long, rectangular building with pillared halls in the front and the altar. Many sacred rooms lay in the back. The whole temple displayed the influence of well laid out mixture of Egyptian and Roman architectural styles. The main sacred room shone as the gold statues of the gods reflected light from the oil lamps. Carvings and writings on the wall depicted the great god, Apedemak in supreme reign. Not too far to the left, schooling of teenage boys went on. Reading and writing were used mostly in religion or government rather than in daily life, and it was the priests who taught these skills.

There was a strange stillness in the temple on this day as they stood in front, underneath a kiosk. Sahid watched his daughter raise her chin slightly and give her husband a smile as the rituals continued. He felt a surge of pride. Perhaps their marriage will serve as a sign of good things to come. Hopefully, the rain would be the first of good things to grace the kingdom with its long-sought presence. He watched as Makarasa got wedded before the priests of the lion god in the traditional union that binds the couple till death.

Rhesa's eyes burnt with tears, remembering her own marriage and how scared she was back then. They had the same kind of customary union. Rhesa knew that Sahid could have as many wives as he wanted but was grateful that he hadn't taken one all these years. She looked back to catch a glimpse of the slave boy but didn't see him.

Samuel stood outside the kiosk, by the rear door. He walked to the other side and beheld the incised sketch of the lion god slaughtering enemies of the state with his bows and arrows, on the walls. Samuel noticed the fluted columns of the temple building, which imitated those used in contemporary Greco-Roman architecture. It seemed the fascination at the civilization here would never cease to him.

The other day he stopped by the master's pottery site and was amazed at what he saw. The laborers would sometimes manually coil up rolls of clay, rub the surface until it was even, and then decorate it with jabs. Others used a wheel to make fine white clay. In just a matter of minutes a mess of clay would be turned to some of the finest poetry ever made in history.

After a while, the whole family came out of the temple, with the new husband and wife. The priests followed, proclaiming blessings on their union with prayers said more for the rain. After the required sacrifices and rituals the priests waited for Sahid, who paid them in gold and took the hieroglyphic writings on a slab that declared the marriage vows as he requested.

Rhesa quietly asked them to burn incense and make sacrifices to bless the marriage again. A passion burned in her to appease the gods to help the marriage work.

Makarasa put up a show that she alone could see through. The poor girl's soul clung to another but it wasn't to be. It's going to take the handiworks of the gods if this union were to last while her father rewarded the priest as blessings were outpoured.

Sahid watched with a twinge of joy as his beautiful young daughter accepted the congratulations and good wishes of their guests when they got home. Bulahau would make a new home with her after the feasting tonight. He planned to move her far away from Meroe, to Alexandria. All he wanted was for Makarasa to start a family, far away from the slow destructive conditions of the weather.

Bulahau's mother, a woman of the Shiluk tribe came closer to bless her daughter-in-law. The tribe was known to wear a row of keloids, which were distinctive tribal marks prominently marked on the face. So Bulahau's mother and those who accompanied her were dressed in silky robes decorated with gold bracelets and large earrings enhanced by keloids.

"So, it's done!" Rhesa, said quietly, smiling up at her husband through her tears. "He is right for our child, Sahid. You've done well for her. Thank you." Now Samuel would no longer entertain anyone but her with his stories, she thought to herself.

The warm smile that spread across his business associate and now son-in-law rested his heart about any concerns for his daughter. Sahid watched Bulahau stare at his bride with adoration. The guests trooped in from the thronging streets of Meroe for the celebration feast. As the host, he purposefully kept the number of those invited small. Rhesa had seen to decorating of their home again and again. Sahid could see joy beyond words plastered on her face. He hoped Bulahau would take his daughter away from this land like he said and get her with child soon. Makarasa would settle away from home quickly as Rhesa must have trained her to do.

In the kitchen, Samuel watched Bithia, the chief cook arrange the lavish appetizers on silver platters. The aroma of exotic and delicious foods filled the hot room and made his mouth water. Bithia carefully placed each goat and cow udder on the tray in a starburst pattern. She added generous dollops of carrot, cabbage and string beans, with vegetables to expand the design. Another tray displayed beef with onion that was simmered with garlic. It's to be served with kisra, a thinly layered food made from flour paste. Samuel had never seen such food before, nor inhaled such an appealing aroma. His belly grumbled every now and then while the other servants small talked about the marriage between Bulahau and Makarasa.

"The master is delighted to have her married off." A slender young girl, with large facial scars, remarked.

"I heard they would be moving away from Meroe."

"Good for them."

His long-lost sister would have grown up to look like one of them, Samuel mused. Maybe not in height but definitely in age. The conversation went on around Samuel but his attention drifted back to the beautiful plump cook who performed wonders with her cooking. Most of the servants wished Makarasa well, for they were well treated by her. All he watched in fascination was what Bithia laid on the wide kitchen table.

"I've never seen food like this," he said, awed by the creations she made.

"That's the third time you've said that Samuel. Thank you. It's not like the palace cooks, but it's the best that I can do." Bithia glanced up as Hammed, the chief servant of the house, entered. He dabbed the perspiration from his brow and looked over the platters with a critical eye.

"Everything smells and looks so wonderful, Bithia." Samuel said again, feeling privileged to have watched her make the final preparations.

Bithia was pleased. "You can have a taste of whatever is left untouched."

"He will touch none of it." Hammed said tersely. He was consumed with disgust for Samuel, hating the foreigner who was gaining favor in the sight of their master as the weeks went by.

"Why not?" Bithia said angry.

Hammed ignored Bithia and signaled to the slaves to take the platters. He looked down at Samuel with an air of animosity. "You'll stay outside after serving this evening. Do you understand?"

Bithia cringed at his bitterness and looked at Samuel with pity. She was a little surprised that Samuel's face was somehow not mottled red in anger like hers was already.

"Take that one," Hammed commanded the young boy, pointing to the beef special, "and try not to pour it on the floor." Samuel lifted the platter and followed Hammed from the kitchen.

The guests were still making their entrances. Samuel steadied his arm as he passed through the crowd. As he set the platter before the central table, Sahid noticed him. He had been having an argument with a Roman historian, who was named after his teacher, Pliny, about an ancient occurrence in Egypt.

Samuel decided to go out as instructed by Hammed. He stared at the display of richness for a minute, soaking in the beauty of the evening. The sight of traditional dancing amused many as the musicians played quietly in the corner. Everything looked grand as people, in their expensive attires and jewels filled the house.

Yet, Samuel could see that for all the celebration and lavishness of this evening, there was little joy on the host's face. Sahid looked pale from where he was standing. Samuel had grown to care deeply for this family he served. He prayed for each of them unceasingly. In this gathering, they looked so happy and yet they were all struggling about the future. Sahid, ever faithful and constantly dutiful, sought solace and blessing from his idols while Rhesa was always trying to appease the spirits of their ancestors thereby going, more frequently, to the Sun Temple at the east edge of the city. Samuel prayed for them all. God had given him this family to serve.

The sons of Sahid, Raja and Calil, came within Samuel's eye view and from where he stood, everyone seemed to notice them. Raja was able to get his warrior friends to all attend except Atlanersa while Calil seemed to be enjoying himself alone. The young lad was very resourceful and always found ways to either amuse himself or those around him.

Sahid still argued with Pliny. He looked across the room and spotted Samuel. He summoned Samuel to come closer.

"Yes, my lord?"
"Stay with me."
"Yes, master."

Samuel had no choice but to listen to their conversation. It was something about a slave's baby who was left in the bulrushes of the Nile hundreds of years ago, then found and reared by a royal princess. Pliny wanted to ascertain from Sahid since he was an Egyptian by birth. The argument drifted to something about the people leaving Egypt to the Middle East.

"Do you know that a different sect of people emerged from the Israelites?" Pliny stated.

"Tell me about it." Sahid replied. In his years of travel, he was opportune to have stop by the lovely city of Jerusalem and saw the spectacular temple before the whole city was burnt down. What a waste it was to destroy something so lovely and wonderful.

"These ones are quite different in their beliefs." Pliny continued. "They say that their God sent His Son to die. As a matter of fact, I was told by one of them that this Son died for all humanity. Have you ever heard of anything so ludicrous before in your life?"

"Yes. As a matter of fact I have." Sahid declared with a quick glance to Samuel.

Pliny looked surprised. "So you have come in contact with this belief? Well, they spread like locusts on a field." He shrugged off with disgust.

"Since you're a historian, let me give you a little story you will find useful." Sahid watched Pliny's aroused interest, aware that Samuel was listening too. "Sometime ago, the eunuch in charge of the Kandake's treasures, traveled to Israel. He made acquaintances with one of the first followers of this faith and came back declaring the same doctrine you speak of."

Samuel couldn't believe his ears and listened closely to hear more. So all this while his master knew more about his faith than he let on.

"He made disciples that went out of Meroe to spread this doctrine."

"What happened to this eunuch?" Pliny asked, curious.

"He left his service of the Kandake to spread his newly found faith and died doing it. As expected, he wasn't able to convert many to his beliefs but his disciples can still be found in the city, if you look hard enough."

"And the Kandake at the time, did she accept this doctrine?"

"You know, it surprises me that you don't know any of this. Your teacher's research is claimed to span across the whole region." Sahid added dryly.

"As you well know you cannot know what has not been told. My teacher went through great lengths to ascertain the stories of the Israelites ever being in Egypt."

"And how do you know then that the information you have, in relation to this case, is true if all the confirmation you get is from one side only? If the Egyptians deny it, don't you still have to ascertain even from them nevertheless?"

"Have you ever been to the Red Sea before Sahid?"

"One of my ships set sail by its Egyptian ports."

"Well, the Israelites claim that the Sea was physically separated by their god at their exodus from Egypt. When Master Pliny got there, the only evidence he found of such an occurrence was the remains of Egyptian chariots on the sea bed, close to the shore."

"So you're saying this is enough evidence?"

"I'm saying that if such remains was from the Red Sea crossing incident, how are we to justify when the Egyptians claim that the findings could range from many sources. A good example given was that the site has always been a trading spot for incoming goods abroad, or that it must have been from many shipwrecks suffered from cataracts."

"So your question is how do you authenticate the true source of your findings?"

"Exactly!" Pliny said with his face lit up. It seems his point was well taken.

"Can I ask you a question?"

"Yes."

"As a historian, how do you ever narrow down the findings you make and even date it if it could range from different sources? How is it you people are able to make a profound declaration stating were an event occurred based on what you discover? If that were the case for all you ever claim, then wouldn't it be right to say none of what you declare can be traced to its original source?"

"That's not always the case with every claim. There are cases where we've made discoveries and actually traced its source because of unique characteristics used to authenticate. I mean correlations are made that are without a doubt identical to its source."

"But how many are these findings fit into the category that you just described? Would I be right to say your work is sometimes based on assumptions even especially when you make a discovery that is identical with more than one source?"

Pliny felt the barb and changed the subject. Their discussions later drifted to the oncoming games. They talked about the upcoming wrestling matches the Kandake usually graced with her lovely presence.

It wasn't long before Sahid grew tired of him and watched what was going on around him with little interest. Some of the female guests displayed their newly acquired rings, nose jewels and bracelets. Many of the opulent came dressed up in materials of great worth, and the myriad shining reflections from common, extracted metals lit up the night more than the stars ever could. Sahid watched with blasé interest both men and women with ornate robes, tassels and sashes that draped from one shoulder. His childhood taste to be elite had waned down to the sweet taste of bile.

The last course was served. It was mainly fruits like pineapples, carrots and cucumbers with fatta, thin bread with lentils, peas, tomatoes and cheese.

A messenger came from the palace with greetings from the Kandake and blessings for the marriage of Sahid's daughter. Sahid accepted the news with a pretence smile on his face knowing that the Kandake wasn't coming at all.

Samuel later returned to the kitchen at Sahid's dismissal. He had seen the look in Hammed's eyes. A flicker of anger that he dare disregard his command to go outside was plastered on his face.

Bithia set Samuel to washing pots and cooking utensils immediately. She sent another two slave girls to clear the tables in the dining room now that the guests had adjourned for the night.

"I suppose you'll have to stay clear of Hammed." Bithia completely understood the bone between Hammed and this young lad. The lad has only been here for a few months and was already becoming the most favored of the master. "You can have whatever you want, Samuel. Help yourself."

Samuel looked at her in gratitude. "I'm sorry, Bithia." He smiled at her.

"You have nothing to be sorry about."

"Everything looked and smelled delicious. They all enjoyed every bite."

Bithia took the pot he had washed and hung it up. "Why should you apologize for what he said?"

"Hammed obviously doesn't have a heart the way you do."

Mollified, Bithia watched him wash the utensils, then dry and put them away, a chore not meant for a personal aide to the master but he did it anyway. She liked this young man. Unlike the others who had to be told, Samuel saw what needed do be done and did it. The others took their time in performing their duties, grumbling over everything. Samuel moved with a characteristic peace on his face always and assisted others when he saw the need.

"There's plenty left." she said. "The other slaves have had their fill and I've ordered them to bed. The harp and flute players and everyone else have eaten. The only one left to eat is Hammed. May he die of envy."

Samuel didn't respond to that as he got water from a vessel on his side and rinsed the utensils.

"Sit down and eat something. All you've taken tonight is kisra. Have some real food." She sat down across the table on a bench. "Try the beef or the goat. I know your taste buds are reeling."

Samuel took Bithia as a mother, and to refuse to sample what she had worked so hard to create would hurt her. She was so generous and free-spirited, telling jokes to the slaves as they worked at times. The food smelled so delicious that his stomach cramped from hunger. He hadn't eaten all day. "Thank you."

"Good!" Bithia said happily. "But you will eat on one condition"

"What is that?" Samuel asked.

"You will tell me all there is about your home and your god."

She served him both the lamb and beef together and returned to washing the remaining utensils, willing to listen to his story about his foreign god. Bithia had always been curious to know the source of the peace always written on this slave's face, even when his face was swollen after Raja lost his senses.

It was one of those days when Raja came home furious and angry. Everyone knew he must have had another fall out with his father. From his childhood that seemed to be the only thing that got him upset.

Raja got home and shouted for Samuel to come to him immediately. Samuel emerged from the room where he usually dined with his father and stood right in front of him.

Raja punched him across the face and began kicking him on the floor. If it wasn't for Rhesa that saved him, Raja would have killed him. Bithia had thought that warriors were meant to protect their own until that day. She heard the commotion from the kitchen and ran out to see what was going on.

Tears came fast when she saw Samuel on the floor almost disfigured. Raja stormed out afterwards and Hammed came in with a smile on his face. How could anyone be glad for another's suffering? What causes celebration at another's despair? Bithia ran to the food storage room to get an herb that had unparalleled medicinal value. The lad managed to get to the kitchen with the help of Calil and Makarasa while Rhesa went after her son.

It was days later before she knew what caused Raja to attack the slave boy. Makarasa told her that someone informed Raja that it was Samuel that was telling their father about Raja's activities; that Samuel was the spy hired by their father to watch him closely. Makarasa overheard her mother begging Samuel not to tell their father about what happened.

Bithia was angry at Raja for what he did. No one needed to be told about his deeds. It was carried by the sands his footprints left behind every crime. She knew the foolish warrior was just looking for who to vent his anger on the same way he did to the slave girls he abused from time to time.

Bithia also prepared another herb that was used to heal swollen wounds. The herb worked like magic. Although it did wonders to Samuel's face, the master still saw the cuts and asked him what happened. Samuel didn't answer even when he was threatened to be beaten by the master.

Bithia turned around and stirred at the poor boy as he ate. His fate in this house was already decided unless he got out somehow. She didn't need anyone to tell her who informed Raja with lies about Samuel. It was the same cold creature that smiled when the boy was in pain that day. It had to be the same evil person who informed Sahid about what Raja did when he was out.

Samuel began to narrate his story about all he had learnt from countless fellowships with the One in the forest and also from the parchment he still carried with him always. The words flowed freely and stole Bithia away from her thoughts.

"So tell me where I can go to see this god of yours?" Bithia asked, coming over to where he sat. She had watched the bright expression on his face as he spoke and held this slave in high regard. Too often times, she had heard him speak of this great god, as his handsome face bespoke of shared experiences with divinity. If this was his source of peace, she might as well try it.

"That is exactly what I have been trying to tell you, Bithia. He is not like the idols made by man. He is Omnipresent! Omnipotent! Omniscient! He gives peace to all who comes to Him."

"Peace." Bithia said with great need. "That's the only thing we all need. Are you saying that the emptiness I feel inside can be filled by Him alone?"

"Yes."

"Well, I guess I have nothing to lose but to try this god of yours. The problem is that I don't know what to do next. What sacrifice is required of Him? All I know how to do is cook."

"The sacrifice has been met already. All you need to do is believe."

"I don't understand." Bithia looked puzzled. He made it sound so easy but she knew it wasn't. It couldn't be. Not from where she stood and how she'd witnessed him suffer in silence because of his faith. She still wanted Samuel to tell the master what really happened that day when Raja almost killed him but he didn't.

"I will tell you Bithia." He rose up and stood in front of her. "Thanks be to God for his mercy." He laid his hands against hers and expounded more on the revealed mysteries of God.

9

Lust not after the beauty in thine heart;
neither let her take thee with her eyelids;
Be not taken by the subtleness; but do as the master bids.

Samuel blinded himself to the fact that the master's wife was taken with him. Since her daughter left Rhesa would request of him duties that made him linger in her presence. The master handed over the pottery site for her to oversee and Rhesa innocently asked that Samuel should help her.

Rhesa taught him how to manually coil up clay and then make vessels out of it. She would then ask him to escort her as she inspected the other workers.

"Tell me about the Serengeti. I heard the animals migrate in millions." Rhesa asked.

It sounded more to Samuel she just asked him to stay with her. He knew one way or another he had to find a way out of being in proximity with her almost everyday.

"It's the most beautiful place you could imagine. In pursuit of the rain, animals like wildebeests, striped animals, among many others, would begin moving from one region to another preyed on by the king of the jungle and laughing four-footed beasts."

Samuel looked distant for a moment. It was indeed a sight to see. "It's been said that the beauty captivates the animals as they move that some would just stand in admiration till wild animals pounce on them.

They welcome death in the midst of the enchanting paradise without a struggle. The cool grass beneath the skin cools the body from the Sun's heat and when the clouds choose to come on the scene carrying loads of rain, the bathe is enjoyed by everything that has breath."

"What drove you away from such bliss?"

"I'm here for a reason. I just don't know what it is yet?"

"There was one time," Samuel changed the subject immediately, "before my journey to Meroe, that I was so hungry I couldn't continue. I came across some large eggs on the hot sand. I looked around briefly to see if the animal that laid them was close by." Samuel broke out in laughter at this point.

"What's funny?" It was the first time she heard the slave boy laugh and her eyes lit up in response.

"I was about to break one of them when I heard loud footsteps coming from behind."

"It must have been the kind of large birds that has broad wings which deceptively aids its run and not its flight?"

Samuel nodded. He had seen a couple of them in Meroe already and learnt from experience not to steal their eggs anymore.

"It was the first time I saw it and what a chase. I tried to outrun it but realized I couldn't. I dropped the egg as I caught glimpse of its long neck brooding over me."

"I want to go there someday." Rhesa admitted. "I mean the Serengeti."

"Maybe you and master can visit someday."

There was a silence between them that spoke of tension on Samuel's part and restraint on Rhesa's.

"So what did you eat after you lost the egg?"

"Actually another bird flew by not too long after and fresh meat fell from its claws not to far in the distance."

Samuel wanted to pique her curiosity to ask him how that came about but didn't say anything afterwards when Rhesa didn't fall for it.

Rhesa wanted to touch him but her heart told her not to. He was a slave and nothing more. She would destroy her years of marriage by just a fad of pleasure. Her body was heavily warring against her mind. Samuel was like her son and he had already been in enough trouble as it was. Raja almost killed him because of a lie and if she did this, the boy would be killed by Sahid himself. But reason began to blur and the craving leavened.

She knew she had to channel her thoughts away from the pits of darkness. How she had gotten to this eluded her and she couldn't put her finger on why her body rebelled against her will. Rhesa realized that she must have denied herself the evaluation needed for her thoughts when it was still day. After the heart dwells on what is sin for a while, it becomes not too much of a sin anymore.

They were about to get home when Rhesa stopped him by slowly holding his hands. Samuel pulled his hands away and ran the rest of the way.

Rhesa watched as the lad disappeared slowly and suddenly she felt slightly faint. She stood alone outside. The air was very dry for lack of rain and so she had to cover herself with mufflers.

Logically, it must have been the weight of gold she wore that caused such heaviness physically. She knew it would weigh her down later in the day with the gold chains, bracelets and the tinkling ornaments on her feet but she wanted to dress to impress. Shame washed over her briefly as she acknowledged the truth that it wasn't for her husband she did all this for.

Hammed slowly walked past her and glanced at her briefly. Rhesa's eyes met Hammed's and she felt chilled within.

Hammed knew!

Tears came to her eyes as she realized that Hammed must have seen the nothing that just happened between her and Samuel.

And that the nothing was going to get the poor lad killed.

* * *

"The games begin today!" One shouted in excitement at the marketplace the next day. In reaction, merchants began packing their goods in for the day. Everyone looked forward to this time with great anticipation and there was practically no reason to stay at the marketplace when every possible customer would be at the games.

Various competitions for the game period would be in horseback riding, archery, wadi, and the most anticipated of all: wrestling. The way of the Romans had already influenced their way of life. The Wrestling bout was no longer for mere entertainment as it was before but to the death. There were rumors circulating that when the Kandake consulted the priests about the change of tactics in the games, it was said the gods would be honored by the blood that will be spilled.

Wrestling is such a wonderful sport engaged in for the amusement of the populace that royalty always graced the occasion.

Sahid made way past the others ahead of him in order to see the arena as Samuel escorted him. "Come quickly Samuel." He said. "We will be shown to our seat." He watched for the usher as he spoke.

"Master, we are here to watch the games?"

"Yes."

"Relax and let the excitement of the games loosen your strung nerves." Sahid assured his personal aide.

Spectators were already crowding around, swarming up and down and into the tier of seats. Samuel noticed that this wrestling ring was far better than the one he saw when he first came to Meroe. Four fluted columns were in superimposed sections. Closest to the grounds is the podium, where the Kandake sits. It was all made of iron and gold. Soldiers were behind every column to protect against the fury of the audience as seats went round.

"When will it begin master?" Samuel said, exasperated.

"The crowd is being handled. Don't worry, Samuel. It's always fun to watch. The Kandake hasn't arrived yet." He handed their ivory passes to the usher. The usher took them to the seats not too far from the Kandake's and handed the ivory chits over so that Sahid could match the writing with the seats.

"The ceremony will begin first, and once the Kandake arrives, the real wrestling fight will begin."

Samuel scarcely heard his master's words. He was so completely enthralled by the crowd. Hundreds were in attendance: from the wealthiest to the lowliest of slaves. How so much people could gather to witness such a gruesome blood fight, he wondered. Even in the midst of increased death among the citizenry, and with the present drought condition, a lot of people believe to relieve their sufferings by watching the games.

Samuel fixed his eyes on a man coming down the steps. He had on a white tunic right to his heels and carried a Sun guard for shade and a basket, undoubtedly laden with wine and delicacies. Samuel looked at the man with interest. The slave must belong to a man of fortune. Gold bracelets rested on his wrists, and large beads on his neck.

Sahid yawned widely as the tedious preliminary proceedings began. A shout followed, announcing the arrival of the Kandake of Meroe.

Everywhere grew silent in salute of her majesty.

It was when she approached them to take her seat that Samuel realized that his master was seated very close to her.

It's the first time Samuel saw the Queen.

She glowed in gold jewels and wore beads around her neck. A gold armlet with colored glass inlays rested around her left arm. On her right arm was an intricately hinged bracelet of gold and enamel, showing a goddess but Samuel couldn't make out the inscribed god itself. Though pale and withdrawn on her seat, her beauty couldn't be overemphasized. A true descendant of the most beautiful of women in Meroitic history.

Many come far and wide just to catch a glimpse of her lovely face. Golden laces accentuated her figure and were held firmly by a tight belt. Her brown eyes glowed in sweet resonance with her skin and thick dark hair rested behind her head.

The gates below opened to reveal the one to direct on a majestic steed. He was splendidly dressed in white and halted before the Queen's platform. With all the dramatic flare of an actor, he honored the Queen. The crowd approved the brevity, and the Queen, its eloquence. The overseer signaled grandly and the first four wrestlers came out bare-chested.

Samuel spotted one whose skin looked a little light, unlike the rest who were Sun burnt. The crowd cheered one of the warriors by his name: Hydaspes. The fairer one was an Egyptian captive.

The whole place shook with the voices from the crowd.

The Kandake nodded and the wrestling began.

The stick fighters were to the left while the Egyptian sparred against the Nubian champion, Hydaspes. There was a mediator on the arena, with a trumpet in hand.

Attention was more on the Egyptian and the Nubian fight. While the other fighters used their sticks they used their hands. The Egyptian was the first to attack. He moved so fast that in an instant, had Hydaspes in a chokehold.

The mediator walked towards the Egyptian grappler and warned him about the illegal move. "Take care. You are in the presence of Kandake."

The sparring went on for a while as each struggled in their entanglement to fall his foe. The stick fighters soon became invisible as all eyes were on the Egyptian and the Nubian wrestler. The mediator separated them every once in a while as they lingered in a lock down while the crowd grew wild and weary with shouts.

The Egyptian began taunting Hydaspes.

"Woe to you, O black enemy! I will make you take a helpless fall in the presence of your people."

"What is this fear you wear on your face and yet your mouth relays something different? Strength is never found in the multitude of words." Hydaspes replied breathing heavily. "Apedemak is with me."

The Egyptian appeared ready for Hydaspes attack. Hydaspes moved in so tactfully and lowered his head as the Egyptian threw the close line. This time Hydaspes locked the Egyptian in a tight grip and pried the left arm while holding him tightly. He drove off his opponent's right leg and twisted his left arm so that the Egyptian's thumb faced downward. This move straightened out the bent arm thereby localizing maximum pressure against the back of the Egyptian's arm.

The captive made a feeble attempt to counter the move by wrapping his left leg around the Nubian's right leg but was forced down with so much strength that both his feet left the ground. Seconds later, he landed face-first in the sand, defeated.

The victorious Nubian stood over his opponent, his hands raised in a traditional winner's pose. The crowd cheered loudly as Hydaspes recite a common victory chant before the Kandake, and the people:

"Apedemak is the god who decreed protection against every land to the ruler. He is the Lord of life! The Lord of the Nubians."

The defeated foe acknowledged his loss by kissing the ground before Kandake.

Only the first and last day of the games survived the bloodshed. The crowd cheered for their own as Hydaspes raised his hands.

The Sun had risen high and hot. The wind refused to stir. Samuel noticed perspiration beading on his master's forehead. The Kandake rose up from her seat to leave. Others rose in honor of her grace. It was obvious she was worried. Her countenance dulled in the light. The continued death toll must bother her greatly after three years of not even a drop of rain.

The whole place was silent until she was gone and then the games continued with horseback riding and archery.

* * *

He had spent three months in the kingdom of Meroe and those that Samuel was free with his beliefs were the cook, Bithia, and the kitchen slaves. Hammed had already poisoned the minds of the male slaves against him. It was something about him trying to win the master's favor and become the overseer and chief servant. This obviously didn't sit well with any of them and he got a lot of rude treatments from the lot.

"Samuel, the master wants you." One of the hostile male slaves informed him early one morning.

Samuel hurried to his master's chambers. He saw Sahid writing in hieroglyph on a papyrus.

"You will accompany me across the city today." Sahid said without looking up.

"Yes, my lord."

"We stop first at Wad Ban Naga. It leads to important inland centers where I need to see someone."

"Yes master."

Without looking up Sahid stood up and walked towards the door. Samuel followed without hesitation and then stopped as he saw the master's wife, Rhesa waiting by the outer entrance.

Sahid acknowledged her presence and stopped right in front of her.

"Is it possible that you can spare your aide to help me on the fields and with the pottery trades today?"

"Maybe tomorrow. He will be coming with me to Wad Ban Naga today."

Samuel breathed a sigh of relief. It seemed that the master's wife was still trying to after him. A certain truth dawned on Samuel that his time was definitely coming to an end in this home. Rhesa never wanted to listen to his stories at all in the first place. A mere child would have figured that out already.

Rhesa looked at her husband and wanted to see if she could read anything from the expression on his face. If Hammed had already told him then this ride to the inland centers was definitely not just a ride.

She would have avoided all of this if she had just tried to stitch up just one loose end of her selfish heart. Apparently, the tear she caused wasn't only to hers but another's.

With horses they rode for hours to Naga and Musawwarates-Sufra, built on the plains beneath a ridge of low mountains, some twelve to eighteen miles inland. Samuel noticed that Naga must be a very important religious center as he counted seven stone temples. A peculiar temple wall showed the soul of King Natakamani and Queen Amanitore doing homage to the lion god.

Water had always been an imported necessity with or without rainfall, and the fields weren't doing well from the underground system that fed them water all the way from the Nile. They rode ten miles north to Musawwarates-Sufra to see the master's friend. The city was enigmatic and awesome to behold, Samuel observed. They galloped through a strange labyrinth of stone temples and courtyards surrounded by walls and connected by corridors and ramps. He was amazed at the tremendous stonewalls that partitioned the complex into twenty separate compounds. The garden of trees there had survived the drought and looked well laid out.

They came to stop not too far from a temple that had carvings of a lion-headed man, dressed in armor and seated on an elephant, bearing prisoners and weapons of war. It was the carvings of their supreme god once more.

"Come with me, Samuel." Sahid commanded.

They came to a large building not too far from another iron smeltery. There was a cripple who sat not too far by the entrance. Sahid and Samuel walked right past him. For a brief moment, their shadows fell on the crippled respectively, and moved away as they got to the entrance.

The guard allowed them entry into the building. He recognized Sahid. He must obviously be well known around here, Samuel figured. They entered a private chamber, and a man rose up from his seat to meet them. He wore a traditional jalabia, which is a long white robe, beads on his neck and gold bracelets that lay numerous around his hand.

"Sahid. It's nice to see you again."

"Same here, Theagenes." They both embraced and held each other at arms length.

"And who do you bring here." Theagenes said staring at Samuel.

"My most trusted servant."

The remark obviously took Samuel by surprise.

"You intend we discuss business with him present?"

"Yes." Sahid said affirming his trust for his personal aide.

"Fine."

Theagenes took his seat and offered Sahid one also. The heave of air that rushed out of his lungs resounded his age. His eyes held a steady gaze of a confident businessman. The only facial hair he had stuck out his nose and ears.

A hot atmosphere hung over the Sun-lit room. Two well-built young men dressed in loincloths and turbans stood on both ends of the room. Theagenes and Sahid sat and began discussing their plans for the exports to the Greco-Roman world.

"You told me that one of your caravans arrived a few days ago." Sahid said. He had the intention of exporting iron at a higher quantity to other parts of the world.

"Yes and it came with the message requesting more gold and iron." Theagenes said.

"Good. That means more business for us in these trying times."

"There will be nothing soon if our ancestors fail to intercede. We have been stretched beyond our limits and the earth is wailing for just a drop."

"Rome's strength increases, my friend. I heard that Jerusalem, the land of the Jews, has eventually been destroyed." Theagenes snapped his fingers and a slave hurried over with a tray of fruit. "The whole race, I heard, is almost obliterated."

"So, the great Israelites have been defeated." Sahid said wistfully.

"Rome is like us in many ways, Sahid. They allow their people to worship whatever gods they choose."

"Provided they worship the emperor, the way we worship Apedemak, and pay respects like we do to the Kandake."

Sahid accepted wine offered to him by a male slave.

"They prostrate themselves before a god they cannot see," Theagenes continued, "and refuse, to their deaths, to bend their necks a fraction to the emperor of Rome."

Sahid glanced at Samuel, knowing that his aide was willing to die for his beliefs.

"Have you heard about the new growing sect of the Jews?"

Sahid nodded.

"They are Jews but they are different in what they believe." Theagenes took a gulp of wine before continuing. "I mean don't get me wrong. This people believe in one god as the Jews but they say that their god sent his son to die for the world; something about saving souls from eternal death. Ha! Such words sicken me."

A vague feeling of unrest and disquiet slowly gnawed at Sahid the same way it does any time he heard about this strange doctrine. He couldn't fathom how a god will allow his son to die as means of redemption. It just didn't make any sense. It defied all logic and reason. To even entertain such thoughts in a preposterous tale sounded vain and imprudent to him. He decided to change the subject and discussed about his investments in the gold mine and iron smeltery.

Sisimithres, the present eunuch of Kandake, and official in charge of the royal treasures, came in with two other men as escorts. He was as young as Theagenes. He smiled as he came in and they rose in honor and took his short hand in turns before pulling him to an embrace.

"Sahid, I see you secure your investments very well or what else could you be possibly doing here?" Sisimithres observed, with a smile.

"As well as you." Sahid replied.

"Ah yes, by all means. I just dropped in and would be off to the Sun Temple."

"Why are you going to the Sun Temple?" Theagenes asked, curious.

"The sorcerers and priests have gathered to appease the gods concerning the drought. A declaration has been made that the rain would fall if the gods are pacified."

"They have been appeasing the gods for three years and nothing has happened." Theagenes said shrugging his shoulders.

"If you ask me, I'd say the gods no longer hear us." A snort of contempt escaped Sahid.

"Then you have to stop by the temple on your way back, if the rain doesn't slow you down, for I tell you it will rain today." Sisimithres spoke in confidence. "Give me the writings concerning my investments Theagenes, and I will go through it on the way."

Sisimithres took his leave immediately after Theagenes gave him what he required.

Samuel noticed the tension in the room. They all knew that if not for the Great Sea in the far north of Africa that fed the Nile, it would have been dried out by now.

"What do you say, Sahid?" Theagenes said, "Are you going to stop by the Sun Temple?"

"What do you think? This I have to see."

"Alright then. I will go with you."

Theagenes ordered one of the slaves to come with him as they took their leave.

Sahid wandered what good could possibly come out of gods that have been appeased over and over again. Will a god try the patience of its creatures by leaving them to rot when they wail and cry out for intervention? If it were a year then it could be considerable but three years it was already since the rain touched the grounds of the jewel of Nubia—the city of Meroe and its neighboring settlements.

People gathered around as they got outside. It seemed someone was addressing them in the center. You could hear the voices of a man in the middle trying to get his story to the ears of listeners and those who pass by.

Theagenes asked a man what happened and the man informed him that the crippled that usually sat down here suddenly started walking without assistance.

"That's impossible!"

"Exactly what I said when told but I've seen him and it is true. He said he felt like the clouds sheltered over him for a second or two. His eyes were downcast before and when he looked up he realized that, as always, two men had just passed by just like people do every day.

"He said strength returned to his body suddenly and the urge to stand was incomprehensible and yet, inevitable!"

"Are you saying that he doesn't attribute his healings to the gods but to the works of mere passer-bys?"

"All I know is what he said." The man walked away after answering Theagenes' question.

"We need to go to the Sun Temple now, Theagenes." Sahid reminded him.

Theagenes just kept quiet trying to work it through in his mind. The former cripple said two men passed him by and then he was healed.

Sahid willed his aide to look at him before they began their ride back to the Sun Temple. It was a good thing they came out early. Didn't sound too far-fetched to think that the two men who passed were himself and his aide yet his mind refused the truth. It was impossible for a cripple to be healed unless the gods show favor. And why would the gods show favor to a cripple when they could have just send rain for the benefit of many.

Sahid reasoned that the cripple must be lying but why would he? He always saw the crippled man every time he came here. A thought occurred to him that maybe it was Samuel's god that healed the cripple but he dismissed it immediately.

Sahid tried to read some truth from his aide's eyes but saw nothing but calm in it. Hopefully, they would have enough time to get to the Sun Temple before the day is done and night is come, and maybe, just maybe, Samuel's god will show up again.

Dust rose from the dry grounds to claim its restless form as they made their way to the eastern edge of the city on horses. Theagenes rode on his beloved camel instead. It was the richest camel in the whole of Nubia. The golden latch that went around it was unmatched in the entire region of Wad Ban Naga. The camel seemed to run with a delicacy and gracefulness befitting a princely stallion.

They past a few rakuba, which is typical desert architectures of sticks, reeds and mats, with the taste of dust in their mouths.

While it was paramount that they all get to the Sun Temple to witness something great, Samuel's heart sorrowed at the sight of pain and deprivation along the way. It was hard to imagine that people lived in the rakubas.

His mind easily wandered away to the free roaming and lushness the carpeted grass of the Serengeti provides. It occurred to him how endless it seems when beauty, so transient and momentary, is being experienced. The deep wounds afflicted by poverty is completely forgotten in the expanse of abundance nature provides. Definitely, these poor people would trade anything just to be lost in such a place as the Serengeti like he was.

After a long time of riding, they could see the great Sun Temple in the distance. It was a grand square building where the sacred sanctuary stood in the center, surrounded by platforms.

Crowds had gathered from everywhere waiting for their gods to come to their aid. The priests and sorcerers, those acclaimed to be gifted by the gods, were making rituals already. Sahid, Theagenes and their servants alighted and walked towards the center for a better view, making their way through the crowd on the flight of steps. The crowd parted for them in respect for the wealthy. They stopped few inches from the south wall of the podium. Samuel noticed several galloping horsemen armed with weapons and wearing peculiar helmets carved on the wall.

Sahid held a countenance of disbelief at the sight of the gathered crowd. If nothing happened today, he might start considering following the footsteps of the animals, for they had migrated far south: the rhinoceros, elephants, and the giraffes. If not down south, he will head north to Alexandria.

Samuel stood beside his master taken by the magnificence of temple structure. He acknowledged the nudge he felt inside about his dream the night before: four hundred and fifty priests, calling the name of their gods and another man who called the name of his God. Now he knew why his heart agreed with Sisimithres when he said the rain would fall today, only that it wouldn't come from the Nubian gods.

Samuel slowly walked towards the priests and sorcerers with boldness, and crossed the line not meant for the ordinary.

Theagenes startled back as Sahid's slave stepped away from them and walked towards the priests. He turned to Sahid and with his eyes told him to stop the boy.

Sahid knew that Samuel would voice out someday, defile their gods, and thereby end his life. He had seen it in his eyes a long time ago that such a day as this would come. It was pointless to try and stop him even when Theagenes told him.

"Let his god save him." We will see who the real god is today, he thought to himself.

Samuel stopped a few inches from the priests and paused for a moment.

Everyone waited in expectation. There was written on their faces desperation and the need for a renewal of hope. Samuel saw this and began to address the people.

"How long will it take for you to remove the folds that blind your eyes to see the truth? Isn't it clear that your gods cannot come to your rescue? How long will you be separated between two choices? If my Lord be God, follow him, but if it be Apedemak, then stay with him."

The people didn't answer a word, baffled at him who dared to defy their gods before the great Sun Temple. The priests and sorcerers had earlier turned to see what caused the crowd to murmur.

All the priests were covered in fine leather garments styled differently as each priest deemed fit. It was well-decorated with printed motifs of the lion god, Apedemak. One of them stepped out angrily.

"You dare defy our gods. The flaming breath of the fierce lion goddess, Sekhmet, caused the brutal heat and drought we suffer from. She has to be appeased with elaborate rituals to ensure that the Nile would rise again.

"What about Tefnut? The goddess of moisture, and rain, and flood, whom we all mankind fear? She has to be appeased with prayers and sacrifices also. And above all, is Apedemak-the supreme god of all, yet you declare profane words on the sacred podium that symbolizes there meeting place. Today, you shall surely die." He looked at the crowd and declared. "We have here a blasphemer who stands before us with a sacrilegious milestone around his neck. He will die for what he has done; for the blasphemies that came forth from his defiled mouth. We will offer him up as a befitting sacrifice to the gods and he will be the perfect appeasement the gods require."

Samuel again addressed the people. "I remain a servant to the only true living God, but you have here four hundred and fifty priests and sorcerers. Let them make their sacrifices and call on the name of their gods, and I will call on the name of the Lord, and the one that answers is the Lord God."

The crowd began to speak in chorus and there rose a loud noise in the whole place.

"Silence!" shouted the priest.

"You may have lost your senses. The drought has plagued more than our cities but do remember where your allegiances lie."

The priest moved further out of the others and stood in front of Samuel. His eyes exhuming hate. His hands tighten in control of the rage building up in him.

"Our gods bring upon us such harsh conditions because we have failed to honor the priests that serve them in loyalty and devotion. Have you quickly forgotten ages ago when our king entered the sacred quarters and slew the priests in disregard of our customary regicide? When our king, at the time, marched into the temple and slew all the priests to avoid being killed, in honor of the gods, our kingdom was destined for doom since then. The drought is one of the punishments from the gods. If you allow this heretic to defile the sacred quarters again by allowing his god to contend against ours, then be comforted by the drought. For worse is yet to come."

"If your gods be true let them come in defense of their reign. I serve the One who will not only bring rain on these dry lands but will deliver all from the plagues you claim destroy these lands when it only resides in your minds. Call on your gods and I will call on mine."

The priest looked at the crowd, the other priests, and finally at the lad. If it was the last thing he did, this boy will not see daylight again.

"So be it."

With that the priests gathered together and took with them a bullock, dressed it and entered the sacred quarters of the temple to offer the sacrifice on the altar. Their cry to the gods to hear them shook the whole temple but there was no response. Not even a blast of wind.

The Sun would soon be setting and nothing happened from the time they called when the Sun was highest in the sky.

Samuel mocked them, and said, "Cry aloud! If Apedemak is God, let him intervene. Either he slumbers from the great task of causing drought, or is far gone in a journey, or maybe he can't hear and needs to be healed."

They cried out the more, and cut themselves with the sacrificial knives till blood flowed among some. Their voices soon faded as their gods failed them.

Words had been sent to the Kandake about what was happening. She came with her chariots and horses hurriedly to the Sun Temple. The crowd parted to usher the Queen to the center. Kandake, just fully aware that the priests had been praying from the Sun's highest, and that nothing had happened, was even more depressed than ever before.

Samuel raised his voice to stir the already weary crowd.

"People of Meroe, listen to me. The only true God shows wonders in the heavens above, and signs in the earth beneath. Though the eyes see and the ears hear the heart of men wander away from the truth: there is only one God. See and believe."

The Sun began to quiet down in such expressive beauty. It was time it boasted of its great light to another earthly region.

"Whosoever shall call on the name of the Lord shall be saved! As you well know that we all are sinners and no matter the amount of sacrifices made to the gods, our sins remain. God knew this and sent His only Son, Jesus to save us from sin and death. He lived among men and was delivered by the counsel and foreknowledge of God; by wicked hands was crucified and slain."

The crowd watched the small lad who spoke with unmatched authority.

"For three years," Samuel continued, "the rain didn't fall in these lands, and it has been the darkest years ever seen in this kingdom."

The people's hearts pricked as they listened.

Theagenes was amazed that the very doctrine they had spoke about inhabited Sahid's slave. Sisimithres had tried to get a word out of Sahid throughout the time they waited for the priests to cause rain but Sahid stared at his aide without blinking. He couldn't make out anything from the stare but followed it as it rested on Samuel.

"What shall we do?" Someone cried out from the crowd.

"Repent and be baptized! Every one of you in the name of Christ Jesus for the remission of sins, and you all shall receive the gift of the Holy Ghost. For the promise is to as many as call on the name of our God."

Samuel looked up to the heavens and prayed: "Lord! Dear God of Abraham, Isaac, and of Jacob. Let it be known this day that thou art God of all the earth, and that I am thy servant, and that I have done all these things at thy word. Hear me, O Lord, hear me, that this people may know that thou art the Lord God, and that thou hast turned their hearts back again by the sacrifice of your only Son . . . . in the name of Christ Jesus."

A strong wind suddenly blew from the Nile raising dust as it came to land. The priests and sorcerers, Kandake, the people of Meroe, all waited for what was making its way to them, on the wings of the wind. It swept the whole land in one swift pace and fear gripped the people as they presumed haboob, a local name for dust storm, was about to overthrow them. Rising to the clouds, the fountains of the deep broke up, and miraculously, the windows of heaven opened.

Rain, from the Lord God fell, and everyone across the kingdom was drenched in it. When all the people saw it, some fell on their faces and cried, "The Lord, he is God! The Lord, He is God!"

A loud shout rose within the crowd as they all embraced the blessing from above. Many ran home to put out their vessels to collect the rain in them.

"Kandake, we need to take you back to the palace. You're all wet." Sisimithres said, himself captivated by what just transpired.

Samuel said unto her, "Go up from here, repent and serve, and savor the abundance of rain."

Kandake hesitated for a moment but later gave in to her guards who took her back to the palace.

Shaking violently, eyes wide, Sahid stared up into the heavens. The Sunset cascaded a beautiful orange-red glow on the horizon. He realized he was shouting and crying and laughing, all at the same time. The glow of the Sun faded into softer colors as the darkness slowly crept in. whatever it was that ailed him within left him at the sight of the power of Samuel's God.

The priests and sorcerers rose from the ground where they had prostrated during the whole occurrence. Some of the people ran away to their homes in jubilation. Those who were left stood awestruck. In the rain, they walked up to Samuel and said, "What must we do to be saved?"

"Believe in the Lord Jesus Christ, and you shall be saved."

And with many other words Samuel testified and exhorted them, saying, "Save yourself from this evil generation."

Then they that gladly received his word were baptized in the Nile, and that same night, there were added a thousand to the Lord, including Sahid. Some walked away with hardened hearts even after witnessing the power of God. Theagenes was one of them. It was only deng. Any sorcerer of the weather could have done the same thing.

Sahid rose, from the waters crying, "Jesus is Lord!" a joyous conviction ringing in his voice that hadn't been there before. The sound of it echoed through the night, driving back the darkness.

That night, Samuel made contact with the surviving disciples of the eunuch of Kandake that went to Israel to worship, the same one that was converted on the way by Philip, one of those chosen to serve tables by the apostles: the one that brought his father into the faith.

"We anticipated your coming." Telipha, one of the eunuch's disciples exclaimed. "Someone prophesied about your coming three months ago." He said laying a hand on Samuel's shoulders. You're much younger than we thought. That's the way God works. The weak he chooses to confound the wise."

"Thank you Samuel." Sahid said as he approached him. "Thank you."

"Your thanks are to God. He alone is worthy, master. He alone!"

Then there was silence. Not like the silence that conveyed messages of drought and sorrow.

This was different.

Everyone stood quiet as the rain claimed its voice. Slowly their bodies felt the chill but their souls welcomed it. Their hearts united in awe and wonder of God. The earth must be drunk by now but the imbuing of body and soul surpassed anything.

It was dark now. The Sun no longer lit the regions. However, they had all the light for this life and the next.

For a moment, the devil left them and angels came to attend man's heartfelt worship of gratitude without an utterance of words.

10

A little sleep, a little slumber may just be too much;
The persistence of the enemy's onslaught, there has never been such.

The new converts destroyed carved images of their gods they had at home. The fear and despair that had so many captive melted away as they turned Sahid's home to a worship place. Rain became a commoner on the lands, nourishing the grounds. What a sight to behold as the fields blossomed once more. As more people came to know the Lord, the land grew fruitful. Wheat and barley, vines and pomegranates, oil olive and honey grew in sweet accord with more than enough for.

Three months passed since that overwhelming event at the Sun Temple.

The Lord was with Samuel, and he was a prosperous man in the house of his master.

The Lord was with him, and the Lord made all that he did to prosper in his hand. Sahid made him overseer of his house, and all that he had. It came to pass from the time that he made him overseer in his house, and over all that he had, that the Lord blessed the Egyptian's house for Samuel's sake, and the blessing of the Lord was upon all that he had in the house, and in the field.

The number of people worshipping in Sahid's home multiplied daily. They came to worship outside his home. While the assembly continued in harmony, breaking bread and sharing with gladness and singleness of heart, evil bloomed in the hearts of some, Hammed being the chief of them. He now answered to the young southern foreigner. The new arrangement sat well with Bithia, the chief cook, amongst many, for Samuel was virtually in control of everything.

"By the gods, I wish him dead," Hammed said, tears streaming down his cheeks. He lay pale on his bed at the slave quarters of Sahid's home. "I see the way they look at him. It utterly disgusts me."

"Why do you worry about this?" Calasiris, one of the young male slaves, said gently, amazed at how Hammed truly felt about Samuel. Samuel never intended harm. Hammed just never thought of anyone but himself, nor did he consider what the results of his actions might be as long as he came out in the end with benefits.

The eventful day had passed when Sahid announced Samuel as overseer, and Hammed as the assistant. He tried one day to get the master to the wrestling arena but as usual, Sahid was listening to Samuel rant about ancient stories past: stories about their newly-found faith. Now accustomed to the doctrinal talk around, Hammed hardly bothered listening to them. He was deep in thought. He pressed in deeper into his dark soul, looking for how to rid them of the lad.

Calasiris, more worried about Hammed's hatred for Samuel, knew something evil would come out of this all in the end. He thought of informing Samuel but shrugged it off as soon as the idea came to his mind. Hammed was always deep in thought, plotting something. Calasiris tried talking to him but he refused. He could feel the silent rage in Hammed as he changed his clothes and went out into the night.

Hammed later arrived just after light spilled all over the land from the intrusive Sun, looking dusty and disheveled. He allowed himself into the house.

The master came out of his private chambers and met him by the passage. "Have the bath filled with warm scented water, and bring me something to eat." Sahid ordered, striding toward his room.

Hammed passed on the instructions quickly to Calasiris, then hastened after his master.

Sahid entered his room followed by Hammed. He noticed nothing amiss about Hammed's gentle face and relaxed manner.

"I've been worried for you, my lord. I hope you know what you are doing."

"What do you mean by that?" Sahid's voice rose in annoyance. "So I now answer to a slave?"

Hammed bowed on one knee.

"I'm sorry master, I forgot my place."

"Why are you worried about me?" There was an act here, somewhere. Sahid sensed it.

Hammed rose up with his head still bowed. "I was on my way home this morning, and then knew something was wrong when I saw people gathered not too far from here." He waited for a response from his master but didn't get any.

"I asked them what was wrong and they told me that they witnessed Samuel speak blasphemous words against Apedemak, the lion god and our honorable Kandake."

"In case you haven't noticed Hammed, Samuel has been doing exactly that since the Sun Temple event three months ago. What did you tell them Hammed?" Sahid perused his face. He was sure there was foul play here.

"I told them that it couldn't have been Samuel, but they insisted and are on their way here. I rode past them quickly to inform you master."

"You didn't tell me before you left this morning." He observed Hammed's face turn ashen. "Where did you go to without my permission?"

Hammed's face bore no expression as his mind flipped in procrastination. He wanted to tell his master about Rhesa and Samuel, and how a fortnight ago, Samuel stormed out of the slave quarters only for Rhesa to leave right after him. Although Sahid wouldn't have believed right away without proof, proof he alone could provide.

But that wasn't the plan he agreed to with Rhesa.

The plan that was now unfolding.

"My lord, my lord!" Calasiris called out from the passage. He let himself into the private chamber. "There are people gathered in front of the house." Fear was written all over his face. "They demand for Samuel, master."

Rhesa entered with her hand shaking. "What's happening? Why are people gathered in front of the house?"

For a second, Sahid envisioned the tension gathering in the room. What will they do with Samuel once they have him? His wife's emotion was already in shambles.

Samuel walked outside as the guards allowed the Queen's guards to come in with the crowd behind them.

"What did he do?" Sahid came rushing out to stop Samuel from being apprehended.

"We have witnesses that said they heard him speak blasphemous words against our gods and against the Kandake." One of Kandake's guards said. "The Kandake commands a hearing between him and the witnesses."

Sahid knew in his heart that Hammed must have suborned men to testify against Samuel. For a brief instant, he hated him, but later felt shame when he remembered Telipha's word at their worship gathering:

'Love those who hate you, and pray for those who despitefully use you and persecute you.'

Sahid was beginning to believe those words were not practical. How feasible is it to love someone who hates you? Wouldn't it be living a lie when your affections are based on pretense? He may try to reason it out but as the guards led Samuel away his mind chose what came naturally to him.

He turned quickly and stirred at Hammed and he was convinced that he could never love this slave.

The sky was clear and the Sun, at its hottest, when Samuel was led to the palace, with the throng of people following. They all stood before the magnificent palace: a golden multi-storied building that spanned about four hundred square meters. It housed not only the kings and Queens, but also their advisors, trade goods, and several craftspeople. It had within its walls a central courtyard, where different doors led to enormous storerooms, some craft workshops, and administrative chambers. On their way to the palace, they passed small houses and craft workshops. The best of the ivory, carnelian, amethyst, gold, amber, copper and other important commodities were brought here first. The palace entrance is admitted by massive gilded doors, proof of security that coupled the high raised walls.

Unfortunately, today didn't serve the majority who had never been through the palace gates to witness the remarkable architecture of unequalled artistry. Descriptions of the palace held no justice to what was true.

The Queen was announced into the courtyard. Sahid squeezed himself through the crowd to seek the Queen's mercy for Samuel's life.

Kandake raised her hand to stop Sahid's pleas before it even left his mouth.

"Let him defend himself." She said taking her seat on the royal golden chair.

The false witnesses stepped out from the crowd saying, "Your highness. This man spoke blasphemous words against the great Lion god, his temple, and against you. We heard him say that this Jesus of Nazareth shall destroy this place, and shall change the customs which was delivered to us by our ancestors."

The crowd fell silent, looking steadfastly at the one arrayed before all to see, the one who defied everything they ever knew by the strange god he declared Lord of all.

"What do you say slave?" Kandake commanded.

Samuel had always wondered what hindered the Kandake from commanding his audience after being a witness to what God did in the Sun Temple. He knew the miracle of the rain falling shook her traditional beliefs. Here he was right in front of her elegance and beauty that knew no bounds. She wore a gleam on her face as she waited for him to answer. Her majesty's clothes matched the golden chair and it seemed she was made with it.

"Men, brethren, and fathers, listen. The God of glory appeared to a man called Abraham, centuries ago, when we were in a far away land." Samuel began his defense. "God said to him, 'Get out of the country, and from thy people, and come into the land which I shall show you'. Then he came out of the land of the Chaldeans, and came to a certain place. After his father died, God sent him to the land of Israel. God didn't give Abraham any of the land, not even for him to set foot on, but He promised him that he would give it to him and his generations as a possession, and to all those born to his name. The ironic thing is that he didn't have any child yet."

Samuel turned round and saw that he had everyone's attention. So he continued.

"God told him that his descendants would live in a strange land and that they would be in bondage, and they would be exploited for four hundred years."

The sound of shifting sandals on the dry ground intruded the courtyard as complete silence served him to speak.

"Some of you know what it is like to be in bondage; to serve someone by force and not by choice." He could see that he had witnesses as some of the people looked down in confirmation.

"God also told him that the nation to whom they shall be in bondage will be punished by him and after that they shall be free to go and worship Him." He looked at Kandake in the eyes and said, "The nation that God punished was Egypt."

That statement alone rose up few murmurings from the crowd. The side talks died down as Samuel went on to narrate.

"God made a covenant with them: a covenant of circumcision. And God brought about his promise by giving Abraham a child. The child's name was Isaac and he was circumcised on the eighth day. Isaac later gave birth to Jacob and Jacob gave birth to twelve sons. There was one of the twelve that was envied by others and hence he was sold to the land of Egypt. His name was Joseph and God, the blessed One, was with him. God delivered him in all he faced in Egypt and made him to find favor in the sight of Pharaoh, king of Egypt. Pharaoh made him governor over Egypt and his entire house."

Kandake knew about the Egyptians enslaving the Israelites. To her, the Jews believed that there was One God and that they were the chosen race, but she had never heard the story in detail like this. With everyone else, she was eager to know what happened to their greatest and fiercest rival of the Nile.

"Now there came a famine over all the land of Egypt and Canaan and great affliction, the likes of which went on for three years in this kingdom. Jacob and his family had no sustenance whatsoever, but he heard that there was corn in Egypt. He hence, sent his ten eldest sons to buy corn from Egypt. The second time they went to Egypt to buy food, Joseph made himself known to them. Pharaoh was told about his governor's brethren and he allowed Joseph to fetch his family from the land of Canaan to come reside in Egypt. It was there that Jacob died and was buried in the cave his grandfather. When the time of promise God made to Abraham was close at hand, the people multiplied and grew in Egypt till another king became Pharaoh." With a slight change of tone in Samuel's voice, the crowd knew they had come to the main part of the story and prepared themselves for it.

"This king didn't know Joseph. He enslaved them and killed their male children. It was during this time that a male child, called Moses, was born. He was a beautiful child and was nourished in secret for three months. They knew he would be discovered and killed so they put him in a basket and placed him along the tall stalks of grass on the Nile River, the same that runs through these lands. Pharaoh's daughter found him and took him in as her son and so Moses was taught all the wisdom of the Egyptians, and became mighty in words and in deeds."

To know such events took place enthralled the crowd. Obviously they wanted to hear more.

"It's ironic isn't it? A child grows up in the arms of his people's foe, nourished and well taught. At the age of forty, he usually visited his people, the Israelites. One day, an Egyptian was beating up an Israelite. Moses got angry and killed the Egyptian. He thought that by now his people would understand that for him to grow up in the hands of the enemy was proof from God, the blessed One, that it would be by his hands that deliverance will come. But they didn't understand."

"So what happened?" Someone said from the crowd.

"The very next day he went out and saw two of his people fighting. He tried to make peace but the one who was wrong pushed him away saying, 'who made you a ruler and judge over us? Will you kill me the same way you killed the Egyptian yesterday?' Moses knew that for them to know what happened the day before, others might know as well. So he ran away to another land where he met a woman and gave birth to two sons."

Samuel didn't say anything for a while. Some slave came to the Kandake and delivered a message she alone heard.

"Go on." She said as she waved the slave away.

"Forty years passed. It was then God sent a messenger on a mountain to speak to Moses. The supernatural being, sent by God, appeared to Moses in a burning bush. Moses saw the bush burning but the flame did not affect the leaves. It was a sight to behold. It was there God, the blessed One, spoke to him saying, 'I am the God of thy fathers, the God of Abraham, and the God of Isaac, and the God of Jacob.' Then Moses trembled, and knelt down. The Lord said, 'Remove your sandals, for where you stand is a holy ground. I have seen my people's affliction in Egypt, and have heard their cry, and have come to deliver them. Now go to Egypt.'"

Samuel turned around and saw Hammed standing not too far from a storeroom, his intent, clearly written on his cold face.

"The same Moses they refused saying, who made you a ruler and judge over us?" Samuel continued. "This same Moses, God sent to be a ruler and deliverer. He brought them out, after so many signs and wonders, the likes of which you must have heard before: the ten plagues of Egypt."

Murmurings grew from the crowd as many had heard about the terrible plagues of Egypt. The legendary tale passed on for ages was actually true.

Sahid listened closely. So that's how the ten plagues came to be, he thought to himself.

"He led them through the Red Sea and into the wilderness for forty years." The crowds quiet down as Samuel raised his voice. "This same Moses told the Israelites that, 'a prophet shall the Lord your God raise unto you, like you listened to me, so listen to him.' This same Moses was with the Israelites in the wilderness, and with the messenger from Almighty God, on the mountain. But the Israelites were rebellious and desired to go back to Egypt, the place of bondage. They said to Moses' brother, 'make for us gods to worship, for we do not know what has happened to Moses, who brought us out of the land of Egypt. He has gone to the mountaintop for forty days and hasn't returned.'"

Samuel turned to stare at the golden image of the Nubian god, Anensnuphis, at the left wing of the courtyard. The whole crowd followed his gaze.

"They made a calf in those days, and offered sacrifice to it, rejoicing in the works of their hands." He shifted his gaze and they all knew that he had defied their god right in their faces.

"Hear me, people of Meroe. God is speaking to you saying. Have you offered sacrifices to images and man-made idols? You all have taken the tabernacle of Apedemak, and the stars of your gods; figures you made to worship. The Israelites had the tabernacle of witness in the wilderness, as he gave instructions to Moses to build as he had seen. They reached the Promised Land and had with them the same tent. They had it till the time of a great king, called David. This king pleased God and God let his son, Solomon, to build him a house. But God doesn't live in temples built with hands, like your gods. Hear this, Heaven is God's throne, and the earth is His footstool. So do you think you can build a house for me? I do not need a place of rest. Remember my hands made all these things."

"You stubborn people!" He declared, "You haven't given your hearts to God. Why don't you listen to Him? You are against what the Holy Spirit is trying to tell you. I was sent by God to tell you that Jesus Christ was killed for our sakes and indeed rose again. Put away your gods and serve Him who proved himself in your midst when He stretched His hands and opened the gates of heaven to pour rain to your lands after three years of nothing. It's not in a man to direct his steps."

Samuel locked eyes with the Queen.

"Neither is it in the gods!"

When they all heard this, the crowds were cut to the heart by these last remarks and started to shout that he be killed. Some even tried to take hold of him but got only few inches close, hindered by the guards.

Sahid stood there, the shout almost drowning his thoughts. He knew it would come to this someday. Somehow, he had waited for it: the day Samuel would sign to his death by his brave words of defiance against all other gods. Now that almost all his households were converts to this newfound faith, fear gripped him as the thought of being in Samuel's shoes crossed his mind. He knew he didn't have the boldness to die for his new faith. Immediately, he looked up at Samuel, and took courage from those comforting brown eyes of his.

"Take him away." Kandake ordered.

The crowd roared in protest.

"We have other pressing issues on our hands." The Kandake added. "My people, war knocks on our doors. I just received a message that the Blemmyes, predatory nomads from the east of the Nile, have attacked one of our cities: Sawba! Tonight I host the Roman emissaries and tomorrow we defend our land against the Blemmyes." With that, she left the courtyard, followed by her personal guards.

After an hour, the last person to leave the courtyard was Hammed. The same smile on the devil's face just after Christ was crucified lined his own.

11

For the lips of a strange woman drop as a honeycomb, and her mouth is smoother than oil;
But see her end as bitter as wormwood, and then watch yourself recoil.

Erotic dancers moved with increasing rhythm to the beat of the drums while the Kandake's guests supped on ostrich and pheasant. The Kandake's heart beat in time to the drums, faster and faster, until she thought she would faint. Then, boom, the dance ended, the drums stopped, and the beautiful female dancers, adorned with colorful plumes, leapt away from the room like frightened exotic birds.

The moment had come. Her breathing still quickened. She raised her hand slightly summoning the guards to bring in Samuel. Everyone noticed him as he was brought in. Kandake wondered what it would take to break this young man that stood before her.

Samuel knew something stirred within the bowels of the Queen or he wouldn't still be alive after what he said in the courtyard. He had come to worry less about what will happen to him and really was taken by the palace's magnificence in the short time he'd spent there. The palace walls were made of bricks well lined together and all covered in gold. He also noticed the roofing beams, well marked at the north and south sides. Statues, fired of gold and iron, native and foreign, were lit up by Roman oil lamps in a sparkle. His chains and fetters were also melted of gold.

The Kandake slipped the towel from a slave and dabbed at her hands delicately.

One of the Roman emissaries leaned close to her, Primus Vindacius by name.

"Who is this before us?"

Kandake forced a smile, pretending nonchalance she was far from feeling.

"What offence did this young lad commit?"

"He is a stranger from the south," she said, "and he constantly defies our gods."

"Go on." His hands touched the golden seal that held his red robe on his left shoulder, and slid down.

"He proclaims that there is one God and claims that this God sent His Son to die . . ."

"Wait." Primus said alarmed. "Are you saying he's a Christian?"

"Is that what they call them these days?"

"You've known about these?"

"I am Kandake. The sands may shift beyond my sands but my feet feel its quaver." Kandake replied.

Samuel felt Primus' gaze without raising his head. The sudden hatred he felt from the gaze was like a tangible presence that surrounded him. His throat went dry and his heart beat like a trapped bird. Samuel then looked up at him.

Primus stared with loathing at the young man in chains. "This cult is restless."

Kandake eyes widened. "What do you mean?" she said and those nearby fell silent.

"We have tried every means possible to utterly wipe out this cult but it seems the more we try, the more it spreads. I can't believe its come this far to Africa." His gaze still fastened on Samuel. "Raging animals.

All of them. Spawn of serpents. They should be exterminated from the face of the earth."

Kandake rose and placed her hand on Samuel's arm. "Are they that bad?"

"Dear gods! You even dare to touch him?" Primus couldn't believe his eyes. Veins surfaced across his bald head.

"Every man has a price." Kandake said, in confidence.

"Do you think so? Perhaps you are too kind and naïve to understand the treachery of this cult. Test him."

"Alright."

"Will you make him worship at the Sun Temple?"

"Yes," Kandake said slowly, as though the admission caused her to think.

"Has he ever cowered before at any threat?"

"Not that I know of, no." Kandake replied and Samuel met her eyes with his.

"Test him as you desire, my lovely Queen," Primus said smoothly, a dark glow in his eyes. "And if he doesn't refute?"

"He will. You'll see."

"You sound very confident. I have to see this." Primus relaxed in his seat. His feet came free off the marble floor as he sat back.

"If you succeed, then you may have discovered a way to wipe out this cult that plagues humanity, and that, I know, my people would be interested in."

Kandake snapped her fingers and two guards came and stood on either side of Samuel. "Release him and make him stand over there by the balustrades."

Samuel went with them on the marble floors without resisting. They left him by the railings, away from everyone.

"Leave." She commanded the guards. Kandake walked over the center of the marble floor where the dancers had just performed.

The guests gathered closer, curious and eager to see what she would do. They whispered among themselves.

Kandake took Samuel's arm and drew him closer to the railings so that no one would hear. She peered out to the starless night.

"Come closer Samuel, and catch this amazing view."

Samuel obeyed without saying a word. He looked out and had to admit, the view was indeed beautiful. He never knew the desert was so beautiful at night.

"Look at the plains stretched out," she continued, "the Nile, ever so boisterous, the little fires burning in the city. Look at how it forms a colorful graphic. Experience the arty qualities of nature that defines the kingdom of Meroe in all its glory!"

She glanced at Samuel and noticed that he was taken by everything.

"And it's all mine, to do as I please."

She moved closer to him and touched his arm.

"I was there when you caused the rain to fall, remember?"

Samuel looked down and wondered what the Queen would suggest next.

"Let me reward you." She looked away briefly and turned to him again. "All these things I will give you. Everything!" she said with a whisper.

Samuel looked between her and the night but his eyes lingered more on her. Her eyes glowed on the terraces of the balustrade like one of the stars glued on the blanket of the skies. The slow caress of his arms by her majesty stirred up desires within. It wasn't an everyday occurrence for him to get so close to maidens let alone the Kandake.

Her coy smile broke through his reserves to resist. Many have stirred into these same eyes and met their demise. The same eyes passed down from generations which have made invading enemies to alternate their primary purpose of assault and assume the Queen's. Tales of a great Greek king who intended to destroy Meroe and take all its treasures still stirred the blood of many. The invading king was totally convinced not to destroy this great city after one gaze at the Queen's eyes.

Though deceitful, it felt good to be touched. Though stolen waters are sweet for a while but death lingered in the foresight. For a second or two, Samuel's heart lingered on the sweetness for a while before slowly moving a few inches away. He turned again at gazed into the breathless night.

Kandake felt his desire stir a while before. She knew she almost had him there.

She let him enjoy the view for a moment more, knowing how spellbound it is to gaze from the height. It felt like you could reach out and touch the sky from where they stood.

If you let me help you, you can have it all."

"What does all entail my Queen?"

"For one whose words bear wisdom you mask foolishness in issues that need no translation. I do not speak in proverbs."

"Isn't it true that Kandake speaks a new proverb each time she speaks?"

"Not tonight. Not when all you need is freedom."

"At what cost? My faith?"

"Not for always. Just for tonight. In the presence of all these people."

"You know not what you ask me."

"There has been no other god I've heard of that offers forgiveness like yours."

"Shall we continue in sin that grace may abound?"

"When we do wrong that affords us the chance to show that God is right, wouldn't it be wrong for Him to punish us? Save yourself and you will have the rest of your life to hold on to your faith."

"To sin willfully after receiving the knowledge of the truth is to insult the Spirit of grace. Will I always deny my Lord every time I save myself?"

"I offer you more than you could ever imagine."

"No."

Samuel closed his eyes as he shook the voice of treason from his ears.

"What you offer me robs me of everything."

"Look at me slave."

Samuel looked at her and only saw, in those dark brown eyes, a depth as deep as hell.

Kandake then snapped her fingers.

The emblems of the gods were brought in and placed before Samuel. He knew he had only to proclaim Apedemak as god, and his life would be spared.

They all watched, waiting for something to happen.

"Do you see how he hesitates?" Primus said with a sneer that made Samuel to tremble.

Lord, help me

"Everything is yours. Remember. Your life is in my hands." she whispered. "Just fall down and worship."

Samuel stepped forward slowly, his hand trembling violently.

Oh, God, strengthen me.

You shall worship no other gods except me.

The guests began murmuring.

Thou shall worship the Lord thy God, and him only shall you serve.

Samuel put his hand by his side and closed his eyes "God, forgive me," he whispered, ashamed that he had almost given in to fear. "Do forgive me."

He that save his life will lose it, but he that loses his life for my sake, will find it.

"Bow down and worship!"

"I shall worship the Lord, my God, and no other."

Astounded and angered, the murmurings grew.

"Kill him." Primus said, and one of the guards struck him hard across the face.

"Apedemak is the god of all," Kandake affirmed. "I want you to say it."

Samuel spoke no word.

"They are unbreakable!" Primus said, hating the young lad the more. I will strike him here."

"You shall strike no one." Kandake ordered.

Her words stopped Primus from fully drawing his sword.

"If you don't say it, you'll surely die." Kandake stood in front of him.

"Jesus is the Christ, Savior of the world, Son of the only true Living God."

"Blasphemy!" Someone whispered.

The guard struck him hard again. Samuel fell down, his face laced with pain. Kandake waved her hand, summoning other guards.

"Take him away."

As they walked from one door to another, light receded slowly. After a while, they led him through a dark passage and the stench that welcomed him leached his sanity.

When they finally came to a halt, Samuel felt a hard hit on his side and suddenly he saw himself standing by the shrubs as Templers beat up his father. Olanana laughed at his father's groan that filled the night. It wasn't long before Samuel's groaning matched his father's.

* * *

Sahid came awake with a deep cry and sat up, his body sodden in sweat. Breathless, he raked shaking fingers through his head and stood. He strode to the balcony and looked outside, catching a glimpse of the Sun Temple from where he stood.

Exquisitely beautiful!

Sahid wiped the beads of sweat from his face and went back inside his chambers. The dream had been so real. He could still feel the world of it. He wanted to shake himself free of it, but it came, night after night in bits and pieces till he knew he would never be free until he understood what it meant. It has been over a month since Samuel had been locked tight and forgotten because of the ongoing war against the Blemmyes. The Blemmyes, predatory nomads, are a small clan of people. Obviously an enemy of the Meroitic kingdom must be helping them out or the war wouldn't have gone on this far. Things were worse now that his first-born son had gone to war, and the believers meetings at his house had reduced in numbers since Samuel's lock up. They'd gone from watch-night gatherings to almost nothing in what seemed like an instant.

He had to see Samuel again, at least one more time. His dreams were sure full of him.

The guard of the lower dungeon dropped the bolt. "We have to move quickly and silently," he said, afraid to be caught by other guards. He knew he shouldn't be doing this: allowing Sahid access to see Samuel, but compassion touched him after so much pleading. They walked through the dungeon stealthily. A look at the rich man's face confirmed his own feelings. He was petrified also, not only about what they were doing but also about the filth of the dungeon.

The sound of the guard's sandals silently on the floor echoed in the darkness. As he followed the guard, the smell of cold stone and human fear made sweat break out on his skin.

Someone cried out from behind a locked door. Moans of despair crept out of some. As they kept walking, Sahid heard some sound coming from the far end of the dank air. There was a sound of life that softened the darkness. Somewhere, deep in the dungeon, a young voice was prayerfully singing.

The guard slowed, tilting his head slightly. "Have you ever heard a voice like that before? In such a place like this?" he asked as the singing continued. They walked more briskly. "A pity he's going to die immediately after the war," he said, pausing before a heavy door. He threw the bolt and opened an inner chamber.

A sickening stench hit Sahid as the door opened. The cell was on the lowest level, and the only vent into the chamber is from another level above it, rather than from the outside. The air, so close Sahid wondered how anyone could survive in it.

"Bad, isn't it?" the guard said. "After a few days, anyone placed here die like flies. It's no wonder some prisoners run out when led to their death. They crave one last breath of fresh air even if they die afterwards." The guard took two stones on the side and struck it. He used it to light up a small wooden torch with an oily hollow tip. The guard handed Sahid the torch.

Breathing through his mouth, Sahid stood on the threshold and looked.

Someone said his name and he saw a thin young lad in rags rise up in the shadows.

"Samuel!"

"Be quick. We don't have time." The guard said.

Sahid watched as he staggered towards him. When he reached the open doorway, he peered up at him with luminous eyes. The prison may have taken its toll on him physically but not for once had it dampened his spirit. The light from the torch reflected in the lad's face.

"What are you doing here, master?"

Heartbroken to see him in such a condition, he took his arm and drew him out into the corridor.

"Please leave us," Sahid said when the guard remained just outside the door.

"We have so little time. Please do hurry."

Sahid nodded. He could hear the sandals on stone as the guard walked away. It was quite a terrible place to hold conversation but he had no choice. He had to put to rest his fears.

Samuel saw his distraction. "How is your household?"

"Fine."

"And the meetings?"

Sahid didn't answer. He looked restless from his thoughts. Samuel placed his hand gently on his arm.

"What troubles you so much that you would come to seek a slave?"

"Many things," he said without hesitating. Why shouldn't he tell him, when it was through this young lad that he met Christ. "I can't get you out of here."

"That doesn't matter, master."

Sahid turned away, anger filling him. "You shouldn't be the one in this place," he said harshly, looking around at the cold stone walls of the dank chamber. "Hammed's the one who should suffer."

How many have waited within these walls to die? And for what reason? To quench the wrath of the Meroitic people and its gods? When he walked through the dungeon gates, he almost turned back from the horror resident in it.

"He should be the one waiting to die. Not you." He hated Hammed so much the feeling sent a rush of heat through his blood. He should have gotten rid of him when he had the chance. All these wouldn't have happened.

Samuel touched his arm, pulling him out of his evil thoughts.

Sahid searched his face. He looked so lean yet he wore that graceful look of peace, only now there was something more; something that surprised him. In this dark place, with a horrifying death facing him, he looked changed. His eyes were clear and luminous.

He felt a throbbing sadness that this gentle young man would soon die as soon as the war ended. Sahid wondered why he couldn't speak as boldly as Samuel. All he did was speak so clearly about his hatred for Hammed. He could still remember the readings of the parchments

Telipha had received from the ecclesia, the fellowship far north. He brought it with him to the meetings. *Love thy enemies* was one of the instructions written in it. Those three words were the simplest to say yet the hardest to live by. Natural causes channeled one to hate freely those who boldly wished them no good. Now it felt like to follow this doctrine is to deny the one thing that qualified one as human: self.

"Oh God, forgive me," he whispered, closing his eyes. "Cleanse my heart and make me see you, Jesus."

Samuel saw his torment. "You must hate this place," he said softly. "What really brought you here, master?"

"I've been having a dream every night now. I don't know what it means."

Samuel frowned slightly. "I'm the least of all to interpret dreams. Mine still haunt me."

"Please, I know you can help me, Samuel."

Samuel felt his anxiety and prayed that God would give him the answers he needed. "Speak master," he said weak from confinement and days without food. "I may not know the answers, but God does."

Sahid began . . . .

"My son."

"Your son? Raja?"

"I see Raja standing in the middle of the desert with other Meroitic warriors. They all draw swords, waiting for the enemy. Then, I see the sands rise a little and then collapse. A second later two small hounds of sands rise to the size of a small heap and two arrows launch out towards the warriors. I run towards Raja and try to warn him. The enemy they look for tirelessly to see through the sandy winds is coming out from the ground.

"I do not get to him on time. The enemy rises up in front of them and the battle begins. I cry out to him every time an enemy rises behind him and for a while he hears me and turn to defend himself. For no apparent reason, I suddenly perceive another enemy rise up from the sands in the distance. There is the strange urge to run and save my son. As I get to Raja an arrow is let loose from the enemy. I stand in the arrow's way to my son but it goes through me and strikes Raja by the side. My eyes close as I call his name.

"The next time I open them, I am in the cave with you; the same cave you spoke about in your dreams. You hold out the parchments and read it for a while. Then you place it in your mouth and chew it all. I try to stop you but you don't let me. You crawl out of the small crevice and face the lion as I follow. I ask you to bring out the sword but all you do is stand there.

"The lion moves out of the bushes and approaches. A loud noise rises from the unknown and fills everywhere. The lion roars in response to the noise. I don't know if I'll ever feel so terrified like the way the noises make me.

"Then it walks majestically from one side to the other coming closer with each turn. Finally, it faces you and starts towards you. As it leaps up, I become you and my fright frees itself through my mouth with a loud cry. The same cry that wakes me up."

Samuel closed his eyes.

Sahid leaned his head back exhausted from the tale. "So tell me. What does it all mean?"

Sahid face tautened with barely controlled emotion. Sorrow filled him to know what would become of Samuel.

"Raja is already on his way to battle." Samuel began. "The warriors will be deceived by the enemy and a lot of them will fall."

"What about Raja."

Samuel put his hand on his arm. "Don't worry. God is in control. You will see him alive again."

"And you?"

"The noise you hear when the lion approaches is the shout of mob at the theatre. You will not die master but you will witness mine."

Sahid took his hand and felt tears rush to his eyes. "God is merciful," he said softly. He could see the bruises that marked his kind face, the thinness of his body beneath the ragged, dirty tunic. He had led him to the Truth-Christ Jesus. How could he walk away and let him die?

"Maybe I can convince Kandake." Sahid said.

"No."

"Yes."

"She wants me to publicly renounce my faith. If I do that, I'm fallen from grace. God will fight for me, and I will hold my peace. He's already won."

He held his hand firmly between his own. "Don't you see? If you don't concentrate on your son and the believers' assembly, a word with Kandake about me might jeopardize everything. Nurture the sheep, and wait eagerly for the time God will take these lands."

"But what of you? After the war, you will . . ."

"God's hand is in this, master. His will be done."

"You'll die."

"As it is written, for thy sake we are killed all the day long; we are accounted as sheep for the slaughter. Nay in all these things we are more than conquerors through him who has loved us. For I am persuaded, that neither death, nor life, nor angels, nor principalities, nor powers, nor things present, nor things to come, nor height, nor depth, nor any other creature, shall be able to separate us from the love of God, which is in Christ Jesus our Lord."

Sahid searched his face for a long moment, taking in strength from his youthful face, and then nodded. "It will be as you say."

"No master, it will be as the Lord wills."

"I will never forget you."

"Nor I you," Samuel said. He instructed him in few words and encouraged him to read and teach from the parchment he brought with him and also from the one with Telipha. "Now, go from this place of death and don't look back."

Sahid went out into the dark corridor and called the guard.

Samuel was already in the cell.

Sahid stood with the torch as the guard came and bolted the door. Samuel spoke from within the cell. "May the Lord bless you and keep you, the Lord make his face shine upon you and be gracious to you. May the Lord turn his face toward you and give you peace," he said with a gentle smile.

After a while, the bolt was dropped.

The sound that filled the dungeon echoed finality.

12

Let the bravery of thy heart strengthen thy shield;
If you are the last one standing, fight on and do not yield

The warriors of Meroe rode to Napata in large numbers to finally put an end to the raging Blemmyes from the east. The air had never felt hotter as they rode on horses and camels. Skilled archers and swordsmen poured out in ranks.

Nothing could be compared to the greener grasses back at Mero city, where the scrub forest begins and where elephants and rhinoceros can be seen in numbers, Raja thought to himself. Now here he was, on a horse's back, thinking about home. How could his father prefer another to his own flesh and blood, he vexed from memory.

The devastation the predatory nomads brought upon their main religious center was utterly terrible. Most of the buildings were destroyed; a temple to 'Jupiter Hammon', which is the god-Amun, lay in ruins. His face cringed in hate for what had taken place here.

They all could notice ruins of houses. The houses must have been built of interwoven pieces of split palm woods, which explained why the houses caught fire easily.

Cagillaris, the chief warrior, raised his hand high, signaling to everyone to stop. He instinctively sensed something wrong. He spat on his hands, robbed it and raised it up. The wind blew sand dust particles all over and some rested on his hands. He brought his hands to his mouth and tasted the particles. He then turned on his horse and looked out into the distance.

They weren't even close to the heart of the city when the chief warrior ordered them to ride outside the city. There they halted and waited.

Nothing moved.

The stillness made Raja's stomach tighten and his heart pound. Arakakamani, Kashta, and Atlanersa walk up to his side and held their grounds as they wait impatiently for the unknown.

A war cry suddenly rose from nowhere, spreading along the horizon as the Sun held its direction right above them. The harsh, intermittent roar rose like an unholy chant, reverberating from the demons of the sands. The warriors held their positions. The roar abruptly stopped and they could hear the pounding of heavy, running footsteps.

"They're coming!" Raja said.

Right out from the sand rose Blemmyes warriors, releasing arrows and spears. The arrows and spears claimed unsuspecting Meroitic warriors.

Cagillaris, chief of the Meroe warriors, raised his hand high, signaling to his men to hold their positions. They waited as the Blemmyes rushed at them. Seeing a horde of fierce, almost naked warriors, armed with spears, and coming at them almost shook them from their ranks. All of them struggled to hold on, just long enough to make them draw close enough.

Seeing the moment was right, Cagillaris brought his hand down. The archers amidst them released their arrows and the spears also went up into the air. Some of the rushing Blemmyes dropped. His golden helmet glistened with every gallop of his stallion. Most of the Blemmyes warriors wore nothing more than a short protective swathe round their waists, and were armed simply with iron-and-leather shields and swords.

Cagillaris threw his spear with brute force. The long-headed spear went through the throat of a Blemmyes and sent the warrior crashing to the ground. Another came close and knocked him off the horse. Cagillaris rolled over on the hot sand and got up quickly. The warrior attacked him instantly. With one swift swing he dodged the spear and broke the attacker's back with one blow of his doubled fists. Snatching the spear from the dead man, he thrust it through another attacker.

Raja's spear snapped as he rammed it through an attacker. He swore heavily and slammed his shield into the head of another. He snatched up a spear on the sands, barely managing to parry blows from another Blemmyes. He knew he had to draw back or get killed.

In the midst of the brawl, swords and spears clashed with a thunderous sound. A courageous Meroitic warrior was making way through the Blemmyes' warriors. Swinging his sword, he cut of a Blemmyes' arm. Another came against him and he blocked thrust after thrust. Using incredible force, he rammed the full weight of his body into an attacker and sent him back into two others.

Arakakamani plowed into two warriors, not even feeling the slash of a small sword graze his side as he cut another down. He blocked blows and used the back of his sword to down one of his attackers. Ducking sharply, he narrowly missed being struck as a spear flew past him.

"Your back, Kashta!" Arakakamani shouted. Kashta ducked sharply, swung around, bringing the sword down and up swiftly, breaking bones as he sliced upward through the groin and into the abdomen of his attacker. The man screamed and went down before Kashta could pull the sword free.

Sword less, Kashta rolled and caught an attacker's leg, bringing him down. Jumping onto him, he gripped the man's head and made a hard jerk, breaking his neck. Grabbing a small sword, he leaped to his feet and charged a Blemmyes who was pulling his spear out of a fallen warrior.

The brave Meroitic warrior caught an attacker across his neck and a fountain of blood splattered all over his face. Dropping the sword, he yanked a spear from the body of a dead warrior in pursuit of another. Roaring in fury, he thrust it through an attacker and grabbed the attacker's small sword, slicing through another.

A different war cry rose again and the Blemmyes warriors retreated. Cagillaris shouted immediately, signaling his men to chase them down. The brave Meroitic warrior was ahead of them in pursuit while others followed from behind, some on horses and camels.

Cagillaris slowed down as he noticed the brave warrior ahead of them stop suddenly. He knew it must be bad. They all came to stop as they noticed they were being surrounded. Face white, it dawned on him that they were trapped. Cagillaris gave a command for all of them to come closer and stay together. Even so, though he had fully expected a reasonable amount of the Blemmyes warriors, he was stunned by the number they were now facing.

The instant he heard the war cry, Cagillaris signaled a counterattack. These foul Blemmyes had played unfair for the past one month now, striking like venomous desert snakes that slithered comfortably through the hot sand. They were definitely helped by another greater foe. Probably Egypt, he thought to himself.

As the horde of almost naked warriors rode and ran towards them, Cagillaris shouted at his men to hold their lines.

The Sun blazed at its hottest.

Fear coursed through Atlanersa, and then was replaced almost immediately by a grim determination. He would fight to his last breath.

Charging straight into the legion, the brave Meroitic warrior used his bloodied sword to strike the first that came at them. Undaunted, they fought back. Having survived the initial onslaught, they stuck together, moving to take what the Blemmyes dished.

Atlanersa ducked as a sword missed his head. Slashing his sword into another attacker, he swore loudly.

A few broke through the lines, but were taken out immediately. Skill and experience was certainly on the side of the Meroitic warriors.

Cagillaris let out a piercing whistle, once again signaling his men to fall back together. He drove the point of his spear into one warrior and brought it back up beneath the chin of another who attacked him from the side. Before he could pull the spear free, another rammed him in the back. Letting his momentum take him, and keeping his hold on the small sword, Cagillaris rolled and came to his feet, freeing the weapon and bringing the razor sharp sword point into the abdomen of an attacker.

Raja saw a flash to his right and shifted, feeling the sting of a sword wound along his right shoulder. Cagillaris let out a feral war cry and drove into the warrior positioned to kill Raja, putting a hard dent into the side of his head.

When another lunged at him he ducked sharply and turned, bringing his heel up into the warrior's face.

A Blemmyes warrior rode right for Arakakamani but he was able to roll and come swiftly to his feet, throwing his hands up and letting out a shrill, warbling scream that made the warrior's stallion rear. Dodging its hooves, he retrieved his iron shield.

It took a while before Cagillaris looked around and realized they had defeated the Blemmyes. After a long afternoon that saw them outnumbered, they still came out victorious but with the expense of many casualties. There was no way of escape for their foes and his men were taking out the few left.

A surviving Blemmyes warrior stepped forward facing him. The warrior shifted his sword and moved around to the right. The warrior attacked him first. Parrying a blow easily, Cagillaris spit in the man's face before shoving him away. Enraged, the warrior charged. Expecting this,

Cagillaris dodged and brought the end of his shield around and into the side of the unwise warrior's head with a hard thud. As the warrior dropped, Cagillaris made a swift slice through the fallen man's jugular. The warrior twitched violently, but briefly as he passed away.

He looked behind him and saw the brave Meroitic warrior attacked by one of the few left. The Blemmyes' warrior swung his sword but he ducked to one side and circled. The Blemmyes was quickly disabled with a deep gash across his thigh. He had one last breath and that was it.

Raja breathed heavily as his last attacker came at him. The Blemmyes brought his sword down hard, clanging against the long metal head of Raja's spear. He ducked sharply and spun around, catching the man in the back of the head with the sword. The warrior fell, face in the dust, and didn't move. Raja looked at the wound by his side. Blood oozed slowly. Lying on the floor, he gripped the small iron sword strongly until blackness overcame him.

* * *

Raja awakened slowly, a while later. Disoriented, he didn't know where he was. His vision blurred and, instead of the clean scent of his home, the smell of blood and dust filled his nostrils. His head throbbed and he tasted blood in his mouth. He tried to rise and only managed a few inches before the stab of pain shot through his temples and brought back the full realization of his demise. Groaning, he sank back.

He could hear the sound of horses' hooves. It seemed he was being transported to somewhere. He blacked out after a while and roused again moments later. He waited for the dizziness and nausea to pass before he opened his eyes.

"Stanch the wound," Cagillaris, in a bloodstained tunic said, gesturing impatiently at Kashta. "He's lost a lot of blood. Leave that one. He's as good as dead."

The day slipped slowly away.

Turning his head, Raja stirred, trying to evaluate his position. His head bumped the side of the caravan as he noticed he was being transported with other Meroitic warriors who had survived.

"Ah, so you've come around."

He recognized Cagillaris' voice. He opened his eyes and grinned at the fierce brown eyes of their leader.

"Good to know you are alive and have some wits about you. You fought bravely, young warrior but your days aren't as many."

Kashta and Arakakamani sat beside him on the carriage to take them back to Meroe.

Raja touched the wound on his side. He looked from side to side, wincing in pain. "Where is Atlanersa?"

No one answered.

"Where are you taking me?"

"Home, warrior. Home."

13

A little time for everything
Is a refrainer from any sin

"It's not my fault," Sahid said, tears streaming down his cheeks. He sat on his bed. "I see it in the way he looks at me. He blames me for everything. I know he does. It's not my fault, Rhesa. It isn't, is it? I didn't want him to go to war." His shoulders fell in mourning.

"I know you didn't," Rhesa said gently, holding back her own tears. She tried to comfort his distraught husband. Sahid never intended harm. He simply didn't think of his sons before Samuel came into their lives and when Samuel did, he seems taken by his new faith. He hardly bothered about anything else but Samuel and his doctrine. Not that it was bad, she thought to herself, only that to every thing, there is a season, and a time to every purpose under the heaven. A time to eat and a time to sleep; a time to break down, and a time to build up; a time to weep, and a time to laugh; a time to mourn, and a time to dance; a time to embrace, and a time to refrain from embracing; a time to keep silence, and a time to speak; a time for family, and a time for sacrifice.

There must be a balance for every time or one would suffer for the other. That's exactly what happened in Sahid's case. He had shut his sons away from himself all their lives, carrying on with his work. Things only got worse when Samuel arrived. Not only was Sahid a changed man, also her younger son, Calil, changed his faith. But Raja wouldn't budge. Raja had never agreed with his father right from time, and to see a stranger take the affection of his father must have been quite unbearable for him. The confrontation between father and son was destined someday to take place. And it did one afternoon.

She was there when it happened.

"I see your affairs are in good hands, father." Raja said entering his father's chambers without invitation.

Sahid noticed the rage in those remarks and decided not to answer. He bent down to read the parchments Samuel gave to him, in his hands.

Raja sought an opening for a conflict.

"Do you know how clever the young foreigner is, father?"

It didn't sound like a compliment.

"He really has the mind of business," Raja continued. A smile crossed his face as he saw he had his father's attention now.

Sahid saw nothing humorous about what he said and knew the smile hid the pain his son suffered.

He said nothing.

"He knew what he wanted and went for it. You see father, he gave you a belief, and got the keys of your business in return. Fine trade, wouldn't you say?"

"That is enough, Raja. You know it isn't true," tired and angry with his son. He lifted his hand slightly and closed the parchment. "You are just wasting your time worrying over nothing."

"Oh really?" Raja said sarcastically. "Maybe I have nothing to worry about after all. Maybe all is well with my father handing over the family business to a total stranger. Maybe it's all good since you've never had time for your family and when you are soon to retire, you give everything away to a gold digger."

Sahid glared at his son in dismay. "Is that what all this is about, Raja?"

"Oh stop the pretence, father. Your career pursuit was all for yourself. Everything you've ever done is for you."

"Raja, Samuel isn't my heir. You are."

"Am I? You no longer know anything that goes on in this house!"

"I know enough of what goes on in this house. Samuel is just my aide, a good one I must admit, but every order, every step, every trade and every purchase goes through me. Now if it upsets you so, then I will retire now and hand over everything to you. Right here, right now."

"You still don't understand do you, father. It's never been about the money, or the business." He moved close to his father and looked at him straight in the eyes. "It's always been about father and son."

Sahid is taken by the admission. He always thought the tension between them was about the family business. Obviously, he was mistaken. It was clear he never knew his son. Come to think of it, he couldn't recall the last time he spent time with him since his childhood. Sahid noticed tears fill his son's eyes. His son had slipped away from him a long time ago and he never knew until now.

"I'm sorry, son. I'll do anything you say." He lifted his two hands to place on his son's shoulders. "I'm so sorry. Come, sit with me."

Raja touched his father's hands and slowly took them off his shoulders. "Time is against us." He turned away and walked to the door.

"What do you mean?"

"I'm going with the warriors to put a stop to the Blemmyes' assault on one of our religious centers."

"You must be joking."

"I can do anything I set my heart on, father, incase you haven't noticed."

"Don't worry. A word in the right ear and you'll be out of . . ."

"Don't you try to get me out," Raja interjected. "It's my choice and I'm going."

Fear gripped him as he watched his son walk away from him. "Please, Raja," Sahid walked towards him. "Don't end your life to spite me."

Raja stopped and turned to face his father. "My life never meant anything to you, father. Besides, you have a new son now. Retire and give him all you have." With that, Raja left the building.

Rhesa stood by the passage, weeping.

Now his son was brought back to him with a fatal wound at his side.

It was his fault, Sahid thought to himself.

Rhesa left his side and went to his sons' chambers to nurture him. Sahid followed shortly.

On the floor was a discarded tunic stained with blood.

"How do you feel son?" Sahid said coming closer to where he lay.

"I will die." Raja said indifferently.

"Let me stay with you awhile?"

Raja lay back on the couch. "No, father. You can go. Mother is here," he said refusing to allow his father any closer. One of the slaves came in with a fresh tunic and a bowl of water. "I don't want to see him," Raja said to his mother at his side. He had spoken loudly enough for him to hear, and Sahid made no protest. He left the room.

Gritting his teeth, Raja fought the rise of pity and remorse he felt. His father looked so wan and thin as though he had diminished since the last time he saw him.

His mother left his side in tears, but later returned. She didn't say anything. Raja started to ask, but sucked in his breath as she peeled the blood soaked bandage from his ribs.

"The wound is still seeping."

"It will mother, until there's nothing left."

Rhesa paused for a moment at that remark. "I will wash it again with wine and then bind it." She took a cup and poured some inside. "Drink some wine, my son."

Raja propped himself up, and Rhesa noticed the wound seep all the more. He lay back once more, and Rhesa soaked a cloth in the fine red vintage. His body stiffened as his mother washed the wound and then bound it again. She gave Raja another cup of wine, noting that his eyes were dark and clouding.

"Don't look so worried, mother," Raja said drowsily. His body relaxed as he passed out, moments later. Rhesa bent over him, unsure whether it was loss of blood or too much wine that caused it.

Calil, the youngest of her children, came in. Rhesa looked at him and was a little surprised how much he'd grown. He was a few years younger that Samuel, but definitely equal in height and build. He hurried to his brother's side.

"The wound?"

"Yes," she said coldly.

One of the kitchen slaves came in to place a Roman oil lamp in the room and left.

"Bring the brazier," she said to him. Calil rushed out and came back with it. She leaned closer to Raja and touched his shoulder. He didn't rouse. She laid a trembling hand against his chest and felt the slow, firm rise of his heart.

Rhesa went out of the chambers and soon returned with a small packet of herbs and a cautery. She placed the end of it in the hot coals of the brazier.

"I intend to seal the wound and pack it with herbs," she told Calil. "You'll need to hold him still."

She took the cautery and drew the hot metal along the wound, searing it closed. Raja groaned, rousing slightly, only to faint again. The smell of burning flesh filled the room, and she reheated the cautery and finished the task.

"I need a small bowl."

Calil brought one to her.

Rhesa mixed the herbs with salt and made a poultice, which she bound to the wound. She sat down on the edge of Raja's sleeping couch and drew her hand across his brow. "I will stay with him," she said.

"Has father been here?" Calil asked.

"Yes."

"Did he speak to him?"

"No, Calil. Raja didn't give him the chance."

Rhesa sat thinking. She put her hand on Raja's bare chest and felt the firm beat of his heart. "See if your father is home, Calil. If so, bring him here so he can see that his son sleeps. It will set his mind at ease."

"Yes, mother."

Sahid came in not too long after. Rhesa rose from the edge of Raja's sleeping couch. She took Sahid's hand and nodded for him to sit.

"He's so pale."

"He's losing blood slowly. The dagger must have been poisoned."

"Will he be all right?"

"I don't know," she said, then added to encourage him, "We cauterized the wound. The poultice should prevent infection." She came close to him. "Don't worry my lord, you are now with him."

"He doesn't want me here," he said, putting his hand over his where it looked strong against his son's white hand. "He doesn't want to see me."

Calil came closer. "You need not fear, father. Remember that the Lord will never leave nor forsake us."

Sahid smiled at his younger son. "Thank you, Calil. He sighed, struggling against the invading weakness. "Your faith grows stronger by the day. Come, let's go to the meeting and pray with Telipha and others. Rhesa . . ."

"I'll stay with him," she said. "Go now."

"Rhesa remained with his son through the night. She passed the time thinking about her lost obsession. Sahid asked her once why she never attended the worship gathering and she told him she needed time. The real reason she shared with Hammed. A truth she intends to take to her grave if the gods let her.

Raja roused once and looked at her with dazed eyes. Frowning slightly, he mumbled jargons.

"What is it, my son?" she said and put her hand on his forehead. It felt cool.

He grasped the edge of here cloth and tugged weakly for a while. Moments later he slumbered again.

Before the night was over, Raja had dreamt three times, moved restlessly and murmured in pain. Rhesa reached out and took his hand.

At his mother's touch, he felt calm.

The dawn sent rays of sunlight into the room.

Raja awakened.

Sluggish and disoriented, he turned his head and saw his mother sitting beside his sleeping couch. He rose slightly and sucked in his breath, immediately remembering the fatal wound at his side.

Rhesa slowly raised her head.

Cringing at the sharp pain in his side, he swore and lay back. She put her hand lightly over his. "Lie still, Raja or you will reopen the wound."

As she drew back slightly, Raja captured his mother's hand and pinned it down beneath his own. "You stayed with me all night. There's nothing like a mother's love!"

"There is nothing like a father's love," Rhesa replied. "Your father is concerned for you."

"He need not be. I'm dying anyway." He loosened his hand.

"You have lost a lot of blood and I have been giving you liquid all night."

Raja said nothing, feeling the least gratitude for being alive. He couldn't shake off the dreams he had in the night.

"You should eat. I'll ask one of the servants to have food brought up to you."

Raja wanted her to stay. He wanted to tell her about the dreams. She turned toward the door as he opened his mouth but nothing came out. Rhesa turned back, her head tilting slightly to study him. She read his expression.

"What is it, Raja?"

"You said father was worried about me?"

"Yes."

"What about Samuel?"

"He's been forgotten in the dungeon." Her heart stirred a little at the mention of the slave's name.

Raja looked up at her again. He noticed it hurt her to speak about Samuel. Somehow, he knew there was something unique about that young slave. He never took out time to talk to him but he could sense it every time he was around him.

"Don't hate your father because of Samuel, Raja. I assure you, Samuel never meant any harm."

"I don't want to talk about it."

"He is a person you know. Don't refer to him like he's nothing."

"Isn't that what he is mother?"

Tears filled her eyes. "Are you at peace with the way things are?"

"At peace? I am dying mother." He said exasperated. "Father has never had time for anyone of us."

"You don't know your father more than I do," she said and came to seat beside him. "From the day I married him, I have never seen a man in search of peace like your father. Not the kind of peace wealth brings. That is only financial security. Nor the one found in conjugal union because he didn't find it in ours."

Raja kept quiet and listened.

"He sought for distractions from his inner turmoil and turned to the next thing in his path: his work! He worked tirelessly, and kept at it."

She felt his brow again to make sure the fever hasn't returned.

"You hold on to your anger against him like a shield when your life is creeps away from you. Your present torment should have made you realize what it is to suffer within."

"What is it you require of me to do?"

"All I'm saying is that he found that inner peace. At least, it seems your father found it in a foreign god. The problem was he couldn't strike a balance for everything, even after his conversion. He became committed the same he was with his work. But not anymore. He seeks a second chance. A chance with you."

Heat surged up in him. He didn't want to talk about it anymore. "Mother, I'm hungry now."

Rhesa rose slowly. "Please, my son. For his sake and yours, forgive him."

"I can't," he said, furious and wishing she would leave quickly.

"Nothing is too terrible that it can't be set aside in the name of love."

"It's the lack of it that I can't forgive."

His passionate words left Rhesa more saddened than before. Only one thing was certain in her mind. "Until you can forgive him, you'll never know the fullness of what it means to be forgiven yourself." Those words left her thinking how much she now regretted plotting with Hammed. She also sought forgiveness for a crime she hasn't confessed.

"Please, think on this. Time fails us as we speak."

Raja did think on it long after his mother left. Despite his desire to put her words out of his mind, they kept coming over and over, cutting him deeper each time. He remembered the dreams he had in the night. He knew he longed for something, for some relief to quench his aching heart. The thought of seeking the same inner peace his father sought all these years scared him. It had taken the words of a loving mother to reprove him.

And he didn't like it.

Raking his fingers through his bare chest, he ached to walk out onto the balcony. He didn't know if he could set the past aside. He didn't know if he could forgive, let alone forget. The loneliness he felt seemed unbearable.

His mother was right, he thought to himself. Peace would elude him until he found peace with his father. He had felt brief tremendous relief in the arms of a strange man in his dreams. Forgiveness received could not be withheld. He must pour it out upon his father, whether he wanted to or not. Yet he still warred with his desire to punish him for neglecting his family, for neglecting him. The desire to make him suffer as his families suffered filled him.

"I can't!" Closing his eyes, he sought the face of the gods to appease but each time he saw the luminous face of a man—the same man from his dreams, with holes in his hands and legs.

"Whoever you are, please . . . help me."

14

The sky is cloudy—a blurry sight of heaven;
Evil sometimes lurks, in things that are uncertain

Tired and exhausted, one of Sahid's slaves, Calasiris, finally got to the home of Theagenes with a message from his master. He traveled by horse with instructions to return with the information concerning his master's investments.

The guards by the gate let him in and being a mere slave, he wasn't escorted into the building. Calasiris made his way through the flight of stairs to deliver his master's message to Theagenes.

When he got the door, Calasiris heard voices in the central chamber where Theagenes worked and decided to wait by the entrance till whomever Theagenes was seeing left.

"You may take over his entire investments as you see fit."

Calasiris immediately snapped out of indifference as the voice struck close to home. He could have sworn the voice was Hammed's.

Theagenes poured more wine, and then thumped the iron pitcher down on a marble table. He looked across the marble table at Hammed, who was lounging on the couch. There rested an indolent look on his face. The young man definitely had a strange air around him. They've been talking for a few minutes and Theagenes couldn't reason with him. Hammed's mind was already made up.

Hammed sipped the Italian Falernian wine and nodded in approval. "Excellent wine."

The compliment was met with a stony glance. He knew Theagenes must be stunned at his briskness though he covered it well. Hammed smiled at him. He didn't come here to negotiate and had clearly stated his terms.

Theagenes seemed somewhat uncomfortable. He normally gave in to fits of anger when he didn't have his way. Doggedly, his demeanor wore calm, which Hammed was well aware is only a facade, concealing the unsettling feeling beneath.

"So, if I'm hearing you correctly, you are saying you have a plan to silence one of the richest merchants this empire ever had; someone who has the ears of Kandake?"

Hammed shrugged and rose from the couch. "So it's true that you've always envied my former master and probably wished him ill?" He turned the conversation at Theagenes with a smile.

Theagenes had never seen someone so cold as the one who stood before him.

"Tempting. Your offer that is, but as much as I want to control all of Sahid's business enterprise, I'm afraid I have to decline."

"As you might have noticed, I didn't come here to negotiate, Theagenes. I have the ears of all the priests, the sorcerers and above all the gods of Meroe. You refuse this offer at your own peril." Hammed dropped the cup on the table, set to leave.

"Give me time." Theagenes succumbed. He was appalled at the audacity of a slave calling him by name but was more concerned about the edge he noticed in his voice when he said it was at his own peril.

"As you know, time is indeed a commodity we all fail to have."

Theagenes realized that it must be true what he had heard about Hammed: that he had solicited for the support of all spiritualists he could find in the city during the war. Idol priests, diviners, healers, exorcists and sorcerers, all supported the one who told them that their duty to their ancestors must be to stop the meetings at Sahid's house. Now he has become someone in reckoning. Very soon, he would have the ear of the Kandake.

"Just because you're now known among the spirituals, doesn't mean you can have your way. Sahid may have been fooled by the sorcery Samuel played on him, but he sure does have people around him who are still loyal. How do you plan to pull this off, and how do we know he doesn't know about this already?"

"I share your admiration of my former master but it seems you really underestimate the support I have right now. I can cause a riot right here if I wanted to. And soon I will have the ear of the Kandake."

Theagenes recalled seeing the Kandake return to Meroe after a brief visit to the remains of Napata. She always looked grand in her special mobile room of glowing stone coverings and rare wood foundation, mounted on wheels pulled by an elephant.

"You haven't answered my question."

"Don't worry about it. Yours is to handle his business and I'll have a share in its profits."

Theagenes rose slightly. "And what value would be your share?"

"I'll let you know once it's all taken care of."

A short, foul curse escaped Theagenes' mouth in a whisper. He walked placidly to the table and poured himself some more wine. He'd had enough shudder of fear course through him from just staring at Hammed's dark eyes. Now that he had his back to him, he felt even worse.

Ah, but business was business, and now a fortune presented itself. He may not like the means, but definitely it would pay out in the end.

"Very well," Theagenes said, his face darkening. I'm in."

Hammed grinned. "A wise decision, Theagenes. You are shrewd when it comes to business."

"And you, my friend, have a black heart."

"Anything to please the gods."

Theagenes was sure Hammed had his own desires at heart let alone for the gods. "Forgive my curiosity but how diligent are those you plan to send out . . ."

"There is no need for anyone," Hammed interrupted, "I will see to it personally."

Calasiris had heard enough.

He went down the stairs and rushed out passing the guards to his horse. With one swift leap, he got on the animal and rode out of Musawwarat.

He left behind nothing on his trail but dust, and the cold dark eyes of Hammed watching him from Theagenes' upper chambers.

The day was drawing to a close and still in Meroe; buying and selling still took place at the marketplace. Men gathered round to watch two men slug it out in the game of Wari. The game is played on a piece of wood with holes hedged into it. Pebbles are moved through a series of holes and the last pebble left is used to claim whatever pebbles in the hole it ends in.

Some children ran around with toys made of wood and straw. A female child held closely to her doll, which was basically a marble-sized clay head fitted to a stick. A plump woman, most likely her mother, sat in front of her round reed hut with an ostrich egg charm on its roof. She held on to her drinking bowls filled by a herdsman with artistically deformed horns.

A merchant, not too far away, coiled up rolls of clay, rubbing the surface smooth, and then decorate the vessel with scratches and jabs. Merchants gradually closed for the day and carefully packed their finest pottery for export round the world. The pottery, wheel-made from fine white clay, was hard, thin, and beautifully decorated. Some were stamped with repeated decorations while others were painted in free-flowing designs. The merchants smiled at what had made them rich for years. Meroe's pottery is known to have reached the ends of the earth.

No one paid too much attention to a man galloping with a horse furiously through the city. The Sun had set by the time he got close to his master's home.

Calasiris' horse stopped abruptly at a distance away from his destination and refused to bid his rider's command to go on. For some reason, the horse turned out of the way. Calasiris struck it by the neck to turn the animal back. The horse turned back to the path but then thrust away again. Calasiris struck it again, this time harder. The horse neighed louder as it was forced against its will each time. Darkness had swept the city.

At one point, the horse threw him off its back and galloped into the night. Infuriated, Calasiris cursed the horse. He walked a few meters he saw flickers of light from his master's building.

He recalled the night before Samuel was taken away by the palace guards, how he had thought of informing someone about Hammed's outbursts. Hammed hated Samuel but he never thought he bore ill-thoughts against their master.

Voices could be heard coming from the building. Obviously another meeting of the believers was going on. He somehow felt safe when he came under the shelter the home provided.

Why did his horse take off like that? He wondered. The darkness was beginning to smear his skin.

"I see you are in a rush, Calasiris."

Calasiris froze for one split second in recognition of Hammed's voice. His heart beat faster with each secretion of adrenalin. He may wonder how Hammed got here before him but that would be time needed to get away from him as soon as possible.

No one told him what to do. His legs cut through the winds in fearful flight.

Hammed caught up with him and hit him hard by the neck.

Calasiris sank to his knees, choking and panting.

Hammed gripped his head and drew it back, glaring into his terrified eyes. "I see wonder mingled with fear on how I beat you to this place. Remember the popular story recorded in Ptolemaic Egypt that tells of a Kushite magician? So powerful he was that he whisked away an Egyptian king in his sleep, flew him through the air to Meroe, flogged him five hundred times in front of the king of Kush, and returned him, black and blue to his bed before sunrise."

Calasiris gasped for breath, struggling to break free as he stared into the coldest eyes he'd ever seen.

"Don't worry, your master and his family will join you soon." With that, Hammed drove the heel of his hand into Calasiris' left side, snapping a rib and sending it like a spear into his heart. Calasiris fell back, blood sliding down his mouth in convulsive throes of death.

After a while, he went limp.

* * *

Restless, the Kandake rose from her bed and walked to the balcony staring outside. Her mind kept wandering to the slave she kept locked up in the dungeons. He seemed to know so much about Egypt than anyone she'd ever come by. Now that the war was over, she knew she would have to make a decision about him. News had reached her, since her return, that there might be a protest soon about the meetings at Sahid's house.

No matter what happened, she had to honor her ancestors and the gods. If there was going to be any ruler to change his or her faith and risk the wrath of the gods and of her people, it won't be her, she decided. Yet she couldn't shake off that nudging on her inside when Samuel addressed them in her courtyard.

What about the miracle of rainfall before the Sun Temple? What about his bold declaration in front of her guests, knowing fully well that his life was in her hands? How could someone bow to a god he doesn't see? How could a god so powerful, yet allow his Son to die? It just didn't make any sense. If this was all sorcery, then whoever taught him must surely be good.

As Queen, she was raised with bedtime stories: stories like that of a long-lived Kushite magician, along with his powerful magician mother, who returns to Egypt for a magic duel with Egypt's magicians. Another story she could remember was of a conquering Greek king who passed through Crystal Mountains, where there were fruit trees guarded by huge serpents. Somehow he survived with his men and did get to Meroe only to be amazed at the marvelously built royal palace, its furniture made of gold and jewels. He also was caught off guard by the beauty of the then Kandake that he shed tears.

The Kandake touched the bead on her neck, musing. She had been told to wear certain charms to ensure good luck and health. On her way back from Napata, she stopped by the royal pyramids. What a lovely sight to behold the great works of men. The sandstone blocks used for the pyramids were quarried out of hills east of the royal cemetery, not too far from the official chapel.

Even as she stood in the rock-cut chambers under the pyramid, remembering her loved ones and their stories passed down, the story of genesis, which Samuel told was some story she'd never heard before. She knew about the Christians but she never got to behold their faith so close. The authority alone with which he spoke was mind-boggling in itself.

Kandake didn't want Samuel dead, and so knew she had to make him renounce his faith before the next games or soon enough the people will ask her to kill him as a sacrifice.

All she has to do is wait it out for the day to dawn and she will formulate a plan.

* * *

"You are welcome."

Telipha smiled at the new ones who joined the believers' assembly for the first time.

The new converts were ushered to the center of the assembly. Many of all ages and different social status came forward.

Sahid spotted a merchant he knew very well at the marketplace among them. Smiling, he walked up to him, touch him firmly by the shoulders, and pull him to a hug. Others close in on the new converts and one by one embraced them in tears and sheer joy.

Everyone present stood or sat on the bare ground. "Telipha. This is the merchant I told you about."

Telipha smiled and hugged him in greeting. "Brothers and sisters," he addressed those assembled, "the heavens rejoice for the salvation of our fellow brethrens." He stumbled forward on his bad leg to hug another convert. A child tugged at his worn out robe. Telipha looked down in response. He scooped the boy into his arms and rested his cheek with the child's.

A sense of peace hung in the atmosphere.

Calil, Raja's younger brother, began the meeting. "Please, brothers and sisters. Our time together is brief. Let us begin by singing praises to our Lord."

They all closed their eyes, letting the music filled with hymnal words wash over them and renew them once more. The song spoke of hardship and faith, and of God's deliverance.

Sahid felt revived and far removed from what troubled his household and the whole kingdom. The region treads in the mire of gods and goddesses. In the quest for happiness and the satiation of their own inner turmoil, people kept finding different ways hoping to lead to peace within.

But Sahid now knew better. Man was never meant to find peace except that which was given by the One who creates. Knowledge will increase most definitely, only that the more you know, the greater the turmoil.

Here, in this modest space, among these people, Sahid felt the presence of God's peace. The gathering embraced freemen of who are slaves, the rich, sitting on the floor beside the poor, and the old with small children on their lap, all existing in such sweet harmony. Smiles and laughs of joy thundered the night. It always felt like homecoming to him and he could only rejoice.

Men skilled in musical instruments took up harps and flutes as a beloved local song about deliverance was raised. Eyes closed, hands open with palms up in offering to God, they sang from their hearts.

"God has blessed us through His Son," Calil announced in elation.

Sahid spread his hands, "Praise the Lord. Praise God in his sanctuary; praise him in the firmament of his power. Praise Him for his mighty acts; praise Him according to his excellent greatness. Praise Him with the sound of the drums; praise Him with the flutes and harps . . ."

Everyone raised their hands again and spoke the well-recited words of the psalms, "Let everything that has breath praise the Lord. Praise the Lord."

Telipha opened a worn parchment. "We will continue our reading of eunuch's memoirs tonight." Calil brought the oil lamp close enough to read.

"It is mindful of us to remind you, as always, how the eunuch of our Kandake, met Philip on his way back to Meroe. He was a God-fearer and had traveled thousands of miles to Jerusalem to worship.

"The angel of the Lord spoke to Philip, one of the seven appointed to serve tables in the ecclesia, to arise and go toward the south, the way that went down from Jerusalem to Gaza, which is desert. It was on this path that he met the eunuch and got him baptized.

"What a wonderful thing to know those that walked with our Savior while He was on earth, made records of his life. Like every night, we continue reading from Mathew's memoir as always. He walked with our Savior-Jesus Christ, the blessed One forever. He even came as far to these regions to preach the gospel, where he met his death."

On that note they all listened as the memoir was read. To hear the written words of Matthew, who had walked for three years with the Lord, made them all tremble. They all drank in the Word and took refuge in it.

After the reading, the parchment was placed carefully in the hands of Sahid. Thin bread and a cup of wine were passed among those gathered. Christ's words were whispered over and over as each partook and passed the Communion feast from hand to hand.

"This is my body . . . this is my blood . . . Take and eat in remembrance of me . . ."

When all had been served, they sang a local solemn song of the redeeming love of Christ, the deliverer. "Are there any new believers among us who would like to share their testimonies?"

A few stood up and shared stories of their conversion while some shared theirs of persecution one at a time. With no polished oratory, men and women of weakness spoke with words of encouragement.

Questions were asked but there was a peculiar one that stood out of all the questions. It was about Christ's crucifixion.

"I don't understand something, brother?" someone asked from the crowd.

"Go on, the Lord has the answers you seek." Telipha replied.

"If it was God's Will that Christ Jesus-the blessed One forever, be crucified then why did Jesus exclaim on the cross, 'My God, My God! Why have thou forsaken me?'"

Many murmured in agreement to the question.

"That's a good question. This declaration of Christ has puzzled many through time. And as much as I want to answer this question now, the night is far spent and such a question needs to be laid out clearly for all to understand. The next time we meet, by the Spirit of the Lord, I will answer this question."

The crowd protested to stay till dawn but obeyed resignedly when Sahid told them to pray for one another and for those who forsook the assembly of the righteous. Intercessions were made for the gospel to someday claim the land, their families, personal requests, and illnesses.

"May I request we pray for Samuel also?" They all agreed to Sahid's request and prayed to God.

The heavens opened and the One seated at the right hand of the Father made intercessions for them.

Trouble might be making its way for the morrow but just for tonight, they all gathered more than enough peace like the Israelites with the manna.

The only difference is that they will need it more than the latter hereafter.

15

O dear darkness! Venture further and be darker still!
Be thick like the clouds but do know one speck of light
will undo the deal!

He remembered when he was taken along a stone block corridor, dragged down stairs, and along another corridor. He was forced to his knees and shoved forcefully into a dark chamber. The door was slammed behind him and a bar dropped solidly into place. The sound still echoed in his brain.

Sometimes he felt like screaming. The walls seemed to tighten around him, the stone ceiling descended momentarily, and the chamber closed in at each passing second. He pushed with all his strength against the darkness but it didn't move. Sometimes he heard the guards as their hobnailed shoes echoed softly by. They came to drop the scrap they call food for him.

That's if they remember to come at all.

Time faded in the darkness. He knew he'd been here for a while now but it seemed like forever. Panic rose in his heart. Samuel closed his eyes tightly, struggling for control.

Gritting his teeth, he didn't make a sound, knowing if he did, he'd be giving in to the terror already filling him. His heart pounded and could hardly form a rhythm. He kicked at the darkness with all his strength again, ignoring the throbbing pain in his heart, and kept kicking the darkness from piercing his heart until his lungs felt bruised.

Samuel panted in fear, sweating profusely. He was so hungry that he couldn't feel his stomach anymore.

Hours equated to weeks, and weeks to months in this place.

All passed in total darkness.

Samuel curled on his side and tried to envision himself in the forests of his homeland but couldn't. Here he had neither water nor food. His eyes had lost its purpose in this blanket of death. Lice took their toll as they crawled on him and bit into his flesh in equal starvation of his own.

"Eli, Eli, la ma sa-bach'than-ni?" he voiced out, barely able to speak. He remembered reading those words in Mathew's account of the Savior-Christ Jesus; the same memoir Telipha had a copy.

Smothered in darkness and drifting in nightmares, he lost touch with time. When the door then opened, he thought he was dreaming, but knew he wasn't when a light shine from the doorway into the chamber.

The Lord has come for me, he thought.

"My God, my God, why hast thou forsaken me?"

Are you a soldier of the Cross-, a follower of the Lamb? And shall you fear to own His cause, or hesitate to speak His Name?

Fear claimed him and darkness within him suddenly disappeared.

"Lord, what will thou have me do?" He trembled all over and his voice sounded distant even to himself.

Must you be carried to the skies on flowery beds of ease? Will others fight to win the prize with sails through bloody seas?

Should there be no foes for you to face? Should you stay afloat of the flood? Is this vile world a friend to grace, to help you on to God?

Samuel's heart began to ache again, this time, for forgiveness. Doubt had sneaked in by the dark door before but now the radiance of the light refilled him with repentance. The Lord placed a word in his heart.

"Sure I must fight if I would reign. Increase my courage Lord. I'll bear the toil; endure the pain, supported by Thy Word.

"Thy saints in all this glorious war shall conquer, though they die; they see the triumph from afar, by faith's discerning eye.

"When that illustrious day shall rise, and all Thy armies shine; in robes of victory through skies, the glory shall be Thine!"

He recited it again and again, with each time enriching him more with confidence and peace.

Footsteps approach his chamber.

The light went out but left a rich brilliance in his heart.
The footsteps came closer.

"How can a man survive such a place like this for a day?" Sisimithres, the Kandake's eunuch, asked the guard behind him."
"No one has, my lord, but somehow this blasphemer lives."
They both got to the chamber and found the door wide open, its bar not in place.
Sisimithres stopped in fear and looked back at the guard. "Do you always keep it open?"
"No, my lord. I . . . er . . . I'm sure I . . . dropped the bar in . . . to place the last time I was here."
The guard touched the door foolishly to check if it was real.

"And when was the last time you were here?"

"About five days ago."

"Are you saying Samuel hasn't been fed for five days?" Sisimithres asked, anger welling up in him. He waited for a response and got none, just like he expected.

"If he's dead, I assure you it will cost you yours . . ."

"Let him be. My God has spared me."

Both Sisimithres and the guard were startled at what they heard from within the chamber. The guard raised his oil lamp and slowly entered.

"I'm hungry. Please get me something light to eat and drink."

The guard was surprised to hear someone who hadn't eaten for days speak with a tone so rich and a voice so warm. He kept staring at this blasphemer with awe and curiosity.

"You heard him." Sisimithres said, "Go and fetch him something light to eat and drink."

As the guard rushed out, Sisimithres had completely forgotten how filthy he thought the place was. He watched Samuel, as he lay on the bare ground, weak and tired.

The darkness may have taken his strength, but not a touch to his heart.

He waited for the guard to return.

The place looked terribly murky. One could scream a thousand times without causing the ants that trudged slimy walls to budge. Human feces induced the air with a pungent smell, convincing him of his lostness. Sisimithres stared at the boy at the corner. The lad's face tried to smile but couldn't keep it for long. Weariness plagues every fiber of his being.

The guard brought a gourd and thin bread with him. Sisimithres held the gourd to Samuel's lips, and he gulped the water that spilled from it. Helped to a sitting position, he slowly started on the bread.

"Who are you?"

Sisimithres demanded for not only the lad's name and background, but about something else. Samuel finished the bread and rested his back on the wall. He stirred into the oil lamp replenishing his soul for the lack of it.

"There was once a king called David, who ruled the Israelites a long time ago. This king's grief for sin was beyond any. Its effect was visible upon his outward frame. No remedy could he find, until he made a full confession of his many sins before the throne of grace."

"A throne of grace?" Sisimithres slipped onto the floor and unconsciously took his seat. The guard listened, wanting to know more.

"David tells us that from time to time he kept silent when his heart filled with grief. Like a heavy pool with no outlet, his soul would swell with torrents of sorrow. He fashioned excuses; he endeavored to divert his thoughts, but it was all to no purpose." Samuel straightened his leg and rubbed it gently. "Like a festering sore his anguish gathered, and as he would not use the lancet of confession, his spirit remain full of torment, and knew no rest."

Sisimithres looked down in relation. Samuel noticed the grief of sin written on the guard's face, the torch still in his hand.

"At last it came to this, that he must return unto his God in humble penitence. So, he hastened to the mercy-seat and there unrolled the volume of his iniquities before the all-seeing One, acknowledging all the evil of his ways." Samuel picked up the gourd and drank deeply from it. He could feel the water wash over his heart with a cooling sensation, while his audience waited impatiently.

"Having done this, he received at once the token of forgiveness."

The guard's countenance changed, enhanced by the torch's reflection dancing on his sin-grieved face.

"The bones which had been broken were made to rejoice, and he came forth from his closet to sing the blessedness of the man whose transgression was forgiven."

"Forgiveness," whispered Sisimithres, " . . . throne of grace."

"Do you see the value of a grace-wrought confession of sin? It is to be prized above all price, for in every case where there is a genuine, gracious acknowledgment, mercy is freely given, not because the repentance and confession deserve mercy, but for the power of the redeemer." Samuel looked up and raised his hands in worship: "Blessed be God, for there is always healing for the broken heart; the fountain is ever flowing to cleanse us from our sins. Truly, O Lord, thou art a God ready to pardon! Therefore we recognize our iniquities."

Sisimithres wasn't the only person watching this grace of worship. The guard looked at the prisoner as well. The need arose in his heart to feel that same way: freedom from his inner struggles. How anyone could have gone this long in such a place like this without the help of the gods, he wondered. Only in this case, it was different. To Samuel, there was only one God, one Creator of all. If this same God stayed with him all this time in this darkness, then he knew this is the God he needed to serve.

"What must I do to be saved?"

"Yes! Where is this throne of grace that we can go find it?" Sisimithres had completely forgotten the main reason why he was here. All he wanted was to alleviate the burden he'd being carrying all his life.

Sisimithres' taste buds resonated with the bile bitterness of sin. His heart yoked heavily with the atrocities his hands had committed. His zest for social status had led him to do things he never thought he could. The lust for money wielded plans that at one point involved taking another's life just to be the treasurer of Kandake. The world didn't know what he did but he knew and that was enough to haunt him insanely. To understand the gravity of the torment that could lie under the radar while the outside skillfully conceals, is to urge the need to dislodge when the chance is offered.

"Beloved! You don't have to go find the mercy seat. It has found you! Right here, and right now the mercy seat remain accessible to anyone who believes with his heart unto salvation by Christ Jesus alone, in His death and resurrection, and confesses with his mouth that Jesus Christ is Lord."

"You mean we don't have to go to any temple to offer sacrifices?" asked the guard.

"The temples you need are yourselves, and the sacrifices you require are your lives. Our Lord Jesus Christ said, 'come to me all you who labor and are heavy laden, and I will give you rest. For my yoke is easy and my burden is light.'" Samuel looked from Sisimithres to the guard. "Are you ready to acknowledge your iniquities?"

Would any believe that in such a shadow of death, two souls would come to know the Lord? The outside will never fathom such a testimony but nothing can be done to convince the without to acknowledge the greatness that lies within. Let there be a thousand years of devastation, and incomparable starvation. Be it so that desolation wears the crown that rules the land. Nothing can be done to ever erode the substance that stems from the death of a seed. If answers are found to explain how life comes from death, as seen in dead seeds before germination, only then is the reason to live without hope unearthed. Samuel instructed them to go to Sahid's home to meet with the believers' assembly.

Sisimithres rose up from the filth a new man and walked to the door to leave. He stood beside the guard, a co-benefactor of immeasurable grace.

"I completely forgot why I came here. The Kandake has a proposal for you," he said turning to face Samuel.

"I know she does. Tell her for me that I will not compromise my faith."

"But you haven't heard what I was sent to talk to you about."

"I don't have to my brother. I'm in the Lord's hand now. Whatever happens is to God's good purpose and for his glory. I'm not afraid."

Looking at him, Sisimithres knew that few hours ago, he would have been puzzled by such remark but now, he knew the same faith like his: a faith that gives resounding peace and unseen assurance. He searched his face for a long moment and then nodded.

The guard looked at Samuel and said, "It will be as you say."

"It will be as the Lord wills."

"Do you want me to take you to a better chamber?"

"No! Darkness is not dark to the Lord and the night is as bright as day to Him!"

He reminded them once more to go to Sahid as soon as possible.

The guard stood holding the oil lamp as he waited for Sisimithres to step out of the chamber.

"Don't worry precious ones. The Lord neither sleeps nor slumbers. He will surely keep me. Go in peace and May the grace of our Lord Jesus Christ, the Love of God and the fellowship of the Holy Spirit, rest and abide with you all. Amen."

16

Behold, and believe, for the dark rescinds;
Will it not at the blast of the four winds?

"It's been three times already," Siaspiqa said and saw the flash of anger in the warrior's eyes, clear warning he didn't want to hear anything from him again.

Akinidad, the brave Mero warrior that fought side by side with his commander, Cagillaris, against the Blemmyes, found himself in another battle to win again: Wari. Many were gathered around them; warriors wearing the normal long patterned robes with tasseled cords and pleated sashes that draped from one shoulder. Akinidad felt rage well up in him as he lost yet again in the game of Wari to Siaspiqa, another co-warrior.

"It seems to me you don't have enough wit in Wari as you do on the battleground.

The audience laughed at that.

Akinidad paled his emotions raw. He continued staring at the pebbles not knowing which move to make, the muscle working in his jaw.

"Don't waste your time. I win with one move."

"No."

"Admit it! There are some things you aren't good at."

"Hold your tongue animal or I'll hold it for you."

"I'm sorry the talisman on your neck ran out of luck."

Swearing, Akinidad stood abruptly, kicked the Wari board and carried Siaspiqa by the neck with his left hand.

The others drew back in fear.

"Now do you still think I don't have enough wit?" Siaspiqa struggled, slowly running out of breath, barely noticing the gleam in Akinidad's eyes.

"I think it's high time we changed the use of facial scars." Akinidad continued.

"What do you mean?" One of the warriors standing asked. "Facial scars are meant for tribal identification, decoration and medical treatment."

"Well I'm about to give him one," Akinidad smiled, "but this one will mean shame."

"Put him down!" Cagillaris, the commander ordered as Akinidad lifted his right hand to strike his prey.

Akinidad hesitated, and then dropped the almost-dead warrior. Siaspiqa struggled for breath and took in all the air his lungs could take.

"What were you all doing, playing Wari this time of the day?" Cagillaris' eyes moved from one warrior to another until it came to rest on Akinidad. He recognized that gaze.

He knew what it meant.

With the physical strength and fearful influence Akinidad willed, Cagillaris tried hard enough to conceal his discomfort. The whole kingdom embraced him as the finest and best of the Meroitic warriors. He also noticed Akinidad's sword slung across the chest as his eyes rose to meet his.

"You all know your duties. I'll let you all go this once." Cagillaris finished.

One by one, they left the courtyard. Not too far away stood the artistic Roman-type public bathhouse.

Akinidad went past some houses made of sun-baked mud bricks, angered more than ever. He bumped into a herdsman carrying dairy produce in a tightly woven reed basket. The herdsman made sure what he carried didn't spill. Akinidad could hear how the herdsman wailed about how important the milk was as he put distance between them. He was sure a man like that would most certainly have quite a plump wife if he fed her on milk.

Akinidad ached for one.

A boy ran past him in pursuit of his dog.

He entered his home and went to exercise. First thing he worked on was his sword.

The morning cool was gone already. He could feel the way the weather grew hot but didn't notice the dark figure staring at him from his own small courtyard entrance.

"I can give you what you want!"

Akinidad looked up at one of the darkest figures he'd ever seen.

"I, alone, can help you, but you have to do something for me."

"Step into the light so that I can see the eyes of the one I'm about to kill." Akinidad took a step closer towards the courtyard entrance. He watched as the dark figure stepped out of the house shade.

"Introduce yourself." Akinidad demanded.

"My name is Hammed."

"Hammed? The one going around soliciting for support from idol priests and sorcerers?"

"I have a task for you."

"Listen and listen carefully. I won't be used for one of your cons, Hammed. Leave now or die." Akinidad said, taking a step closer, his sword raised up slowly.

"It's a pity you won't become a commander of the Meroitic warriors after all.

That remark stopped him in his tracks.

"Oh! I'm sorry I to let that out. I know how much you want to become a commander, and that you want Cagillaris dead if that would be the cost."

Hammed laughed watching Akinidad turn pale. He loved the power he had over people when he revealed their darkest thoughts to them. He did the same with Theagenes, the idol priests and had just had the ear of the Kandake-Queen Amanikhatasan. "Now you listen and listen carefully. A week from now is the games. The wrestling match will hold the best wrestler now in the kingdom, Hydaspes, against the strongest warrior: you."

"What!" Akinidad couldn't believe his ears.

"The winner," Hammed continued, "will be crowned chief commander of the warriors, earn his freedom, and would also have the privilege of destroying the one who blasphemes against our gods."

"What then happens to Cagillaris?" Akinidad muttered. His sword lowered already.

"He's been taken cared of, even as we speak."

Akinidad always thought he had a dark soul but now standing in front of Hammed convinced him otherwise. Hammed's face didn't hold any expression.

"Practice warrior. You'll need it." Hammed turn to leave.

"And if I refuse?"

"Then I'm afraid you'll suffer the same fate as your commander now does!"

Hammed walked away leaving a brave warrior in rage. Akinidad's hand tightened on his sword with a scowl resting on his face.

* * *

Raja laid on his leather-strung wooden bed, decorated with ivory inlays. A cool clothe rested over his brows. Rhesa had left to speak with the cook about preparing him a broth that might soothe his stomach. He hadn't been able to eat in three days, not since he had those three dreams again. He couldn't stop thinking about his father and how things are between them. He put a trembling hand over the cloth, pressing it against his throbbing head. Wishes to die now and have the pain and misery of his life over and done with owned his thoughts.

Someone entered his room and close the door.

"I don't feel hungry, mother," he said bleakly. "Please don't press me to eat. Just sit with me and tell me another story."

"It's not your mother."

Raja froze at his father's voice. He lowered the cloth, thinking he might be imagining him here. "Father," he said in tentative greeting.

Sahid watch his son sit up shakily in struggle with the coverings and cushions. Raja's hands tremble by just pushing the cloth back from his face. He sat thin and white as death.

"Can I sit, please?" Sahid begged.

Raja gesture gracefully toward the seat his mother usually occupy.

Sahid sat down slowly unable to tell anything from his son's face. Raja seems more withdrawn every time he saw him. Sahid, on the other hand, feel himself grow worse daily. He felt like weeping. His son detested him and had every right to feel that way. Yet, his heart hungered for him—for his soul, now that he drifted farther as the day passed. His emaciated body looked so white his bones showed. The fever was upon him again, wilting his strength and making him tremble like an old man.

Raja smiled up at him sadly. "You must be ashamed of me, father. It doesn't matter anymore." His mouth curved ruefully.

Sahid's heart beat heavily with dread at his son's words. "How can I be, son, when you are the one that should be ashamed of me."

"Oh! I see you've had a change of mind concerning me, father but when I die, you are going to throw my body out and forget that you had a son."

"Don't say these words, son. Please." Raja spoke of his death so matter-of-factly that it chilled him.

Raja glanced up, hurt by what he heard in his father's voice. "Your hatred is preferable to your pity."

Sahid let out his breath and bowed his head. "I see you've set your mind against hating me."

"A difficult resolve, father. Did you expect more?"

Sahid had no strength left for self-defense. He tried to find the right words but none came when needed the most.

"Why do you come to me now, father? To see what's befallen me?"

"No." Sahid couldn't hold back the tears anymore.

"I am cursed," Raja said, fighting tears. "You can see how accursed I am."

"The gods I called upon once don't exist, Raja, but I serve a new One, the only One. The same, yesterday, today and forever!"

Raja looked away. "So that's why you've come. To remind me of your new god." He gave a bleak, humorless laugh of despair. "You needn't. I look back upon my life with loathing. I see the wretched things I did as though the scenes are painted on these walls I stare at every day." He placed one thin pale hand against his heart. "I remember, father. I remember all my sins. I wish I didn't."

"So did I, son, but there is still hope."

Raja looked up at him then, eyes dark with anguish. "Do you know why I despise Samuel? Because he is everything I'm not. I've never seen anyone have so much impact in such a little time."

"Oh, Raja, forgive me! I didn't know what I was doing."

Raja's eyes flashed. "You knew," he said coldly, "when you chose another over your son."

Sahid closed his eyes, his mouth trembling. For once he was honest with himself. "All right," he said in a choked voice. "I knew, I knew, but I was so consumed with misery myself that I didn't care what I did to anyone else. All my life I sought for inner peace. I had it all: wealth, fame, slaves, but not peace. It eluded me. Most times we are not what are perceived of us. I thought if I buried myself in my business, my inner struggles will disappear." He looked at his son desperately. "Can you understand that?"

Raja stared at him coldly. "And did it?"

"You know it didn't." He looked away from his cold face. "In return I lost the most important thing in my life. I lost my family! I lost you!"

Raja struggled with what he saw in his father's eyes. Somehow he felt he shouldn't forgive him.

At least not yet.

Sahid stood up and came close to the bed. "I'm sorry."

"Sorry?" Raja said, eyes blazing.

Sahid turned and walked toward the door. "I don't expect you to understand. How can you? When all I did best was ignore you from your childhood. It must have been better not to have a father than have one who was never there for his family."

"We all have inner struggles too, father, and that's why we are a family. We would have made it together. It's a little late now."

If he couldn't reach his son with any means he knew, he would lose him forever. That would be a burden he would carry for the rest of his life.

"There is a dream I've been having."

Raja looked at him, and thought also of his dreams.

"I'm walking through a garden," Sahid begin, "full of large, beautiful trees with branches that wedge above to form lovely canopies. I take a step forward and feel the softness of the grasses beneath my feet, gentle, sweet, and delicate. Feelings of weariness and the lure to lie down explore my senses. The ambience makes forever seem like fleeting moments." He looked at Raja.

Raja urged him to go on with his eyes, his heart aching terribly with his wounded side.

"My eyes open from the brief drift away. I look up and notice something strange about all the branches of the trees. They point to the same direction. I then hear a noise coming from one of the trees. On top of it, a man, with his back turned to me, makes a clean cut of one of the branches. I forbid him to leave the branch alone lest he destroy the explicit splendor of nature. The man lifts up his head and without looking at me points to the same direction with the other branches.

"Another garden, more beautiful than the one I'm in forgives my gaze at its awe. My eyes stare long enough to lose words befitting its description.

For I cut of this tree, beautiful but wild by nature, and take it to the garden beyond to graft it in. it shall die before it bring forth fruit.

The man on the tree speaks up.

"Immediately, I see him in front of me, going to the garden beyond. I run to follow him and then stop behind him. He slowly moves away and I see a young lad in front of him, standing before a large abysmal pit.

"I look at the man standing by the side and ask him without uttering a word, and he answers me that the branch is the young lad. I turn back and the once lovely garden is gone."

Taking a deep breath, Sahid wiped the sweat off from his forehead.

"The young boy faces me and tears are streaming down his face. I cry out for him not to do it, but he bends over towards the pit that separates the two gardens."

Raja couldn't believe what he was hearing.

Shaking, Sahid rose.

"I run as fast as my leg can carry me and catch his leg. My other hand holds the cliff and as I begin to slip. I cry out in pain, no longer able to support his weight, as well as mine.

"The man speaks up again and tells me to let go of the cliff. I hope for help but he stood there and bids me to let go. A shout rushes out of me in cry for help. Finally I slip with the young lad and when I think that all is lost, a hand holds me and my feet feel the ground beneath it. The young boy stands beside me and then a man approaches, holding out both hands. He says he will take us to the other side, to the real garden, not the counterfeit we're from. His hands stretch out, not to me, but . . ."

"To me!" Raja interrupted, finishing his father's words. His heart ached even more as he continued where his father stopped.

"He comes closer and his hands and legs are pierced."

Raja watched his father sink wearily down to his knees, obviously in shock. Raja himself couldn't believe that he's being having the same dream with his father.

"Do you take his hand?" Sahid asked, pleading. "I always wake up when the man gets close enough."

"I don't know," Raja said bleakly. "I don't remember."

"Neither do I." Sahid said hopelessly.

"That is the first of my dreams."

"What do you mean?"

"There is two more, father." Tears unstoppable rolled down his cheeks. "These three dreams come in successions every night."

"Please, son, will you tell me the other two?"

Raja closed his eyes for a while. The images in his dreams flash through his eyes. He never felt darkness close in on him so strongly like it did now. It choked and sapped his strength. His heart feels like a milestone placed on it. With every breath he inhaled, the milestone seems to press closer, crushing him. For a while, Raja struggled to breathe. He struggled again but the more he struggled, the more pressed he felt.

Sahid looked at his son, and noticed his face grow white by the second. Sahid close his eyes and pray to God like never before.

A blast of wind from nowhere rushes through the balcony, carrying with it warmth from the four winds. The soft breeze brush over Raja's body and feelings of refreshing and release bathed father and son. Raja let out a breath as he feel the milestone lifted.

Sahid thanked God for his son.

"Father!"

Sahid hold his son's hand close to his heart. "Tell me, my son. The other two dreams."

Raja stares at his father for a while. Like a river overflowing his banks he tries to narrate the events of his other two dreams but the words came out in soft gasps of inaudible sounds.

17

When the Lord commands something that seems unwise,
Obedience is better than sacrifice

Alexandria, the shining pearl of the Mediterranean, capital of Egypt for centuries, flooded once more with people all over the world. The city was an outstanding cultural and academic center. Its importance was ever rooted in the beacon: a long lighthouse tower that radiated its culture and heritage to the world at large. For sailors, it ensured a safe return to the harbor, for architects, it was the tallest building on earth, and for scientists, it was the mysterious mirror that fascinated them the most.

While the beacon's reflection served as a guide over thirty miles offshore, attracting people all over the world, all Makarasa wanted was to flee from it. As she peered through the window of her home, she could still remember when Bulahau brought her to this great city to live. Many expectations overwhelmed her at the thought of a new beginning and the sheer delight of living the rest of her life in wealth and status.

Bulahau seemed to be wealthier than her father, she discovered. Well known in a city that served as the principal port of Egypt, located on the western edge of the Nile delta. Many tired travelers by land found comfort when they came close to the peninsula that separated the Mediterranean Sea and River Mareotis, on which the city was built. The city is divided into sections with a substantial Jewish quarter, the Royal area, the Neapolis, and a necropolis to the far west. They moved into the Royal area, which held firm to its name. It was indeed royal in every way.

She noticed a cloud rise out of the west. There will definitely be a shower today, she thought to herself. She had everything she needed: servants at her beck and call, escorts through the crowded port whenever she wanted, and lack for no material thing. But it wasn't enough.

"The life of a man isn't found in the abundance of his possessions," she said to herself as she walked away from the window. How will she be able to go on living now that her husband had forbidden her from meeting with the believers in this city? She tried to support her weight, a hand on her side. Her belly showed in slight protrusion.

Makarasa took her seat slowly, trying to fight the tears. It has been a month now when Bulahau struck her hard across the face, yet her cheek ached from remembrance. Bulahau only cared for her safety, and for the safety of their unborn child, now that Christians suffered persecutions greatly in the city.

She had come to know some believers who were present when John Mark was here. John Mark was a man faithful in his co-laboring with apostles Barnabas and Peter, and later a strong and faithful co-worker with Paul. At the great solemnity of Serapis, the city's main god, he was dragged and torn to pieces by horses.

Grave expression overcame those who shared the story with her, bringing tears whenever she recalled, yet somehow the believers assembly had grown with increase in their persecutions. The good news in John Mark's death was that the gospel was written in Egyptian before his passing.

She knew she couldn't live without the fellowship and thanked God for the one who planted the seed that led to her salvation—a young lad that served her father back in Meroe.

Go home

Makarasa looked up, startled by the still small voice. Suddenly she had the feeling that something was wrong at home.

Pray for Raja on your way

"My brother? But dear God, what about my husband?"

Trust in me

"Dear Jesus. Have my family come to know you? How will they handle the idea that I left my husband's home to travel down because I felt something was wrong?

Lean not on your own understanding.
Heed my call

Her mind wrestled with her heart as reason challenged her faith. How was she going to make the journey in her condition? What was wrong with Raja anyway?

Don't go! She hears her mind say. She had to. It was either she stayed or do God's Will.

"Precious Spirit, what are you up to this time? What is your purpose in this?" she waited for an answer but none came. She relaxed a bit trying to think it over. Her eyes swept the elegance of her chamber. Handmade pottery from Meroe and Faras were placed beside the table and at both ends of the door, while the tapestries, decorated with seated figures of the Amun from Qasr Ibrim, overshadowed the window. A beautiful cloth was laid on the table with painted bowls of different sizes placed on it. The mud-rendered internal walls stood in white, with the edges of the niches and windows picked out in red, imitating frames of wood.

Her mind drifted to how much she cherished looking up to her new home when returning from the market. Its external wall was enlivened with pilasters and vertical semi-circular moldings, variously painted in blue, red and yellow. The color varieties gave it a striking effect against the white background.

She could hear Philus, the chief servant, admonishing one of the servants at the passage. The soft tears of a child stirred her heart and she knew whom he was scolding. Analmaaye was the youngest of their male servants who always ran away. Strangely, Philus would go get him back and scold him without telling his master, her husband. The consequences would be grave if it touched the master's ears.

"How many times will you run away?" Philus reprimanded. "I can't keep up with this anymore. If you run away one more time, I'm afraid I'll have to inform the master."

The child begged Philus with promises not to do it again.

"Obedience is better than sacrifice."

Makarasa came to her feet abruptly as the baby in her belly kicked. Those words spoken by the chief servant weren't meant for the runaway servant. It was meant for her. She was wasting time and God used her chief servant to speak to her.

"Dear God, I'm sorry. Please, forgive me. I'll go now. I'll go now." She said into the air.

How was she going to get to Meroe on time?

A ship

"Yes Lord." She said. With good winds, she will be in Meroe before the week ended.

"Take care of my husband, Father, who art in Heaven. He's been too kind. Watch over my family, especially Raja."

Makarasa took her shawl and headed straight for the port. Without food or pass for the ship, she realized that if God directed, he will surely get her to Meroe safely.

Bulahau got home few hours later, hungry and exhausted from work. He called for one of the slaves. Philus sent Analmaaye to go attend to the master. "Tell the cook to get me anything. I'm famished."

"Yes, my lord." He took a bow and headed straight for the kitchen.

Bulahau collapsed on the leather bed, feeling drained from the day's work. He needed a hand to work on his shoulders and suit his temples. The best hand there is.

"Who is there?"

Philus came in. "You called master."

"Yes," Bulahau said, wiping his brow, "please call my wife."

"Yes master."

"And tell the cook to hurry up with whatever she's preparing, will you." He added before Philus exited his chambers.

"As you wish, my lord."

Moments later, Philus came in with Analmaaye carrying a tray of prepared Falafel. The meal is made of deep fried beans, drained and minced with dill, coriander, onion, garlic, parsley and leek, well spiced with sesame seed on the side. It came with hot tomato salad and hibiscus drink.

Bulahau heard his belly growl in hunger at the mere sight of it. He looked up at Philus and his hunger disappeared. "What is wrong?"

"It's your wife, master. She's not here."

"She must have gone out. Didn't she tell you where she was going?"

"No, my lord. She was in her chambers earlier today."

"Are you saying my wife left this house without anyone knowing?" Bulahau could feel his muscle tense. Rage burnt his eyes as his mind worked. He knew that things hadn't being going well between Makarasa and himself for a month now. Since the moment he struck her and forbade her from going to that cult meeting. But that wasn't a good enough reason for her to leave him and besides, she was heavy with child. Where could she possibly go? "Call me the guard at the entrance."

Philus rush out to call the guard while Analmaaye watched how his master's appetite vanished in an instant.

Maybe she's at the secret meeting again. Anger rose in his heart but was immediately overtaken by fear. What if she is captured with the cult members? What will happen to her, and their unborn child? The painful thing was that he knew. She will be burnt alive or worse—thrown to beasts. By the time Philus came in with the guard, Bulahau was already pacing heavily across the passage. "Did you see my wife leave today?"

"Yes, master."

"And you didn't stop her or escort her?"

"I tried to but she said I didn't have to since she was going home."

"What! Home? Meroe? And that alone didn't hit your senses to prevent her from leaving?"

The guard kept silent as sweat broke in his brow. He should have stopped her but the calmness in her eyes convinced him otherwise.

"Which direction did she go?"

"The port, my lord."

Bulahau couldn't believe this. She went by ship. "By the gods!" he whispered. In a time of the year when it's unsafe to venture through the dangerous cataracts around Aswan, the first of a series of rocky stretches along the Nile that made travel between Kush and Egypt difficult.

"Come with me, both of you."

Why did she have to leave? What could have prompted such an impulsive act?

The rain fell heavily as Bulahau rushed out with his servants to the port. They got to the port only to find out there will not be any ship sailing again till the next day.

Philus stared at his master in sympathy. In the midst of the heavy downpour, he still noticed tears streaking down his face.

Not too far away, caught by a strong wind, the ship on which Makarasa boarded, was making a swift yet safe passage to Meroe, its first stop Thebes. Her heart beat fast on thoughts that had nothing to do with Raja or her family or her abandoned husband. Guilt came swiftly as her whole body quivered, not to the rain, but to thoughts of seeing Atlanersa again. Maybe after she attends to Raja, she will tell him the truth at last: the truth about who fathered her unborn baby.

18

The end is near and hopelessness evident,
But do not fear when a glimmer is imminent

Five days passed since Raja went dumb. Sahid walked the flatlands along the river with burdened thoughts. He walked all morning and couldn't help but notice the acres of millet, vegetables, dates and cotton, growing. The Games is tomorrow and visitors from far and wide arrive in hundreds.

Tomorrow's games usually marked the end of the year. Rich merchants risk coming to the city, traveling from afar to sell their products and later leave with Meroe's finest produce. The rich visitors ride on elephants; others on caravans, while the majority treks on foot.

Ships made way to the ports in such a difficult time of the year to navigate through the dangerous cataracts. The cataracts hinder foreigners from other parts of the world to visit one of the greatest civilizations ever achieved by man.

Sahid walked through the grasslands, savoring for a moment in the beauties of nature all around him. Wildlife of elephants, ostrich, and cattle roam a good distance away.

It was only yesterday he found out Calasiris was dead. The poor lad he sent out to meet Theagenes about his business affairs was found dumped behind the city walls, a part to the east reserved for the common people's burial. His son just lay somewhat lifeless. He prayed and fasted. Questions that needed to be addressed in the believers' assembly were suspended while prayers for Raja, Samuel and for the whole region of Nubia intensify.

In the midst of all his trials, peace lingered to this morning. Although, Samuel is to be killed tomorrow and Raja might die any time yet his heart rested.

Before Rome ever dreamed of becoming a world-conquering empire; before the people in the far northeast ever built their great wall; before the tribes of those afar learned to write; before mining ever began anywhere, the African people of Kush had raised a great civilization. Kushites developed their own writing that only could be read by them, made durable artifacts and built lasting monuments, controlled a vast territory; made exquisite pottery, entertained complex legends, and mastered a technology that brought change to the whole region.

All this, Sahid prided in. If not for the almost inaccessible route to Kush, the whole world would have known and carried their praises beyond.

Someday, these legacies will almost be wiped out

Sahid tried to listen intently to what God told him.

The greatness of this race will not be taught, as it should.

"Why lord, why? Sahid was deeply saddened. He couldn't comprehend the mere thought that this entire splendor will be swept away in oblivion. "Father, what must we do? Please, help us."

Teach your children, and tell them to teach theirs. The greatness of the sun-burnt people doesn't lie in their civilization, but in their salvation.

The salvation God spoke of was not the physical but the spiritual. It was based on how much they come to know and live by Him.

A sound came from behind. Sahid looked back. A chill coursed through his body. Something was wrong. He could feel it. He looked to his right and could see a Dinka man singing praise songs to one of his animals, not far away.

Go now

Heeding those words he almost ran to the Dinka man. When he came near, the herdsman invited him to join him in the praise but he declined. He looked back again towards the spot he felt the chill but didn't see anything. It must have been an animal, he thought to himself. Somehow, he couldn't shake off the feeling that it wasn't an animal but someone in the grasses.

While his eyes held the spot, somewhere by the riverside, the ship carrying Makarasa arrives.

* * *

"I hear you are to fight the great wrestler, Akinidad." Siaspiqa smiled, cynically.

Akinidad sighed in exhaustion. Not from his practices but from the constant acerbic remarks he suffered from the hands of Siaspiqa.

"I see your skin is taut and your body has taken more workouts for tomorrow's encounter."

Akinidad tried to swallow up his hatred but it was one acid taste in his mouth that burnt his throat every time he took it in.

"Are you dumb warrior, or you're scared?" He laughed in contempt. "You should know what tomorrow's outcome will be."

Akinidad drew his sword from the sheath hung directly on his chest and started practicing with it. He tried to keep his mind off from doing what he had always wanted to do-shut Siaspiqa up for good. Tomorrow's match isn't going to be a mere wrestling encounter. It is to the death. Hammed told him. Now the whole city was already buzzing with the news, and also of the news that the blasphemer will be killed by the one who triumphs.

"I happened to visit the bed made for the one who dies tomorrow," Siaspiqa continued, enjoying the sting of pain he inflicted on Akinidad, "and it was the exact fit for you." He noticed Akinidad turn around, all covered in sweat. The rage in his eyes was beyond description. Siaspiqa noticed Akinidad's struggles to control his temper. His stomach lurched and his mouth went dry under the gaze. "I think I've spent enough time with a dead man already." With that he left.

Hammed stood not too far in the scorching Sun watching the warrior turn pale with hatred. Akinidad will be too glad if his opponent for tomorrow is changed for Siaspiqa. The hatred he bears for Samuel matched the warrior's. At least comfort will come tomorrow from the lad's death but he still had Sahid to worry about. He wanted above all else to make him pay for the pain he caused him, demoting him and giving his former position to Samuel. He came close to killing him on the flatlands. Somehow Sahid suspected something. Hammed's hands clenched into a fist at the thought of failing.

Later that day, Akinidad noticed Hammed approaching him. He went on swinging the sword in practice. Hammed stopped a few feet away from him.

"If you are victorious tomorrow, I promise you the pleasure of killing Siaspiqa." Akinidad's face lit up. He turned and looked at him. "Besides, the anger you hold against him will aid you in combat. Your opponent, Hydaspes, may match your skills, but not your hate. Now you have another reason to win."

"Remind me of the first." Akinidad stated as he went back to practice.

"The office of Cagillaris."

Akinidad took out his bronze dagger, by the gilt handle, from his side. He looked at it for a moment and smiled.

"So be it."

* * *

The guard of the lower dungeon threw the bolt. Sisimithres was thrown in and the bolt was put back in place. A torch lit up the room slightly at the side.

"I see we have another blasphemer sent to join those sentenced to death by the morrow." Cagillaris remarked. He had only spent six days and couldn't still imagine how any man could survive this place of death for a week, let alone a month. He even welcomed the idea of facing death the next day, that's if he survived another day in this hole. Somehow, he wondered how this young lad beside him was still alive.

"My brother! Sisimithres." Samuel said joyfully.

Sisimithres walked to the far end of the dank chamber. "Samuel. It's good to see you again."

How these two men could find joy in such a place, Cagillaris wondered. The sickening stench hit him so readily he almost vomited his intestines. All his strength had dissipated. No food. No water. For three days now. His weary eyes strayed to the faces of Sisimithres, the Kandake's eunuch, holding the young lad. Words of encouragement passed between the two.

Samuel peered up at him with luminous eyes. "What are you doing here, Sisimithres?"

"The Kandake has sentenced me to die with you tomorrow."

"Ha! Aren't we all?" Cagillaris laughed in disdain. "At least you two have a reason to die, but I don't have a part in this, yet I'm to be slaughtered. This is all I get for serving the kingdom."

"Cagillaris," Samuel looked at him in pity, "we may not be able to change our fate but we can change the reason we face them."

"You are saying that I should change my faith? No way! The gods may have abandoned me, so also have yours."

"I know why I'm here, great warrior. Tell me why you are here."

"Yes," Sisimithres added, "why are you here?"

"I don't really know." Sorrow washed over him. Why was he here, really? He wondered. All he ever did was serve, and serve, but this is the thanks he get.

"I was arrested by the palace guards six days ago. When I asked them the charge, they told me, conspiracy and blasphemy.

"And you Sisimithres, the Kandake's personal eunuch, keeper of the kingdom's entire treasury. How did you, of all people end up here? Were you caught stealing from the treasury?"

"Nothing out of the ordinary." Sisimithres sat down on the filthy ground, his back against the wall. "Samuel."

"I'm listening." The young lad replied.

"The first time I came here to speak with you, the Kandake instructed me to reason with you to renounce your faith. Only on that basis will she be able to save you from condemnation. As you well know, that wasn't the case when I got here." He laughed readily.

"Instead of you to convince him to deny his faith, you got yourself convinced and accepted his, right?" Cagillaris sneered. He tried to hold his gut from throwing up the little left in him. He had been vomiting for days now and nothing but liquids came out.

Samuel joined Sisimithres in laughter.

Cagillaris couldn't believe this. How could anyone find anything amusing in these conditions? He was beginning to believe this young lad was indeed a sorcerer. He turned his eyes away in fear of being charmed by the young imp.

"Brave warrior," Samuel said, "I'm not a sorcerer as you think. I'm just a child with even greater weaknesses than you have. The difference only is I believe in the only true God."

Cagillaris was a little shaken by Samuel's words. He rightly guessed what was in his mind. "If you can know what I'm thinking of, doesn't it confirm all the more that you are indeed a sorcerer?"

"It sure should, but that isn't the case her." Samuel replied. "Such works that have been wrought through me is taken as the act of sorcerers. Also for a warrior who believes in what he sees, and trusts in the strength of his hand in times of battle, you are indeed entitled to that opinion." He relaxed his legs and slowly rubbed the aching in his thighs. "Some trust in chariots and some in horses, but we trust in the name of the Lord, our God." He knew it would take an act of grace to convince this man to change his ways. All he was used to was the discipline of training schedules and regimes. The only way he knew how to live was by the sword, and that was what worried him. It was a shame for him to meet his end like this. Worse! He didn't meet his end in battle but in bondage to the kingdom he served. The wish of any great warrior is to live and die by the sword. That is what is considered honor in their eyes. It's the basis of their training, and the ultimate goal of their exploits.

Cagillaris turned his face away from where they sat, like he wanted to avoid them in the thick darkness. He never felt so desolate.

"Did you happen to go to the assembly, Sisimithres?" Samuel asked.

"No, but I sent someone to them. I sent the guard that was here with me the first time I came here."

"Thanks be to God." Samuel weakened again. His mouth tasted like bile as feverish heat rushed through his blood. "Tell me your ordeal with the Kandake."

"Well, she asked me what the outcome of our meeting was. I told her something else. I witnessed to her about my new found Lord and Savior."

"No wonder she feels that I'm a sorcerer," a happy tone in Samuel's voice, "when all she asked you was to deliver a message."

"So tell me, sorcerer, what magic do you have planned for tomorrow?" Cagillaris asked.

Samuel kept quiet for a while. Thoughts of his sister flooded his heart. He had only a year left. His sister, Loiyan, will be fifteen years of age two years from now. He thought God had plans for him to return to his land, and to his people. What will happen to Loiyan?

Put your trust in me.

"Or your God has a hand in your death?" Cagillaris added.

"I have a champion already, Cagillaris. The battle is over. He's already won." Samuel reached out and held Sisimithres' hand firmly between his own.

"If your god was so powerful, he should come for you." It was more of a question than a statement. Cagillaris had suffered this boy for six days. He had heard him sing songs to his God, a sound so sweet that it drew him every time as he listened. He had heard him pray fervently.

Surprisingly, the prayer was for the same people who will derive pleasure in his death tomorrow. Somehow, he felt pity for him.

"When I came here, I thought I would soon return to my homeland to save my sister."

"Tell us about your family, Samuel." Sisimithres asked.

"My father was a disciple under the former eunuch of Meroe."

"The same one who left his office in proclamation of the god he met in the land of the Jews?" Cagillaris asked.

"Yes!"

"And the god he proclaimed is the same one you believe in?"

"Yes! My father traveled far south and settled with the Tabora tribe. It was there he married my mother, a native of the tribe. They had three of us." Samuel felt pain as he recalled the sacrifice his brother paid for his life. "Oh Caleb."

"Who is Caleb?"

"My brother. He died because of me. Now my sister is in the hands of a priest who intends to kill her in two years time if I don't return."

Cagillaris couldn't imagine a young lad like this having gone through a lot in his life. Despite his age, there was a kind of strength and peace attributed to him. This he humbly claimed not to be his. All, he acclaimed to his God.

"I have one question for you. How can your god watch his son die and do nothing about it?"

"The prince of this world has blinded the minds of unbelievers so that they don't see the light of the gospel of the glory of His Son." Samuel shifted to speak directly to him. "Cagillaris, His Son didn't just die. He rose again! Don't you see? He died and rose again thereby defeating sin and death."

"He rose from the dead?"

"Yes."

Cagillaris seemed to dwell on the idea. Since he came to know about this god, he never knew of the resurrection. He always thought this god's son died and that was it.

He rose again . . . He rose again

The words kept coming to his ears, pricking at him like a knife through his stone heart.

"We all celebrate when one of us dies, believing he or she has gone to a better place," Samuel continued, "yet we all are afraid of it. We all try to live a good life, believing in laws against malpractice, yet we all are guilty of it. 'For all have sinned and there is none righteous.' We even mummify the dead, but that doesn't change the fact that we'll die someday. We set up new laws against evil, but that doesn't mean we ourselves are not beyond its influence." Samuel took Cagillaris' silence as consent. "Do you now see why He had to defeat sin and death?"

"Now tell me," Sisimithres added, "How else could God defeat sin if He didn't remedy the thing within us that make us do what we do not want to? Or how could he defeat death if He didn't face it Himself, only to rise again in victory?"

The words went straight into Cagillaris heart. It all felt too good to be true, but there were questions that ailed at him, a lot of questions he needed answers for.

"I know you have many questions." Samuel said.

"Stop doing that." Cagillaris answered.

"What?"

"Reading my thoughts before I voice them."

"I'm sorry."

Samuel and Sisimithres waited for him and the wait was a long one.

Finally, Cagillaris spoke. "Tell me! Everything. Don't leave out any details. From the beginning."

19

Do you possess a contract with evil that none can rescind,
Your Savior comes on the wings of the wind

Makarasa and Calil entered the room. The red light from the Sunset crept over the wall. Rhesa glanced at them noting how pale and strained Makarasa's face looked. She also noticed the small bulge below her abdomen. Their eyes met, and Rhesa understood. Calil must have briefed Makarasa about everything. They both would talk later. She rose from the seat beside Raja's bed for Makarasa to sit beside him.

"How is he?" she said.

"Not very good. It's been six days," Rhesa said grimly. "He hasn't eaten all day and has been awake most of the night." She tried to swallow a tear. "Come Calil. Let's give your sister some privacy with your brother."

Makarasa sat down wearily. Rhesa felt her distress and put her hand on her shoulder, pressing lightly.

"I trust in the Lord, mother. We're all in his hands, and He's assured us all things will work to his good purpose."

Makarasa reached up and covered her mother's hand. She withdrew and watched them walk toward the door and go out. Depressed, she rested her elbows on the edge of the bed. Raking her fingers through his hair, she touched his cheek. "Jesus . . ." she said, but no other words came. "Jesus . . ."

Raja slowly turned to her. It surprised him to hear his sister call that name. She must have somehow gotten converted in Alexandria. This god seems to have his arms everywhere. Seeing her was enough joy for him to take to his grave. He tried to tell his father the other two dreams but couldn't. Now, in the grip of death, he recalled the story his younger brother, Calil, told him the day before. The story was an exact retell of his second dream.

In his second dream, there was a great and mighty king who wished to settle accounts with his slaves. When he began the reckoning, one who owed him ten thousand measures of gold was brought to him; and as he could not pay, his Lord ordered him to be sold, together with his family and all his possessions, and payment to be made. So the slave fell on his knees before him, saying, 'Have patience with me, and I will pay you everything.' And out of pity for him, the Lord of that slave released him and forgave him the debt. But that same slave, as he went out, came upon one of his fellow companion who owed him a hundred measures of gold; and seizing him by the throat, he said, 'Pay what you owe.' Then his fellow companion fell down and pleaded with him, 'Have patience with me, and I will pay you.' But he refused; then he went and threw him into prison until he would pay the debt. When his fellow slaves saw what had happened, they were greatly distressed, and they went and reported to their Lord all that had taken place. Then his Lord summoned him and said to him, 'You wicked slave! I forgave you all that debt because you pleaded with me. Should you not have mercy on your fellow companion as I had mercy on you?' And in that anger, his Lord handed him over to be tortured until he would pay his entire debt.

Raja's heart ached heavily. Obviously, he was the slave that was forgiven yet he hung his father on his past offence and didn't forgive him.

'So will my heavenly Father do to every one of you, if you do not forgive from your heart?' Emptiness kept on digging through his inside. How many times had his father knelt down to plead for his forgiveness and all he did was to cast him off.

You are not worthy, Raja. God will not forgive you.

Those words taunted him. If there is a true God now, He will never forgive him. The thought of being lost forever broke his heart and spirit in ways inexplicable. He never cared about anything or anyone but himself. Pride and arrogance were his companions from childhood. He always thought he'll never be capable of feeling. However, when death knocks on your door, and goes as far as to turn the knob, fear of the afterlife seals you in and even the strongest is becomes the most vulnerable. Unfortunately, this feeling spares no one.

You are lost forever . . . never to return home.

Raja drank this poison from the dregs of evil.
Makarasa wiped tears from Raja's face. Her heart ached for him. He was drifting away slowly. Jesus . . . , her heart cried yet again.

Tell him a story

She heard it clearly. What story, her heart cried. A story came to her heart.

"There was a man who had two sons. The younger of them said to the father, 'father, give me the share of the property that will belong to me.' So he divided his property between them. A few days later the younger son gathered all he had and traveled to a distant country, and there he squandered his property in dissolute living. When he had spent everything, a severe famine took place throughout the country, and he began to be in need. So he went and hired himself out to one of the citizens of that country, who sent him to his fields to feed the pigs. He would gladly have filled himself with the pods that the pigs were eating; and no one gave him anything. But when he came to himself he said, 'How many of my father's hired hands have bread enough, and to spare, but here I am dying of hunger! I will get up and go to my father, and I will say to him, "Father, I have sinned against heaven and before you; I am no longer worthy to be called your son; treat me like one of your hired hands." So he set off and went to his father. But while he was still afar off, his father saw him and kissed him. Then the son said to him, 'father, I have sinned against heaven and before you; I am no longer worthy to be called your son.' But the father said to his slaves, 'quickly, bring out a robe-the best one-and put it on him; put a ring on his finger and sandals on his feet. And get the fatted calf and kill it, and let us eat and celebrate; for this son of mine was dead and is still alive again; he was lost and is found!'"

Raja closed his eyes unable to stop the tears. It was the third time he had heard his dreams told back to him. Who would dare doubt the love of God who reveals all the ponderings of his heart? Is it true he could still find acceptance from this great God?

A gentle wind came in from the balcony and, like a whisper of kindness, brushed Raja's brow. He drew in a soft breath of it and exhaled. Opening his eyes, he looked straight at Makarasa sitting beside his bed. He reached out weakly and brushed his fingertips against hers, wanting to give comfort.

Makarasa looked at him. "Raja," she said hoarsely, staring at him. "My little sister."

Makarasa's blood warmed with delight at the sound of his brother's voice.

"I'm glad you came back," he said softly. She grasped his hand and held it tightly, kissing it. Tears filled his eyes that he hardly could see her face.

Sahid came in with an oil lamp and was surprised to see Makarasa with Raja.

"Father!"

Sahid placed the lamp on the floor and rushed to his son's side, his face lit up in joy.

Raja looked up at his father as he took the place Makarasa was. He did love him after all. Oh, God, he did love him. A breeze brushed his face, oddly comforting. He felt so weak and light, as though that soft wind could lift him and carry him away like a leaf. But it wasn't yet time. He was afraid where it would take him. A repressive darkness seemed to be closing in around him, and the heaviness within his heart had not eased, even for a moment.

"I'm so sorry for everything, father," he whispered.

"I know. Forgive me, son."

"Oh, if it were only that easy."

"It is little one. Listen to me, son. I've wronged you, and I must tell you."

"No, father. I have wronged you." He then spoke of endless escapades that led to innocent bloodsheds, debauchery, and the abuse of female slaves. He confessed all he had done to sate his insatiable hunger. Yet nothing satisfied, nothing filled the empty aching inside him.

Rhesa walked along the upper corridor from her chambers. As she neared Raja's open door, she heard words indistinctly. She entered quietly, her heart leaping as she saw Raja talking to his father. Sahid listened intently to Raja, who kept on.

Rhesa sat down happily on the other side of the bed. Raja went on talking to his father, and at the same time searched for his mother's hand and found it.

"You didn't do what I did," Raja said sadly. "You never sinned the way I sinned."

"We all sin, Raja, and no sin is greater than any other. God sees all sin the same. That's why he sent Jesus to atone for us. For each and every one of us."

Raja blinked back tears and look up at the ceiling. He turned to Makarasa as she lifted his head and sat at the spot, placing his head on her laps. He returned to the ceiling again, feeling wretched and lost.

"How do I go back to God? My three dreams were retold to me by each one of you." He looked up at Makarasa. "Like the prodigal son, will he take me back despite my sins?"

Makarasa laughed softly in joy. "Oh yes! That's the almighty God he is."

Sahid took Raja's hand firmly between his.

"Despite ourselves, He loves us!" Sahid said in haste. "You've confessed your sins, Raja. Will you confess your faith in him? He's called you all your life. Answer him, beloved. Please, Raja. Let him in."

"How can I not?" Raja said, holding tightly to his mother's hand and seeing the love shining in her eyes. "O God, dear Jesus, please." As he voiced those words, it was as though something rushed into his very being, filling him, lifting him, and overwhelming him. He felt lighter. He felt free. And he felt weak, so very weak. His hand loosened. "So easy," he said with a sigh. Raja held his father's hand against his heart. "It shouldn't be so easy, father."

Makarasa stroke her brother's face. "Jesus did all the work."

"He must be baptized," a voice said from the open door. They all saw Calil standing with tears-stained face.

"Rhesa, tell the brethren at the meeting to meet me at the Nile." Sahid carried his son along the upper corridor and down the stairs. He crossed the opening, which was filled with the moonlight, and headed for the Nile. He held him in the caravan while Calil drove it all the way to the Blue Nile. Without removing his sandals, he went straight into the river. The cool water rose around his legs and hips, dampening Raja's body.

He lifted his son slightly as he bent his head and kissed him. Then he lowered his son into the water immersing him. "I baptize you in the name of the Father and the Son and the Holy Spirit," he said, raising him up. Water streamed from Raja's face and hair and body. "You have been buried with Christ and raised again in the newness of life."

"Dear God," Calil exclaimed, "Thank you. Thank you."

"Why would the son of God ever cry forsaken when power is availed to him in abundance? What hope is there for any if the son of God could be abandoned by his father?" Telipha's words silenced the crowd that gathered around Raja. The recovery of Sahid's oldest son spread so fast that not only the regulars came but also strangers to the believers' assembly.

"The gospel according to Matthew's account of our Lord stuns us all with this eternal question. I also have the Spirit and will thus delve into this."

He had everyone's attention.

Calil came close to Telipha, and at his nod started reciting the twenty-second psalm in tears. The boy's voice exuded authority as he proclaimed the psalmist's treasured words. When he finished he took his side by his family.

"These words of Jesus have puzzled many and, sometimes, like a seed that sprouts with no roots, caused some to slip back. Will it surprise you all if I said that it was a question that was never meant to be answered by any one person?"

A whisper began to grow amidst the crowd.

"The answer has already being provided."

"Where?" One shouted.

"Tell us." Another added.

"Like many of his proverbs, it confounded those who fêted in the banquet of unbelief but for those of us who believe, it is the power of God unto salvation. This very last proverb Jesus quoted cannot be appraised from the cross alone. Calil, our son and brother, redirects us from the wisdom source. The twenty-second psalm tells us why.

"Jesus cried to God to let us see, and know, and understand the only reason why a father will abandon his son, why a creator will let go of his creation. Do be warned that the answer is not for the wise but for the fool, not for the lawful but for the sinful. So lay down your expectations and receive with meekness this engrafted word able to save your souls.

"Here it is! I will re-state some of the psalmist's words: For God has not despised nor hated the affliction of the afflicted. Before your weary minds travail to wander on endlessly in search of the afflicted, look at yourselves. If you have basked in liberty in all that you think, say, and do, and still feel the clutches of sin like chains around you like the milestone weights of anguish, then tell me who is the afflicted? Care to define it your way? If you do not realize how afflicted you are or have been then I say all is lost.

It says in this psalm that none can keep alive his own soul, but how sweet that a seed shall serve Him.

A seed that will do all it takes to redeem everyone. How many of our ancestors, and even us, give voice to afflictions? However, God, who is not confined by time, heard it all and met our need.

So why, oh God, does it sound like you forsook Jesus on the cross?

"Simple!

To provide a seed that will save the rest.

A seed that will bring those lost in time past and time to come, back home.

A seed, which is Jesus, to bear the sins of you and I. A seed that will stand for man and reclaim what was lost.

A seed that needed to face sin and death alone for the saving of other seeds.

"How many times do we embellish the stories of heroes who achieve the impossible? We all know that the heroes that are revered the most are those, who with a company of none, faced the impossible on their own and returned in triumph. So if you celebrate such local heroes, will God fall short of the same standards and not save us all from what ails the entire human race?

And do it alone?

"That is exactly what He did through his Seed. The Seed called Jesus.

Jesus wasn't questioning the Father's love when he said why have thou forsaken me.

He affirmed it!

'Why have thou forsaken me?' A prayer said by Jesus to redirect to the Psalm that holds the truth of it all!

The truth revealed in our atonement and adoption as sons and daughters—lost seeds of God

He is with the father right now. Therefore, we know that God didn't abandon him but let him face the darkest evil man will ever know. So when Jesus rose again, all of mankind was saved, once and for all!

It may have sounded like the cries of thousand souls coming from the cross when he went through the travail for us; it may seem to have housed the afflictions of a failed Messiah; it may send quakes through the foundations of your faith . . .

But above all it showed a high priest who can empathize with the feelings of our infirmities and reclaim all that was lost in the beginning, at the end.

So when you hear it read to you 'why have thou forsaken me,' when its thrown at your face that your Savior wailed on the cross in pain, then hail your hope on mounted shoulders and wield your faith like a warrior's shield, and raise your love like a proud child . . .

My God came. Died. Rose. And Conquered.

And do not forget to end it the way Jesus did.

IT IS FINISHED!

This is much of what has been given for our understanding. The rest we'll come to know in eternity.

"The last verse of the twenty-second psalm says that 'they shall come, and shall declare God's righteousness to a people that shall yet be born, that God has done this.' This I have done and I charge you to do by telling others this gospel."

Tears flowed freely down the faces of every one present, in understanding. More people came out in response to accept Christ. The whole assembly raised their voices in prayers, praises and thanksgivings to God, till the first rays of light from the Sunrise hit the horizon. Finally, prayers were made for the whole kingdom of Nubia, and finally for the young lad-Samuel.

By dawn, Raja was finally asleep.

20

What glory awaits God in the end!
When his children resolve not to bend!

A tempting day for inhabitants of Nubia to go horseback riding, drive chariots, hunt fishes, and practice archery, but no one gave heed to that. It was the day of the games-a special celebration by the Kandake herself, in honor of their god-Apedemak.

Citizens of Meroe, visitors far and wide, and historians sent by the emperor of Rome, surrounded the games arena. The games began in a procession of praise by the local priests calling out, "Lion of the South! Strong arm! Great god who will not be hindered in heaven and earth, providing nourishment for all men; who hurls his hot breath against the enemy. The one who punishes all who commit crimes against him, who prepares a place for those who give themselves to him, who gives to those who call to him, Lord of life? We salute you today." The sounds of harp and flute filled the air.

Afterwards the rituals followed the display of skilled archery by the Kandake herself. She moved gracefully, wearing a long patterned robe with tasseled cords of gold and pleated slashes that draped exquisitely from her shoulder; her wrists and legs overwhelmed with gold bracelets, and pure emerald graced her neck. The insatiable hunger of the mob for spilled blood robbed the queen from being appreciated. No one was skilled in the entire kingdom like her when it comes to archery.

The harps and flute sounded again when the Kandake took her seat. Then the local priests paraded lions before the spectators in religious procession. The musicians serenaded the wild animals for a while before leading them away.

Dancers ran out and moved in beat to drums that shook the earth's foundations. Their bodies enthused rhythmically. Shouts broke out from the crowd for blood and no more distractions from the main event.

The Kandake later raised the golden staff, an image of Apedemak associated with a lotus and a snake, signaling the opening of the lower gates to allow the wrestlers to come in.

The whole believers' assembly stood together at one side of the arena, in agony of the aftermath of today's games.

The sacrifice of Samuel.

After one hour, the whole crowd grew bored and cried out for the main match. The Kandake raised her staff and the wrestlers left the center arena.

Hydaspes was the first to come out. The crowd cheered in praise and honor. He walked straight towards the Kandake and took a bow. The Queen raised her staff in salute. Afterwards, Akinidad stepped out onto the arena. The crowds cheered again. The match would leave its mark on their memories for the greatest wrestler is squared against their finest warrior. Both men were dressed in an iron helmet, their left arm cast in iron shield, a small waist tunic, and wore hobnailed sandals. Well-built and skilled in swords, they stood facing the Queen. Rumors had been that Akinidad killed a thousand Blemmyes in the recent war.

The fighters both waited for the signal to begin. Hammed came behind the Queen and whispered something to her ears. In response, the Queen nodded her head to one of the guards below. He immediately threw both fighters two swords. The Queen raised the golden staff and dropped it. A sign to begin.

Both men picked up a sword and faced one another.

Hydaspes launched at his foe strongly, swinging the sword heavily. Akinidad moved back, almost losing his head.

The crowd cheered in support.

Bellowing a cry, he charged after Akinidad again. Akinidad blocked the sword with his and plowed into his opponent, not even feeling the point of a sword graze his side as he rolled away. The first drop of blood brought cheers again.

Hydaspes blocked blows from Akinidad and punched him hard. He followed with his sword but Akinidad ducked sharply, narrowly missed being decapitated. He brought his fist up into Hydaspes chin, a direct hit.

The crash of blade against blade claimed the arena from all sides, as well as cries from both fighters. An hour sped by like minutes.

Akinidad tired slowly. He looked at his opponent who seemed to grow stronger by the second. Then Hydaspes did the unthinkable. He threw away his sword and opened his arms wide, in challenge. Akinidad thought to take the advantage but knew it was not a thing of honor to fight an unarmed man with a weapon. Besides, what if he attacked with it and got disarmed. The shame would be unbearable. The shout from the crowd deafened logical reasoning.

Akinidad decided to drop the sword.

Immediately the sword left Akinidad's hand, Hydaspes came at him with heavy blows. One caught him by the jaw and sent him crashing on the sand. Akinidad rolled and got up before Hydaspes could smash his feet right through his skull.

Hydaspes didn't wait for him to catch his breath and came at him strong again, ramming his shoulder into him. A deep cry escaped Akinidad, one hand of his held his side. He was sure a rib or two was broken. In an instant, Akinidad's head was locked beneath Hydaspes arm, choking him slowly, but surely.

Akinidad's eyes met someone in the crowd. He recognized that face. It was Siaspiqa's. There was a gleam of triumph written all over it.

Hydaspes tightened his grip. Akinidad looked at the Queen and caught sight of Hammed as he struggled for breath.

My bronze dagger, he thought himself. He lowered one hand down to his sandals and pulled out the dagger he hid there and plunged it into Hydaspes neck.

The whole place went quiet as Hydaspes released his grip and struggled for breath. The dagger must have severed an artery. Blood gushed out in freedom release.

Akinidad watched him collapse on the sand. He held his side as the crowd cheered in excitement. "Akin! Akin! Akin!" the crowd went on.

Akinidad pulled out his dagger and faced the Queen. He took a bow in honor and lifted his head. His eyes met Hammed's again. Hammed smiled at him and leaned over to whisper to the Queen.

The Kandake raised her staff again. One of the guards ran towards the arena gates. Not to long afterwards, three prisoners emerged, bound in gold chains, to be executed. A young lad, the chief warrior of Meroe, and the former treasurer of Kandake were led out.

The sight of the lad drew sweat from the Kandake's brows. She hated him more than when she loved him. She sent her treasurer to talk some sense into him. The only way out of death at the games is to perform another miracle just like he did at the Sun Temple. The one to convince became the convinced and returned a changed person. Kandake rather Sisimithres die first but to please the crowd Samuel will be first. What a terrible waste, she thought. He could have had it all by the warmth of her bed.

In the face of death, Samuel couldn't get his mind away from last night's dream. He recognized a unique shout from the crowd. He tried to look up at first but closed his eyes in pain. Staying in the dungeon for months worsened his bad eye sight. He opened them slowly and saw Sahid in the theater. Tears welled from his eyes.

"Your son?" Samuel managed to say as one of the guards pushed him to the center.

"If it be His Will, you'll see him soon." Sahid shouted through the crowd.

Tears of joy fell down Samuel's face. Hobnailed sandals came down the dungeon to bring them to their execution. It was time, he thought then. One of the guards ordered the rest to take them out. Pain jolted through his body as he was led through the passageway of death. He could hear around the dark corners cries of anguish in his head. Now here he was in front of thousands. His eyes hurt so much that images around him blurred. It burned him in the blazing Sun.

Last night's dream was another chapter that he had lost hope of having. The dream continued from the point where his master stopped. The lion pounced on him and immediately he finds himself on a narrow path. Relief overwhelmed him. He is safe from the lion. Samuel comes to two paths. One leads to his hometown and sister. He turns to the other and sees a young lady begging him to come. Tears flow from her eyes and she kneels to plead him over. His heart aches for home again.

Not too far away, the cries of Telipha snapped him from his thoughts. "We will follow the example you have left us. We will carry on."

Kandake rose up from her seat. She had no choice. Samuel chose this path, and in the interest of her people, he has to die, she reasoned. Besides, Hammed will turn her people against her if she tries to intervene. She nodded to the guard below. The guard turned and took the sword from the priests that stood by the side. He walked up to Akinidad, and gave it to him.

Immediately the priests shouted, "This is the one who blasphemes against our god. May his soul never find rest!"

As Akinidad limped towards the young lad, a small wind stirred the sands at a spot close to the center arena. With every step he took towards the lad, the wind grew stronger, carrying with it dust into the air.

"Sorcerer!" Hammed whispered behind the Queen.

The hot Sun caught the blade of the sword. One mighty shout of praise by Samuel . . . and then the sands rose up into the air blinding everyone present.

From the center arena, everyone heard these words:

"The torch! Take the torch! Be keepers of the flame!"

The winds then suddenly dissipated and the air cleared in an instant. Everyone looked around, and then down at the center arena.

The priests were there. The guards stood in awe. Cagillaris' chains were off of him. So also was Sisimithres. Akinidad still held the sword in his lowered hand, one hand to his side. A ship had just arrived with Bulahau alighting in haste. A lost warrior, from the war with the Blemmyes, just made it to the city gates.

It was Atlanersa.

Aside from all of these, other things were as it was before the sands rose into the air.

But the young lad was gone.

EPILOGUE

"But the eyes of the Lord are watching over those who fear him, who rely upon his steady love. "He will keep them from death..."
Psalm 33:18

The story isn't over!

Don't miss the exciting and moving sequel of the story of Samuel, and the thorn of his flesh, Hammed in Book Two: the Eyes of the Storm, the second book in the Lion of Africa series.

Eyes of the Storm

Samuel strutted into the city of Axum. The food and water he had from the city of Gondar sustained him three hundred and sixty five kilometers walk northeast. He walked around in the marketplace for a while, not knowing what to do.

"God, help me in this place." He prayed silently. A man walked past him, his shoulders hitting him hard. Samuel stumbled over, cutting across a merchant's table. The merchant shoved him off hard onto the floor. He said something in his language that Samuel didn't understand, but from the fierce rage on his face, it must have been a curse.

He picked his way through the market looking for a quiet place he could rest. He was extremely tired from the walk. God have been merciful, he thought to himself. One instant, the blade was soon to hit its mark, and in the next, the Spirit of the Lord snatched him away. He found himself in the city of Gondar, and as he was passing through the region, he proclaimed the good news to those in the town. He didn't make much progress. All he got was a plate of Metin shuro, a meal of local mixed vegetables and water from a kind man. The man couldn't make out what he said but took pity on him because of his lanky appearance. He found a small pond and knelt down to wash his face.

Makeda was restless. Her spirit felt distressed by the longing of something she couldn't place a hand on. Suitors had come from far and wide to seek her hand in marriage but she had somehow convinced her father, the King, she wasn't ready yet. Seasons had come, one after the other, and now her father was terribly ill. She shivered in the comfort of the castle.

The towering castle stood in beauty and radiance of architectural varieties. Designs from faraway lands of Egypt, Kush, and Rome stately dignified it. Makeda was on the upper storey that offered panoramic views of the whole land. Many princes and rich merchants had sought the hand of this beautiful princess in exchange for golds, silvers, and riches beyond description or magnitude but none won her heart.

Makeda stared out of the window, worried about her father. His condition was getting worse, she thought to herself. The gold bracelets scratched her brow as she wiped sweat from it. "By the gods!" she uttered, feeling weighed down by these customary dressings. The gold bracelets on her wrists, and ankles, the rare emerald on her pierced nose, and many large bangles on her neck, her long hair weaved down artistically, all seem to weigh her down. "I'm tired of all these. I'm tired of everything." She burst out in tears and buried her head in her hands.

What will she do, she worried. She couldn't afford to lose her father. Not now. He had no male heir. Her fifteenth birthday was less than a year away and she dreaded the day from coming. How could they appease the sorcerer that brought this illness on her father? She pondered. It was all because he demanded something that his father couldn't give up-a sacrifice. Not any sacrifice. He claimed the gods requested a sacrifice of a royal child. And she was the only one. The whole city was in disarray that wretched day when the sorcerer made the proclamation. Hot color flooded her face. The thought of it maddened her more.

"If it's a sacrifice he wants, then a sacrifice he'll get." She said into the air. It will not be her life. It will be his. If anything happened to her father, she would have his head. She swore it. She turned to walk away but her long fine apparel caught a small protrusion on the window. She turned back in anger and yanked her cloth from it.

Then her eyes caught a movement just at the pond below, close to the palace. She peered out and caught sight of a young man in an attitude or worship. Who could be worshipping by the pond at Sunset? She wondered.

Samuel lay with his face down, close to the pond. His heart sang praises his mouth couldn't utter. He knew God brought him here for another purpose. God must be building a foundation for the future. Someday, He will reign through these lands. He was sure of it.

Look up, son.

Samuel looked up and his eyes met with a lady in one of the storeys of the towering castle. He held her gaze. She would be younger than him, he thought, but her beauty was captivating. "This one, Lord?" He whispered. He had never seen such beauty in his life.

Makeda looked at the dirty young lad by the pond. He must be very poor from his looks, but his eyes. She couldn't place it but she felt her heart call out to him.

Your longing is over.

She heard a still small voice say to her.

"Your highness?"

That startled her. She turned around and saw that it was her favorite nurse, the same one who raised her when her mother died at her birth. "You scare me, Magda."

"I'm sorry, my princess. The King requests your presence in his chambers."

"Please tell him I will be with him shortly."

"Yes, my lady."

Makeda smiled at her and waited for her to leave before she hastily turned back towards the pond below. He was gone. She looked up the path and back again. No sign of him.

Makeda moved away from the window. Something in her heart told her to find him. The notion was pressing. She walked quickly to the corridor and called one of the guards. "I need you to arrest someone for me."

"Who is it, my lady?"

"He trespassed over the palace walls and I want you to bring him to me, first. Do you understand?"

"Yes, my lady." He ran away and came back immediately. "How do we identify him?" He hesitated at the princess' words. Those descriptions weren't possible, and if it was, darkness was closing in on the land.

"Do as I say. Take all palace guards if you have to."

The palace guards searched the length and breadth of the city but found many that met the all description the princess gave except one. They looked through the dark alleys, the dirty corners of the marketplace. They left not a scribble part of the city unearthed but found nothing.

The dark cloud rose from the west and a stormy rain was upon them before they knew it.

"We have to return back, my lord." One of the guards said.

The guard that was instructed by the princess stood there hopeless. He knew he was right. They had to return or risk their lives. He turned to leave and was about to mount his horse when he saw a small shimmer of light coming from the rear dark side of a mud house. He moved away from the horse and walked slowly to the place.

"My lord, we have to go."

"Wait!"

The guard couldn't see clearly in the storm but he made way to the mud house. He found, at the side, a body shivering terribly. He reached out and grabbed the torn tunic on him and turned the face of the loner. He jolted back in surprise at what he saw. This pauper matched the last description. For in the midst of the storm, he saw the face of a young man, shone like that of an angel.